R. B. Gartrell

Reliving the Dark

Homicide Detective John Francis Kelly Series
Book II

Copyright

This is a work of fiction.

Names, characters, places, and incidents are products of the author's imagination and are used fictitiously and are not to be construed as real. Any resemblance otherwise is purely coincidental.

Library of Congress

Registration Number TXu 2-212-120

"Reliving the Dark" Copyright © 2020 by Richard B. Gartrell

All rights reserved, including the right to reproduce this book or any portion thereof in any form whatsoever without the expressed written permission of the Author.

Dedication

To My Fellow Veterans

Regardless of the theater/campaign, combat zone or era

Thank you for your service and ongoing sacrifice

We served with honor

Welcome Home

1

Five hundred American flags-red, white and blue-proudly wave in the soft breeze, each on a 15-foot pole, staked in the ground in a semi-circle of rows, located at one end of the huge base parade grounds, part of a colorful memorial garden; the "Flags of Honor", as they have come to be known, each bearing multiple names of soldiers who had fallen on the battlefield, were, on this warm day, a very moving and appropriate outdoor backdrop for the medal ceremony. The center piece of the garden is a bronze statue of a solider, in combat attire with a rifle, kneeling on one knee in a prayerful manner, looking at a buddy's grave marker.

In front of the garden was positioned a large metal collapsible platform with a red carpet, and a mahogany podium at its center bearing the Army's emblem hanging on its front facing the audience; a collection of microphones were rigged on the podium along with several chairs on the platform to seat Army brass. Facing the podium were multiple rows of chairs for the invited family, friends, and other dignitaries. A company of soldiers, in their crisp tan camouflage combat uniforms, had marched in formation onto the parade grounds, positioning themselves behind the guests' chairs facing the podium. The setting was spectacular, the weather perfect, and the excitement electric in the air.

"Attention!"

The sound of heavy boots coming to attention, the scramble of bodies sliding off chairs in response to the loud and strong voice of the Command Sergeant Major. It took less than 5 seconds for the area to be in complete silence. The Base Commander led his guests of honor onto the podium, including the Base Vice Commander, a Colonel, each stopping in front of a chair. Each officer was in full-dress uniform, with chests full of vivid medals and stars or other rank insignias on their shoulders. To make these medal presentations was Army Lieutenant General Cornelius Walker, straight from the Pentagon; he walked his large 6-foot-3 frame onto the platform, taking a seat, waiting to be introduced by the Base Commander.

"At ease." The standing soldiers relaxed their posture while invited civilians sat back down.

"Good morning and thank you for coming. I'm Brigadier General Scott Hansen, Commanding Officer of Joint Base Lewis-McCord. I'd like to welcome all the families and friends here this morning. I know this is a special moment in your lives, as it is with your loved ones. We're here to commend several outstanding soldiers for their commitment and sacrifice while serving in a combat zone overseas. To make these heroic presentations, it's my honor to welcome, from the Pentagon, Lieutenant General Cornelius Walker."

With that very brief introduction, General Hansen turned to General Walker, shook his hand, and stepped aside so General Walker could step to the podium.

"Good morning, Ladies and Gentlemen. What a beautiful day. I'm honored to be the one, on behalf of our Nation, to recognize these outstanding soldiers. They're among the few who have returned to be recognized for their extraordinary gallantry. Every soldier knows what it's like to be in combat, to see their buddies wounded or killed, or even themselves. Combat tests the best of each soldier; how they're trained to respond is the ultimate test, being able to fulfill their mission and support their colleagues."

On the large platform, to the right and slightly behind the General and facing the audience were four Army enlisted personnel in their dress blues. Sergeant Alberto Drury sat, holding a cane; next to him was Sergeant First Class J. Francis Correa, in a wheelchair, noticeably missing part of one leg. Standing at opposite ends next to those seated, like book ends, were Staff Sergeant Frankie Plank, an arm in a sling; and Staff Sergeant Anthony Franklin, whose wounds were extensive but not visible.

"These soldiers," continued the General, "have demonstrated their intense commitment to their men and to this Nation. Their bodies now bear the marks, wounds received in the line of duty. Only they know the depths of their sacrifice." He paused. "It's my honor to award each of you, Sergeant Drury, Sergeant First Class Correa, Staff Sergeant Plank and Staff Sergeant Franklin, the Purple Heart for wounds sustained in combat."

With that, the General stepped before each of the men, with the help of the Command Sergeant Major, speaking softly with each soldier, reading their individual commendation, and personally conveying his congratulations; pinning the Purple Heart with its purple ribbon onto the proud chest of each courageous soldier, he shook their hands and exchanged salutes.

Stepping back to the microphone, the General continued. "Each soldier is also being recognized for his heroic service while under intense enemy fire and commended for their efforts to support and protect their fellow soldiers. On behalf of our Nation, it's my honor to award each of you, Sergeants Drury, Sergeant First Class Correa, Staff Sergeant Plank and Staff Sergeant Franklin, the Bronze Star." He stepped away from the microphone and, once again, stood before each man, pinning the gold star, hanging from its red ribbon with a blue and white stripe down the middle, onto their chests, reading to each their formal written commendation, shaking their hands and mutually saluting each one. Though there were no expressions on their faces, their military bearing spoke of their pride, let alone what the medal meant in the way of sacrifices. And if you could look closely at their eyes, they were glistening. The faces of family and friends were aglow with smiles as tears dropped from many eyes. Then they broke into unexpected applause, with hoots and howls, for their loved one's sacrifice and recognition. On stage and in the audience, the tears flowed.

Returning to the podium, General Walker continued. "One soldier's efforts were brought to the attention of the Pentagon and the President of the United States. He's not unlike these others honored here today. They all have seen the worst of combat. He may not look like he's wounded, but I can assure you, Staff Sgt. Franklin's body bears many scars and in fact, he's still here at Madigan recuperating from those wounds. His heroic selfless acts saved his platoon while under severe enemy crossfire, a firefight that could have wiped out his entire platoon; because of his courage, he returned devastating fire, killing many of the enemy. Severely wounded, yet still able to go above and beyond, he returned and dragged out two of his comrades, salvaging their operation. Then as if that wasn't enough, driven, he repeatedly returned to the firefight to rescue his comrades, until his own wounds finally took him out of action. A fierce fighter, he exemplifies the quality of intense Army training and execution of his orders and responsibilities to their fullest degree. It is with great pleasure, and on behalf of this Nation and the recommendation of the President, that we thank you, Sergeant, for your commitment and heroic efforts."

The General turned to Staff Sergeant Franklin. "Each of these awards are based on documents submitted by Staff Sergeant Franklin's commanding officers, outlining the merits of his performance during engagements with the enemy. Staff Sergeant Franklin, I present you with two additional decorations, among our Nation's highest military honors; this nation's third highest decoration, the Silver Star, is awarded for valor and gallantry in rescuing your platoon under extremely fierce combat conditions." The General turned and pinned the star hanging from a red, white, and blue ribbon on Franklin's uniform and shook his hand again. "Congratulations." They saluted each other.

"Staff Sergeant Franklin, I now present you with the Distinguished Service Cross, our nation's second highest award, for your heroism, courage, and unselfish risk of life, under enemy fire in a deadly combat situation, behind enemy lines." The General again stepped forward, pinned the gold cross hanging from a blue ribbon with white and red vertical borders onto Franklin's uniform, read to him his official commendation, shook his hand again, congratulating him. They crisply saluted each other.

Looking at the four sergeants, the General added, "Each of you has demonstrated the highest achievements under extreme duress. You have faced unimaginable danger and carnage; these awards are symbolic of what you have sacrificed and earned. Your families and friends should be enormously proud of your sacrifice and recognition. The Army and our Country salute you for what you have given and accomplished. We hope your full recovery is quick."

Unexpectedly, he stepped back in front of each soldier again, spoke directly to each one and shook their hands, to the sound of muted applause in the background.

Returning to the microphone, General Walker said, "Staff Sergeant Franklin, you remind me of Audie Murphy, a fierce combat soldier who, during World War II, committed similar acts of heroism under severe enemy fire. He is one of the most decorated soldiers from that war." He paused. "Each of you standing here today have given much; you should be proud of these accomplishments. Thank you for inviting me to award these honors. These proceedings are now closed."

"Attention!" Soldiers snapped to attention and the civilians rose from their chairs. Shaking Franklin's hand again and responding to his salute, the General shook the hands of the other recipients, mutually saluted and departed. The quiet was broken with applause and yells of glee; families and friends flocking to hug and shake hands with their proud soldiers, while Staff Sergeant Franklin walked quietly back to his barrack.

2

"Kelly, have you seen these reports from the ME's office?"

"What's he into now?"

"Ha, ha! Seriously, he's sent this folder with the autopsy reports on five recent murders, all homeless men, each with a single gunshot wound."

Homicide Detective Bob Conway and me, Homicide Detective John Francis Kelly, are part of the Violent Crime section of the Seattle Police Department. We've been partners for several years. My being a 12-year homicide veteran, Conway was partnered with me and we just clicked. Sharp, talented, perceptive, energetic, runs 3 miles around Greenlake every day, rain or shine, and married to his high school sweetheart who is expecting their first child; we're more family than just partners. I value them as they have seen me through some strange and tough personal times.

"What are his conclusions besides 'they're dead'," I asked with a slight smile. Got to have some humor, ever so slight, to combat the sobering and often depressing side of solving murders.

"Funny man," responded Conway. "As I said, he confirms death by a single shot to the head. Each victim is homeless; fingerprints and DNA are being run to identify them. When identified, we'll have the depressing job of family notifications, if there are any in the area."

"That's exciting! You know I remember seeing one of his reports under the piles on my desk while we worked our recent murder case. I forgot about it."

"Yeah, we've been a little preoccupied."

"In his reports, is there anything that stands out besides the single wound?" I asked.

"He did note ballistics have the slugs and should be able to identify the weapon. He says there're no shell casings found, which he fines interesting."

Just then the Sergeant called, growled really, and told us to get ourselves into his office. Sergeant Matthew Ivan Troy, a big man at 6'5" and 260 pounds, African American, has been with the department nearly 30 years and decorated for exemplary performance of duties several times. Tall and impressive in stature, a former All-American running back from the University of Washington, he suffered a career ending injury during his second year with the pros. The brutal damage to his knee never allowed him to regain his agility, so he retired and joined the PD. He and his wife Camille have been good friends over the years, sharing dinners, time on his sailboat "The Library" and hacking at golf. He can be gruff, especially when bureaucracy overwhelms him. Actually, he's a lot more sensitive but doesn't like to show it. He's direct, wants to know what's happening and what we're doing to solve the worst of all crimes. Incredibly supportive, he'll rally the resources we need to make things happen or to protect others threatened by an unknown perpetrator.

"What's up, Troy?" as Conway and I entered.

"You've seen the ME's report on the homeless murders? Well, street advocates have been calling the Chief for action, asking what she's doing to solve these deaths. Her next call, well you know the command structure, now my call to you."

Pressure trickles down!

"So, we have protestors pounding on our doors claiming we're not doing our job quickly enough?" I asked.

"Something like that. I know you're just surfacing from your last extremely complicated murder case but that's our job, solving murders. You did a commendable job by the way; now we have five new murders and guess what, this case is all yours. Need results yesterday."

"I love delegation," said with a smile. "We were talking about the deaths just before you called. We'll see what the ME has and will talk with CSI too. We'll keep you posted."

"Please do. The Chief is breathing down my neck for results," as he waved his large hands, pushing us out his door.

Conway and I arranged a visit first with the ME and later with Tucker Locklear, head of our Crime Scene Investigators.

The Medical Examiner (ME), Dr. Charlie Bain, MD, nearing 70 years but you wouldn't guess it based on his youthful "Dick Clark" appearance, "Dick Van Dyke" stature and high energy level, has been on the job thirty-five years; his credentials are impeccable and his performances before a jury awesome, giving them an education in forensic pathology and for him, almost an academy award nomination.

"Charlie, we've got your reports but want your impressions beyond the paper," I began.

"Okay. Haven't really got much," he said with a smile. "Each of the victims came in as a 'John Doe'. None of them had any identification or money. They were not clean; meaning hadn't showered for some time. Their clothes were dirty and ratty. We've taken fingerprints and DNA samples which are being processed. Two of the victims were dead in their sleeping bags at least four or more days. Pretty gross."

"You'd think someone would have noticed," I commented.

"How were they found?" asked Conway.

"Dead." He paused, straight faced, then smiled. "Just joshing. The latest one was found by another homeless person who saw the sleeping bag thinking it was empty and was going to take it; instead, he found a dead body. He doesn't like authorities, so reported it to one of the missions."

"Which mission?"

"The Bread of Life in Pioneer Square. This victim was found near the viaduct, hidden in a stairwell. With all the construction in the area, I'm surprised he wasn't found sooner; maybe seen and ignored like so many do with the homeless."

"How were the others found?"

"Same way. The homeless wander upon their own. No one else seems to care, want to get near or awaken them. One said he saw blood on the sleeping bag, another said the dead guy stunk. They went to either Bread of Life or the Union Gospel Mission, told them what they saw and where, then faded back onto the streets. The missions called us, so Locklear may have more."

"We're planning on meeting with him after we leave you," I replied.

"So, what else do you have?" Conway prodded.

"None of the victims were near one another. As I said, one was found near the viaduct. Another underneath the I-5 behind the jail, lying behind an impounded car against the cyclone fence that surrounds the parking area; the third found near the waterfront park behind some bushes; the fourth found 3 days ago underneath the freeway off Rainier; and the fifth found in a stairwell on the back side of the theatre building at Seattle Central College. All were killed by a single gunshot to the head. There were no shell casings found at any of the sites. As I said, ballistics is working on identifying the weapon from the slugs I removed from the victims. No one seems to have heard or seen anything and if they did, they don't want to come forward or get involved. A cultural ethic I think, like 'no hear, no see and no say'. Even those who reported the murders wanted to remain unidentified."

I made a mental note that we needed to map the locations where the victims were found. I doubted this would be a meaningful effort, but it's something we need to do in the event someone asks us about the locations and any related connections.

"Charlie, the times these victims were killed?"

"Based on our current victim, between midnight and 4am. Because of decaying factors, I can only guess on the days the others have been dead but can't give you exact times," replied the ME.

"What about dates or a timeline for these murders? Is there any kind of a pattern?" I asked.

"I'd say the murders probably occurred every week, days vary. Conditions of the corpses don't suggest much more than within the past 4-5 weeks. The MO leads me to believe we can expect others will happen."

"How's that?" Conway asked.

"Whoever is doing this knows what he's doing; killing someone with one shot is not easy, especially when they're wrapped in a sleeping bag. The removal of shell casings is another sign of a professional, trying not to leave any evidence behind. The perpetrator has done it five times already without being apprehended, so there's no reason to think he or she will stop."

"You're suggesting a serial killer?" I asked.

"Possibly. If this keeps up, the answer is 'yes'," he replied.

"And you're suggesting some kind of a professional, a well-trained killer?" I probed.

"That would be my preliminary assessment," he responded.

We thanked the ME and went to visit CSI Team Leader Tucker Locklear. A quiet, intense, and methodical technician, he's been doing this job for a good many years. An imposing figure at 5'11" with long black hair pulled into a ponytail with leather ties, he's a master at sorting out the mysteries of a crime scene and finding evasive or obscure evidence. I don't envy him or his team working and cleaning up a bloody scene. Then again, I don't handle seeing dead bodies very well either.

"We got the ME's technical information. What can you tell us about these murders?"

"Five dead 'John Does' at this point. Homeless men. Ballistics has not returned their findings. Each victim was alone. No one was camping near them. Each location was isolated, so the killer had to do some observing to find out where they hid. One shot to the head. This is worthy of note. It was only one shot, and the victims were wrapped, if not partially buried, in a sleeping bag. Without disturbing the victims, not knowing which end of the bag was the victim's head, it would take some skill in making that one shot and hitting the head. So, it's not just someone off the street doing the dastardly deeds."

"That seems to gel with the ME's assessment," I contributed.

"Second, there's no noise reported, so I'm suspecting use of a silencer. A single pop. And third, no shell casings. The perpetrator knew what he or she was doing. The area was policed. We've dusted for fingerprints and DNA; but don't hold much hope beyond what we got from the victims."

"And your assessment?" I asked.

"A professional expert with the weapon. He knows what he's doing and plans ahead. I have no clue why he's targeting the homeless."

"You say he?" I asked. "Could it be a female?"

"Right now, I'm using 'he' as a generic for the perpetrator. No clues either way," responded Locklear.

"Anything else?" Conway asked.

"No. I'll be interested in what ballistics says. That might give you more to work with."

We were at that proverbial spot in any investigation: Dead victims, in this case five; no observable motive; no weapon; not even a person of interest. No one sees or hears anything. We're off to another exciting start, and people are already nipping at our heels wanting to know why we haven't solved these murders. Give us a break, folks!

3

Patti Hancock and I became engaged following the successful conclusion of our last murder case. We were high school sweethearts and had gone separate ways for too many years. Several years following the murder of her FBI agent-husband, Neil, she came face to face with his murderer, a result of the convoluted nature of my previous case. She's currently up to her pretty elbows, along with Interpol, shutting down an extensive international drug smuggling, money laundering, and federal murder case as the FBI's Special Agent in Charge for Seattle. She's agile, strong, trim at 5'9", my love, and one incredibly talented cop.

"What do you think we need to do now?" I asked.

"We've just about got it all taken care of. Goodwill comes tomorrow and takes it all away. Our designer arrives in 20 minutes. Let's see what she recommends then tweak it to fit our own needs and desires."

We'd agreed to remodel my aging houseboat, now ours, something I had felt no urgency to do until now; we want to create our own new memories, and this would be our first major effort.

"Is Snowball going to survive all this change?"

Snowball is Patti's cat, a short-hair white Persian furball of warmth, who likes to cuddle and let her purring engine work overtime; she has now acquired and is training another master; I guess I can say she's grown on me, and maybe vice versa.

"She's pretty mellow but I'll put her in my car when Goodwill arrives. Don't want her to think she goes too," said with one of her contagious smiles. "She'll be frightened with the movers so it will be wise to remove her from the scene."

"She is adorable and I'm slowly getting attached to her," I commented.

A knock on the door signaled our designer had arrived. Entering, greetings aside, she slowly looked around, turned, and said, "I'm going to have fun with this makeover."

"How's that?" Patti asked.

"Never worked on a houseboat; this is a fabulous gem. Now, tell me what it is you want done."

"Here are the floor plans. We have 2200 feet between downstairs and up," Patti began.

"Yeah, and never remodeled in over ten years, from the day I bought it," I interjected. "So, what we want is an open, airy, colorful setting."

Patti continued, "Our bedroom on the first floor is a priority. We want double-paned windows that overlook the lake, sliding doors, remote controlled motorized curtains both sheer and black out, and a walk-in closet. The current second bedroom can be integrated into the one master bedroom downstairs. We'd like, on the narrow deck outside the windows, a potted garden. In the bathroom, double sinks, and a small hot tub for two; the hot tub needs to accommodate our sizes and it's an absolute priority. Upstairs we want some of the open space converted into another bedroom and bath giving us one up and one down, and an indoor loft like a family room just off the deck."

"That's easy to do," she responded.

"The deck upstairs is where we retire to and enjoy watching the activities on the Lake. We'd like new decking, new clear glass on the railing making it easier to see the activity," I contributed. "The deck is where we go to unwind."

"What about your kitchen and front room?" she asked.

"Modernize the kitchen. Again, open, and airy. We'd like the narrow deck off the front room to hold potted plants. And the furniture must be comfortable. I don't always think modern stuff is that practical," I chirped up.

"The bottom line is open and airy, colorful and practical. We want a homey home, not a showroom display that's cold and sterile," added Patti.

"I get your message. It'll take a few days revising the floor plan. I'll get the permits and have our contractors begin within 72 hours. While that is in progress, I'll order the carpets and furniture, and kitchen appliances," the decorator added. "I'll have it scheduled so carpets and floors are done before furniture and appliances arrive. Don't need a traffic jam."

"Patti and I will find the beds we like and will advise you so they can be delivered when you need them."

"That would be great. Anything else you think I need to know, or you want done?" she asked.

"Not particularly. We're a little old-fashioned and a cold sterile home is not what we want. Harsh colors are not wanted either, maybe look at pastels. Kelly is arranging to have the bottom of the boat checked; should there be any repairs needed, we'll have the association call you directly to fit what might need to be done into your timeline. It's a requirement to have divers check the hull every 2-3 years, and it's now due."

"What about the exterior?" the decorator asked.

"It needs new siding and a new roof. I suggest using cement board for the siding and aluminum for the roof. Those will handle the weather and water well. Chose colors which are consistent with the interior. No black, purple, or bright reds please. And while we're discussing the exterior, I'd like the insulation checked in the walls and ceiling. As we live on water, it gets very damp. An R-factor 22 in the walls would be preferred and at least R-30 in the ceiling. That should make the house healthier and warmer," I said. "And I'm wondering about a plumber installing a water system to wash down the glass on our deck and the windows in our bedroom. I have seen them used at a restaurant that sat on the ocean. It would ease having to clean them."

The decorator wandered around the house, again checking both floors, measuring where necessary and making notes and diagrams. Using her measuring tape, she marked the now old carpet, we assumed delineating new corners and walls. It was fascinating watching her do her thing knowing when we return, she'll have performed her magic, giving us a new home. After about 30 minutes, she asked us if there was anything else.

"There is one small item and it relates to cost. We're not sure what the costs will be, but I'm giving you upfront money toward the total." Handing her an envelope, "Enclosed is a cashier's check for $25,000, that should be helpful in getting the work started."

"That's appreciated and unexpected. My first estimate of this job, based on what I've seen and what you want, suggests this will cover about a half or even more. When completed, I'll give you an itemized bill including the money you're giving me today. I'd like full payment within 30-60 days of completion."

"Sounds reasonable to me," I responded.

Once that had been clarified, we gave her the keys, shook hands and she departed, planning to return tomorrow afternoon and begin the makeover. Once all the work was done, I would have the task of updating our home insurances. We float on water, but insurance companies want everything set in concrete, so to speak.

"Now our decorator is gone, what packing do we do next?"

"You've got to be joking," smiling with a wide grin.

She didn't hesitate, just walked over, put her arms around my neck and began a ritual of passionate kissing, soft, long, deep. I scooped her up and carried her into our bedroom. We were slow and passionate about making love; our bodies tense with the excitement of feeling the other. The afternoon light slowly dimmed, and we didn't even notice evening settling in. Her head was snuggled next to me, her hands rubbing my chest, one of her legs over one of mine. Sleep did periodically come, but we were too excited about each other to let that interfere.

Whispering in her ear, "When would you like to get married?"

"We still have to tell our offices and most importantly, our son."

While assigned to their San Francisco office, Patti's agent-husband had been on an undercover assignment in Southern California where he was fatally identified as the law. Their son Neil Jr. had struggled through the many years his dad was away on assignments. Then his dad was killed and Neil Jr. was devastated. During my last case, she and Neil Jr. came face to face with the killer. Those conversations were traumatic but ultimately allowed healing in their disrupted lives.

"You touched my heart again."

"In what way," she responded.

Choked up, I struggled with my words. "You referred to 'our' son. I now have family, something I've always wanted."

"Yeah, I know, and it's our family."

"I just don't want Neil to see me as an interloper or someone taking his mother away from him. I want you happy, and I want him happy, and to know he is genuinely loved by the new man in your life."

She twirled her fingers through my chest hairs, "You are and always have been my only true love. Now we build what we want the way we want it, beginning with our home. We're catching up on the years we were apart."

"I know."

"Neil will love you for loving me."

We hugged and kissed and drifted off. When we awoke, it was another day. Sleep was on the thin side, but not our passions. The morning was going to be short as we had to finish packing, stuffing what we needed in our cars, including Snowball, and wait for Goodwill to arrive and clear out the old. Out with the old, in with the new. The timing was fun, as the interior decorator would arrive in the afternoon and begin the transformation.

We opted to stay at the nearby Silver Cloud Hotel. They agreed we could keep Snowball in our room, with an extra deposit in case of an accident. The hotel is a high-quality chain in the Seattle region. Family owned, it's cautious where it opens its properties and as a result, it's extremely successful. It's not far from our home and overlooks Lake Union, giving us easy access to monitor progress on our home. We wanted a room with a hot tub, but those did not overlook the Lake. Had to sacrifice something!

"Snowball's not been with me long but she's grown on me. I like having her around."

"See, your life was dull compared to what you have now!" said with her seductive smile.

"No argument and no regrets."

4

"Kelly, Tucker here. Ballistics has returned their findings. The slugs are from a military Sig Sauer Mark 25 9mm weapon. Ballistics believes a silencer was used, based on markings. That would explain why no one hears anything."

"That helps. Know who might sell such a weapon? And you say military, so someone is likely to have served or is currently in the military?"

"I'd say yes. Since guns of all types are sold by gun shops, I will have to narrow down the field to determine where it was bought and by whom. That might take a little time. Shops will have a log regarding purchase. Then we might have a clue about whether someone has a military background. Hard to make that judgment at this time. Now, here's the not-so-good news. We've just got another call about a dead homeless. Will get back to you as soon as we've checked out the scene."

Conway walked in just as I finished my call with Locklear.

"That was Tucker. They've identified the murder weapon as a military type issue Sig Sauer Mark 25 9mm. He says ballistics believes a silencer is used. And he just got a call about another dead homeless; he'll get back to us once they've checked out the scene."

"The good news and the bad. I guess that gives us our first serious lead. A military weapon with a silencer. What are we looking at, Kelly? Someone with a military background?"

"Initially, Tucker had agreed with the ME that the shooter was well trained, almost some kind of a professional. Add in what he just got back from ballistics; I say he would agree that our killer may have had some military training. Beyond that there is little more that can be surmised. Maybe we need now to plot where the killings took place to see if that might give us anything new."

"I don't think we need to waste our time doing that; we know they're spread out which, at this time, makes no sense," Conway injected. "Bluntly, the homeless are all over our city and they walk the streets, hide at night where they can't be seen, well most of the time, and go to food kitchens and missions to get warm meals. I'm not sure there's any logic to the killer's pattern if that's what it's called."

"Okay. Maybe we should visit the missions and see what they know about the murders, or at least whether there's a communication network among the homeless so they can let them know to be on the alert."

"Not a bad idea. The homeless need to partner up and not be alone at night," Conway added.

"*Real Change* is the newspaper project where homeless vendors sell copies at various locations primarily around the downtown; part of their profits support them as they work their way out of homelessness. We need to let the editor know and have him advise his vendors. They're on the street and will likely know others and can pass the word. They'll have an immediate network. They might even hear something helpful for our investigation."

We got on our computers, identified the missions, and called the editor of *Real Change*. In a few minutes we had what we needed and were about to check out when CSI called us.

"Kelly, you're not going to like this, but I think you need to come and see this. We've got four dead, not just one, all four at the same location, asleep in their bags. The encampment is located alongside the interstate. Getting here is a bit of a challenge. City personnel, who are helping with this mess, will meet you at 11th

Avenue South and South Atlantic Street and guide you along the Mountain to Sound Greenway Trail. As I said, the camp is well hidden."

"You said four? Same MO?"

"Yep!"

"Who found them?"

"That's the interesting part. Another homeless apparently looking for a friend came across them, got distressed, exited and found a lady walking her dog and asked her to call the police, then disappeared."

"Fortunate, I guess. Give us a little time, we'll be there."

"Don't hurry. This is a mess well beyond the four victims. City personnel will be helping us, and the ME, move the victims, and then our decon team will clean up and dismantle the camp. A lot of junk and garbage; and it stinks, feces type, let alone the stench of dead bodies."

Conway and I departed via the Sergeant's office.

"What's up?" he growled as we entered.

"Well good news and bad news."

"Give me the bad news first," he grumbled.

"CSI called. Four homeless found dead near the interstate. All victims in the same camp. Same MO. Sounds as if our killer is feeling more confident and upped his number of targets. CSI says it's a mess, smelly and trashed, so City personnel are being asked to help with the evacuation of bodies and the final cleanup using a decontamination team."

"How were they found?"

"Another homeless found them and asked a woman walking her dog nearby to call the police, and then immediately disappeared.

We'll visit the person who called it in."

"Okay. What's the good news?"

"CSI says ballistics has identified the weapon as a military handgun. They're going to try and identify gun shops that sell the weapon."

"Does that mean we're looking for someone in the military?" Troy asked.

"Not sure, but most likely former military."

"Keep me posted. The Chief 's not going to like this," he said grumpily.

5

"Gees, Tucker, you weren't kidding. This is a mess and man does it stink. Had no idea this is how the homeless live, more like barely survive. It's disgusting."

"Yeah, I warned you. I thought you needed to see how remote and difficult the access to this camp was, too. I'm not sure what we'll find, if anything. Regardless, this one is truly a stinking mess. Some scattered food, so I'm wondering if one of them would go out and panhandle or dumpster-dive."

"What I think is interesting," began Conway, "is how our killer knew about or found this camp. It certainly wouldn't be listed on Zillow.com."

"No, but he might have seen it from the interstate," added Tucker. "We'll keep digging; if we find anything, we'll get it to you. My report will carry all the other relevant information."

Realizing his team had plenty of work to do, we departed and walked back to where we parked. The nearby area was rather quiet with several apartment buildings, a small neighborhood food store and a couple of dumpsters at each apartment building.

We found the person who'd made the 911 report. She had been walking a small black and white dog. About seventy, short, she had a blue bandana on her head, wearing powder blue sweats and white tennis shoes. Interrupting her doggie walk, we showed her our badges, introduced ourselves and asked if we could visit. She agreed.

"We appreciate you waiting for the police to show up. May we ask your name and where you live?" pulling out my digital recorder.

"You don't use a notebook?" she inquired.

"No. Technology." smiling. "You don't mind us recording our visit, do you?"

"No."

"Our first question is, we need your name."

"Just call me Bee, Bee Wright, like opposite of wrong," smiling. She pointed. "Live in that building and was walking my little dog here, Macho."

"Our understanding is someone approached you regarding the camp. Who was it?" I asked.

"This scruffy guy, dirty and smelly ran up to me, out of breath, and pointed in the direction of those trees and said, 'call the cops, there's a dead person down there.' I wondered how he knew, but he was gone in a flash. So, I called 911."

"Just call the cops. No other information?"

"None. Just call the cops," she replied.

"Had you seen him in this area before?"

"Nope. We don't usually see anyone who doesn't live in these apartments."

"A little surprised? Weren't you scared by this confrontation?"

"Not really. Macho would protect me."

I couldn't figure why she named her little dog Macho. He was no Macho to my mind, more mellow, but she felt he would defend her and he probably would have done a decent job of at least scaring a potential attacker.

"Didn't get a name or anything?"

"Nope. Just asked me to call and said I'd be stupid going in there to see if what he said was true or not. That's a jungle in there!"

"We thank you for not going in there too. Can you describe the man any further than being scruffy, dirty and smelly? For example, how tall, weight, ethnic background, hair, eyes, anything?"

"Well, it all happened so quickly. Let's see. He was taller than me and I'm less than 5 feet 3 inches, so maybe 5 feet 9, dirty black hair, dark skin but it just might be from being outdoors as his hands were weathered and chapped. Clothing was this and that, nothing matched, jacket brown and dirty, his jeans the same. Scruffy boots with caked dirt on them. Might have been brown but with the dirt, hard to tell. Brown eyes, beard lengthy and knotted, one tooth missing the rest yellow and dirty."

"That's pretty good for such a quick encounter."

"Use to work with the police as a volunteer. Was trained to remember features."

"That's surprisingly good. If you saw him again, would you recognize him?"

"Don't know. Probably."

"If we got a sketch artist here, would you be willing to describe who you saw again to that person?"

"Can do my best. You know, memory failure, but will give it a try. Never done that before. Might be fun."

Conway meanwhile had stepped to the side and radioed for a sketch artist to come to our location, as it would be time-consuming to bring the witness to the station.

"Bee, the artist will be here in 30 minutes. Can you wait outside, or do you wish us to have him come to your apartment?" Conway asked.

"It's a nice day so I'll keep walking Macho. He likes warm weather like I do. I'll stay close to my apartment building so he can find me."

"Another question, Bee, who lives in these apartments?"

"Mostly seniors or low income, and I qualify as both. Some of us have pets and walk them a couple of times each day. Of course, we prefer sun over rain."

"There're a couple of dumpsters over there. Have you observed any of the homeless doing what we call dumpster-diving, looking for food?" Conway asked.

"Not directly but my neighbors and I have often talked about the banging of the lids at night, not a time the city is picking up trash. Maybe that's what it was."

"Okay, Bee. Conway and I have another daunting chore, interviewing everyone in the area, knocking on doors. Please excuse us. The artist will be here shortly."

Bee walked slowly off with Macho in tow. Interesting lady. Conway and I discussed how we wanted to handle the door-to-door calls.

"Usual questions? Do you think we'll learn much more than what Bee has told us?" Conway asked.

"Not sure, but we have to do it anyway. Part of the drill. We've got some large apartment buildings, though; let's call and see if we can get some help," I added.

Conway made the call. Two patrol officers were redirected to our location and would be given the task to ask if anyone had seen anything unusual over the past few days, if they were aware of the homeless camp nearby, did they see anyone dumpster-dive or were there any suspicious cars or persons in the area.

"You know, Kelly, that encampment is well hidden. I think the killer stalked the victims, determining how he was going to get in and out without being seen by all these apartment dwellers."

"Agreed, and we need to let the officers know if they find out anything about a strange car in the area, to identify where it was seen. It'll be hard knowing whether it was the killer's car or a hiker's car," I offered.

"Even if someone saw a car, hearing that is interesting, but unless we have a description and a license plate number, it's rather a useless piece of information," Conway concluded.

We chatted briefly with the officers about the car issue and bid them well as they embarked on their laborious interviews. Bee connected with the sketch artist; she took him to her apartment so Macho could get something to drink. We asked the artist to let us know when he had a sketch. Thanking Bee, we embarked on knocking on doors in her apartment building; the other officers took the other two buildings. The usual questions were asked whether they had seen anyone suspicious around the area at night, or a suspicious car. The answers were unanimous; no one had seen or heard anything at any time at night, except the dumpster lids periodically being banged.

On our way back to the office, Conway observed, "If Bee is good at giving the artist a good likeness, maybe other homeless will recognize him."

"That's my hope. We need to find ways of getting the artist's rendition into the homeless network."

"We should start with the *Real Change* newspaper and their networks, then the missions. Maybe someone will recognize the guy we're looking for."

"Then to find anyone who saw anything at that hour of the night driving along the interstate; the camp site is hidden and the killer no doubt wore black. In other words, invisible. Doubt that would be a productive avenue to explore," I observed.

"I'd agree with you on that one; however, we still need to ask the media to broadcast an appeal, essentially to cover our search for the killer. I think it's a waste of time but needs to be done."

"Dot those I's and cross those T's."

"Kelly, I keep asking myself what is driving this person to kill? And why the homeless?"

"Those are tough questions; killing's an insane act regardless of who the victims are."

"Do you think he's targeting the homeless because they are homeless, some kind of irrational motive to reduce homelessness in our city?" asked Conway.

"Possibly but unlikely. The killer's irrational and rationalizes or fabricates a reason for doing what he's doing. What's happening makes no sense to us at this point and may not make sense to him either."

"We now have nine dead men in what, a little over a five-week period. This incremental jump killing four; what caused such a change?" added Conway.

"That I can't answer. But since CSI has identified the kind of weapon being used, we at least have that as our first possible lead. Motive unclear but the MO similar, just the number killed at one time changed. We have nothing else to work with," I surmised.

6

There are several smaller missions in the City but two major ones serving the homeless, well, the operative words are "really trying." The numbers are overwhelming with well over 7,000 each evening living on the streets, in cars, tents or RVs. The missions are full, with just over 3,000 beds. And the situation is only getting worse; Seattle is ranked third in the U.S., behind New York and Los Angeles, for its homeless population. Daily, the missions serve hot food and, in the evenings, provide a sleeping area. For those wishing to regain their lives, missions provide temporary housing as residents progress through rehabilitation and job training programs along with counseling and support groups. The Seattle Union Gospel Mission, for example, has volunteer dentists caring for their residents' teeth as well as lawyers offering pro bono services to help the homeless with whatever baggage they carry. The Gospel Mission has a different location to accommodate women with or without children. These missions are a haven from abuse or homelessness while they work on regaining their strength or finishing their rehab. Many in rehabilitation are successful, while others stumble and don't make it.

Church groups and nonprofits gather warm clothing for distribution. Some provide warm food or sandwiches and water to those on the street. In the inclement winter weather, the City of Seattle asks many of its downtown businesses that have large lobbies, no businesses or shops on the first level, and security personnel, to open those lobbies and get the homeless out of the freezing cold. There are plenty of efforts to find or provide shelter for the homeless, assist with job training or reach out in other humanitarian ways to heal the many wounded walking the streets. Many cities, like Seattle, have these outreach efforts yet the homeless populations continue to grow with no easy explanation as to why.

Addictions consume many lives and overcoming those habits only complicates restoring lives. They can't stay sober, don't have an ID therefore don't qualify for social services, have dirty clothing and lousy hygiene, few job skills or just can't find work because they drink, are undependable or mentally ill. Their futures are bleak. Like the Biblical story of the Good Samaritan, most walk on the other side of the street to avoid contact with the homeless. Boy, that makes them feel good; doesn't help their self-image or self-esteem either. Now a killer is ravaging their population for unknown reasons.

Conway and I met up with the gospel mission director.

"We're grateful," I began, "for what your mission is doing to mitigate the pain and hunger in the lives of the homeless."

"Thanks. It's not an easy task nor do results come easily. They're humans to be valued, even if they are in the grip of addiction or mental illness. We try to encourage them, motivate them so they can become self-reliant," said Reverend Carlos Fernandez, head of the Gospel Mission.

"Seeing so many homeless daily must be discouraging," I responded.

"Yes and no. We know we're keeping them warm and fed. We're here to answer their questions or address a specific need. For those who enter our programs to tackle their addictions, we see great resolve on their part to clean up their act, find employment and get their own place. They confront their personal demons and from those battles comes hope and personal achievements. The others are just not ready to address their issues. And of course, we have few facilities that can handle those who are mentally ill."

"That has to be frustrating?"

"No question. For whatever reason, the homeless find themselves on the street in a battle to survive; they have all kinds of issues and find themselves ostracized because their illness cannot be easily treated without their own commitment to make changes. Some have resigned themselves to the street. We have one older guy out there who pushes a cart and says he's been on the streets for 15 years, and more than likely, will die there too. So many give up and feel it's easier than having to tackle their personal demons."

"What kind of a success rate do you have rehabilitating them and their not returning to the street?" I asked.

"We work hard to find jobs for those in our program so when they leave our facility, they have someplace to start rebuilding their lives. Specifically, if we can retain a client for at least 9 or more months, get them sober, clean up their teeth, teach them job skills and employment interviewing, dress them for success so to speak, and address their baggage, we see about a 95% success rate in the homeless no longer continuing their homelessness or being captive to their addictions. Another way to look at it is only 5% ever return to the street. Reasons are not always clear, but have a lot to do with their self-confidence, self-esteem, things we try to work on when they're in our program. Some are simply scared of success, successfully finishing their rehab and finding themselves on their own again."

"That's amazing!"

"Yeah, but we see more and more new faces. We wish we could see a decrease in those being homeless, but as soon as we graduate some, we see 5 new faces. It's an unending cycle of despair, hopelessness, brokenness in body and spirit. But Jesus asks us to feed those who are hungry, give water to the thirsty, and clothe those who are naked. We try to fulfill that, as do all the other missions."

"You're to be commended. What we want you to know, if you have not already read about them, that homeless men have been killed over the past week by an unknown assailant. We have no clue why this is happening, or why the homeless."

"Yeah, I've seen the stories in the newspaper. Any idea what's going on?"

"No. But we have a witness working with a police artist, regarding a homeless person who approached her while walking her dog, to say there had been a murder back in the woods and to call the cops. She did just that. Now we're looking for that person so we can interview him, see what he might have seen."

"Sounds promising," he added.

"It's if we can find him. He's not a suspect, just someone we need to talk to about what he saw and why it spooked him. We'll get the composite photo to you to pass around. We need a name and where we can find this man. So far, no one seems to have heard or seen anything. We know the killings take place in the early morning hours, but nothing more. That's why we are stumped."

"We'll give it a try. But I can assure you the homeless often use nicknames, don't like giving out their real name, and seldom tell you where they're living, or more like camped out. So, it may be difficult."

"We've got to give it a try," I responded.

"Safety among the homeless in light of what's happing is a concern to us," began Conway. "We would like to ask you to share with your clients the need to pair up and be alert to anything abnormal near or around wherever they camp or sleep, if not here at the mission. Those who crash away from the others, in hidden or isolated sites, may be the most vulnerable."

"We can do that."

Having completed one visit, we had to cross to the other side of the downtown area to sit down with the editor of *Real Change*.

"We need your help, and access to your networks," I began. "As of right now, we have 9 homeless murdered by an unknown assailant for unknown reasons."

"We've been watching those stories; a little scary. Any idea who's behind this? And what is it you want from us?" he responded.

"No clue who's behind these murders. But that is why we are here, to first ask you to run a photo, a composite sketch we're getting from a woman who was approached by a homeless male while walking her dog, asking her to call the cops as there was someone dead within the nearby trees. No name, nothing. We don't want to arrest him; just need to talk with him to ask what he saw and whether he might have more to offer. We'll get the sketch to you as soon as it's available."

"We can do that. Is there a name attached to the photo?"

"No; we understand they go by nicknames more than their real name. No clue who this person is or where he lives. We are working with little and need all the help we can get at this point. Maybe someone who reads your newspaper will know this guy, be willing to arbitrate a meeting. Our perpetrator is using the homeless as targets for reasons we do not understand."

"We'll let our vendors know what's happening and will run the photo in our forthcoming issue, front cover," he offered. "We'll use our office as a contact point for anyone who knows this guy or for that matter, should the guy wish to contact us directly. That's safer than calling the cops."

"We agree. No need to spook him."

We left his office knowing he was going to help in whatever manner he could. He said the safety tip would also be part of his communications with his vendors. Double up, be alert, and be on the lookout for anything out of the ordinary.

On our way back to the office, Conway raised a critical point.

"Kelly, we've had some great and insightful conversations about the homeless and homelessness here in Seattle. But we aren't any closer to identifying the killer than we were yesterday. I think we need a profiler! We need our friendly Forensic Psychologist to take what we have and see what she comes up with that we can work with."

"And your thinking is?" I responded.

"We don't know who we're looking for. Simple. No clues except dead bodies, and what the ME and CSI have found, and now the ballistics result."

"Rather thin stuff for sure."

We got back to the office, called our Sergeant, putting him on speaker phone.

"Sergeant, we'd like to ask Dr. Caitlan Ward for her help in profiling our killer. Can we get approval to engage her services?"

"Your reason?"

"We don't know who we're looking for. The only evidence we have is what forensics has told us about the weapon being military. Thought her insights might be helpful with what little we have. It always seems like my cases have little to nothing to begin with."

"Sort of the nature of homicides. They don't autograph their work, well usually. Okay, let's see what miracles Dr. Ward can generate," he agreed.

The Sergeant arranged a meeting with Dr. Caitlin Ward, a Forensic Psychologist from the University of Washington. We've used her before on several baffling cases. Her research and expertise focus on the mental state likely to contribute to homicidal tendencies. Well credentialed, a full professor, published and a frequent consultant, she's been on the University's faculty for nearly fifteen years. With brilliant red hair, she's tall and beautiful, disarming her intellectual depth and intense talents. We agreed to meet her at her campus office the next day.

7

The University grounds, filled with brilliant vegetation, trees, flowers, grasses, and a magnificent Arboretum, are wedged between Interstate 5 on its west side and Lake Washington on its east side. 634 acres accommodating over 30,000 students. Its football stadium is one of two in the United States accessible by boat; game day brings a multitude of yachts tied to a boom giving boaters access to the game site, and, of course, tail-gating parties.

"Dr. Ward, thank you for agreeing to work with us again."

"My pleasure, Kelly, and good to see you again too," she replied. "Please call me Caitlin."

"I love it when I have to walk across the grounds to get to your office. Beautiful and serene. But we're not sightseeing as you well know." I continued.

"So, what do you have for me this time, or maybe I should say what don't you have?"

"We're puzzled by the murders of the homeless men, and as to who might be committing them. You've no doubt seen the stories in the newspapers. Six things are apparent in our summary sheet (handed to her). First, the targets are homeless men. Why exclusively them we don't know, and there's no visible pattern to the killing sites either. Second, their individual locations are hidden, as are their encampments. The homeless try to remain invisible. The recent encampment of four homeless was found near the interstate next to the Mountain to Sound hiking corridor. The killer had to really look for that site and scope it out. Third, the victims were wrapped in their sleeping bags. Our CSI people feel that in some cases knowing which end the head was positioned would have been difficult, yet the killer hasn't missed his mark. Fourth, each victim was killed with one bullet to the head. The shooter is accurate and lethal. Fifth, no one has reported hearing or seeing anything, so we're suspecting the use of a silencer, which forensics now confirms as well. Sixth, no spent shell cases were found at any of the sites; the sites were policed, nothing was left behind; and finally, based on the ballistic tests of recovered slugs from the victims, our CSI guys believe the weapon is a military type handgun. This is not public information at this time."

"I agree, isn't much to go on; but let's look at several things. First, the homeless. As of two days ago, the coordinated "point-in-time" count identified over 11,000 homeless in Seattle and King County, and it just continues to grow. The ones on the streets at night are vulnerable, exposed, and defenseless; some consider them trash, the worthless dredges of our society. In fact, there're those, I am sure, who've seen the news reports and are saying good riddance. Sad, as they're humans, too. Why he's narrowed in on the homeless is currently unknown. Strange as it may seem, our perpetrator may see his actions as a solution for homelessness; however, I'm inclined to believe he's simply targeting them for some delusional reason."

"The numbers are bigger than I thought. Not very encouraging," I commented.

"No, it's not," she replied.

"We've thought about what you said, which is rather farfetched but unlikely," responded Conway. "We're leaning more toward the delusional reason. Do you think this is a conscious or subconscious act?"

"That's hard to know but if delusional or irrational, my suspicions are subconscious. He or she is obsessed with the homeless, making them the brunt of his or her irrational behaviors. You said the weapon was a military type handgun. With the other data you have, my guess is the user is familiar with its weight and when fired, how it reacts. If, as you suspect, a silencer is used, he's familiar with that tool as well. Knowing how the weapon responds, he's able to keep track of the spent shells and with only one shot per victim, he doesn't have much to retrieve."

"Are you confirming the perpetrator is military?" I asked.

"No, not necessarily. Anyone trained with firearms could shoot this weapon with a significant degree of expertise. It's possible the perpetrator may have learned his skills in the military. The combination of hidden encampments, one shot and no shells left behind might suggest someone who is highly trained, lethally trained, maybe with a black ops background in the military."

"What are the 'black ops' you're referring to?" Conway asked.

"In the military, these are operations they usually don't speak about publicly. These missions are usually classified, off the record, not spoken about much. You're aware of the Green Berets and Airborne; well, there are units, similar in nature, assigned to do serious damage to the enemy, usually behind their lines of operation. We had such secretive units operating during the Vietnam War, in Laos and Cambodia, and no doubt have them today, in Iraq and Afghanistan. Those in such units have had special lethal training. And their orders are to commit actions to disrupt enemy endeavors, whatever those are. Their missions are secret, and for the enemy, deadly."

"And you surmise that from what little we have?"

"In a sense, yes. I'm confirming your perpetrator is well trained. His or her actions and accuracy are indicative of a highly skilled assassin. He's trained to be a stealth operator; no one sees anything, hears anything, or finds anything except dead bodies. Your perpetrator is dangerous."

Jokingly I said, "Doubt that'll make me sleep any better

tonight. So, why is this perpetrator doing what he or she does?" I asked.

"Kelly, I can only suggest and try to profile a likely scenario for what is happening. But I don't know why per se, currently. My thinking is your perpetrator is most likely mentally ill. Why he or she picked the homeless may be tied to a reenactment of what they've done before, elsewhere, during black ops or similar settings. He or she is probably delusionary, living in a world in which they cannot adjust. And if mentally ill, doing things they can't explain."

"You're suggesting someone who is now or was military trained to be some kind of an assassin?"

"Possibly. Until you capture your perpetrator, who really knows who he or she is or what kind of a background they have, or what has made them go on a killing spree. He or she will continue to do whatever it is that's driving them."

"You're saying others may be targeted as well?" asked Conway.

"Yes. Your perpetrator is ill. He or she is a killer, 9 down, more to come," she replied.

"That's not encouraging," I injected.

"No, it's not. I think you can expect him to strike again. The killing sites are random, spread around the city. The killer may see this as a means of keeping you off balance, not knowing where he will strike next. From that point of view, he's being successful. You know he strikes in the early morning hours. But you have no way of finding where he is. You're working blindly against the clock. There's nothing good about what he's doing. For the moment he's focused on the homeless; let's hope he doesn't change his target audience."

"Why do you say that Caitlin?"

"Kelly, if the killer changes populations, we have a major complication. One targeted audience allows us to focus but if he opens up on others within our community, we have the potential of mass hysteria and the ruthless evasiveness of 'why'."

"Are we dealing with a deranged serial killer?"

"Yes. You have multiple murders over several weeks; I would call that the work of a serial killer. He may not see himself that way. He's a deadly threat, pardon my pun," said with a faint smile. "As I said, he or she knows what they're doing, and it's planned down to the minutest details."

"Suggesting?" I inserted.

"Linear, methodical, obsessive, focused, destructive thinking and behavior. They've done it before and will continue to do it. They're motivated for whatever reason. As I said, they get in and out, and do what needs to be done, or at least what they think must be done."

And the weapon?" I asked.

"I don't think just anyone gets a military type weapon and is as accurate as this with their hits, unless they were military, professionally trained to do that kind of killing. That's why I mentioned black ops training or something just as lethal."

"Why couldn't it be almost anyone as earlier noted? Conway asked.

"It could, but I don't think it is. Too much pointing the other way."

"So, we're looking for someone, at this point we've not determined if he or she, in or out of the military, trained to do some nasty stuff."

"That's one way to look at it, Kelly. You need to look for someone currently in, or who's been in, a combat trained unit with these kinds of demanding skills. Like sniper training. My guess would be Delta Force, Special Forces, or SEALS. We found that those who were highly trained to crawl through the tunnels in Vietnam, simply put, it messed with their heads. After being in dark tunnels with enemy soldiers passing almost at arm's length, they were easily spooked, and adjustment after the military was horrendous, exceedingly long and difficult at best. Those trained for such operations go behind enemy lines, carry out whatever their orders dictate, which usually is pretty bloody, and leave unseen. Only the dead are left behind. As I said, we did it in Vietnam, Laos and Cambodia. So, it's possible we've had the same occurring during Desert Storm, Iraq, and Afghanistan."

Being a smart-aleck, I replied, "Well that leaves us with a few hundred thousand soldiers to investigate in the Northwest."

"It may not be that bad, Kelly. Joint Base Lewis-McCord had Delta Forces stationed there in the past. I'm not sure about the present. I'm sure their Commanding Officer would be open to finding this person who's bringing discredit to the Army, assuming the killer is former Army and not Marines or Navy or something else. I just hope he doesn't get tied up with having to go through the Pentagon. That would be a timing disaster. But I have another thought. Many soldiers who've returned from combat are being treated by the VA for what's called PTSD, post-traumatic stress disorder. PTSD can be caused by a physical, emotional, or psychological trauma. Contact their administrator, I'm sure he'll put you in touch with their medical staff handling those cases. The treatment of PTSD became a serious effort beginning around 1989. Research prior to that was done at Dartmouth on returning Vietnam vets, but not until 1989, nearly twenty years later, did it get full attention. It's a complicated ailment and not easily diagnosed nor treated. And that's the key word, 'treated.' It can't be fixed or cured, as the events from which the person suffers remain with them, physically, mentally or emotionally, the rest of their lives."

"How does PTSD affect those individuals?" I asked.

"That's the complicated nature of the disease. Trained

psychologists use therapy groups to work with those diagnosed with PTSD, to help them express their frustrations and anger, and then guide them with resources and skills they can use to structure a more productive life. In civilian life, they don't have the structure of the military to reinforce them. For those physically injured, the trauma is real, and rehabilitation takes time. Without a visible injury, the challenge is even greater, as what's being suffered is in their heads and hard to get at, recognize or resolve. The veteran will often say 'you don't understand' or 'you didn't see the horrors I saw' or 'how can you understand something you can't feel.' As I said, it's complicated."

"How do you see this playing out?" I asked.

"Not good, until you capture the killer. Capture him then treat him; the latter will take the rest of his life. And you may never know why he did what he did. We're talking irrational, delusionary actions from a mentally ill person."

"That's not much encouragement."

"Remember, Kelly, if the killer is former military, the military and its veteran services have a responsibility to do what they can to heal those devastating wounds. We always talk about war and combat, but being there sometimes is no different than being here. They just can't escape the grip of what they did and saw. That's PTSD; it cripples veterans, ruins lives and marriages and in some cases, hospitalizes the veteran."

"When I was an MP, I saw these guys come home all messed up. It was hard to describe or explain what I saw except messed up lives."

"So, you've had a glimpse at what might be the issue. Now as for Lewis-McCord and the VA, I don't know what you'll find but I'm hoping they'll be cooperative. Regardless, I can assure you the killer will strike again; my guess is he's playing out something terribly dreadful and using the homeless as his targets, possibly reminding him of what he saw and did overseas. If he's military, former or present, my professional guess is he's mentally ill, delusionary, isolated, and unpredictable, not a narcissist or psychopath. Nothing indicates that. Not a lot of help I have no doubt, but you're up against a killer working within a mindset none of us have experienced. As you said, Kelly, you've seen the worst exposed in those returning from combat."

"Yeah, and that scares me too, for he'll strike anytime, anywhere against anyone. 143 square miles of City can be a challenge."

We thanked her for her candidness and analysis and departed.

"Wow, what a bleak prognosis," began Conway.

"She's focused and to the point. We've got a crazy killing people. She's definitely given us more to work with, however, in suggesting we're looking for someone with deadly military training," I added.

"What do we do with this profile now?" asked Conway.

"I think we take her recommendation and contact both the Army and the VA and see what we can find," I replied. I knew full well we had a challenge in trying to find an elusive killer with no obvious reason or pattern to what he or she was doing except using the homeless as their target.

I then called the ME.

"Charlie, what did you find from these four dead homeless?"

"Nothing new. All dead. One shot each, to the head. I've removed the slugs but guess they will be like our previous finds. Not dead that long, maybe 8 to 12 hours before being found. Could've been longer had someone not found them. They sure did stink, too, dead and decaying. But they stunk like their encampment, feces smells. No hygiene habits."

"Thanks," I replied and clicked off.

We had a message from the sketch artist: the composite drawings were on our desks. He confirmed Bee Wright felt the composite was "right on". I suggested to Conway we distribute them to the missions and *Real Change*; I also suggested we put out a BOLO (be on the lookout) to our patrols. Maybe someone would spot him, but I wasn't holding my breath.

8

His physical wounds were healing nicely, though there was a profusion of scarring from bullet holes and shrapnel damage. For months, he'd been cared for by the hospital, given no duty, but enjoyed three free meals a day, a roof over his head, and a soft rack to sleep on. The bed certainly was better than sleeping on the desert floor. When it was time, there wasn't any celebration; he was given his discharge from the Army and wished well. They said he would be embarking on a new dream, a new journey as a civilian; now, though, he was lost in a world he didn't recognize. He found a place to live and took a week to find a job at Costco as a greeter, a little below overseeing a platoon.

He walks a long distance to work to get his exercise, and each day returns to his quiet one-bedroom apartment. He does little outside of work; he has no friends, no family; he doesn't even like to chat with his work colleagues. He's still not well, but in a manner he is unfamiliar with. He was ordered to enroll in a therapy group at the VA when he left Lewis-McCord, to handle the trauma of his physical wounds. He did what they ordered; he's with the program and though his physical wounds are healing, no one understands his nightly agony.

His head explodes with vibrant flashing lights, visions and sounds bouncing off the walls 24/7 in his tormented brain. They're not to be silenced. Restless at night, he finds sleep an evasive commodity. He's no longer overseas but the craziness and insanity, the haunting quietness of killing in the dark, remains with him. No one knows or understands what he's struggling with. No one hears the voices, the commands, or sees his visions. No one can perceive what's happening or explain it away. All their medical terms and hocus pocus do nothing for him. No one gave him advance warning, when he joined the Army, his life would forever change. It sucks!

Learning his lesson from past bloody missions, he now carefully and methodically stalks his enemy targets and observes their comings and goings. Cognizant of the elements and surroundings, he weighs the risks he's taking, mapping a way into their operational zone, doing what he must do, and exiting without a sound; it's a stealth operation, and he knows he's good at it. It was time to focus, make ready for moving out. Until then, he stares at the wall in his command center where combat maps hang, markings of successful missions and pending maneuvers, identification of enemy strongholds and choke points, future evasive strategic maneuvers, and notes about other targets under surveillance.

Once his mission is complete, he'll return, and as with all his operations, discard the retrieved shells, put his field clothing in a bag to be washed, and take a shower.

9

My cell rang, the screen telling me it was Patti.

"What a pleasant surprise. What's up?"

"Are you sitting down?"

"Well yes. We just got back to the office."

"Coming in tonight on a flight from San Diego is our son. He called to surprise me and asked if I could meet him at the airport. I'm not sure what to do! He's coming!"

You could hear her excitement. A long-overdue reunion, considering the past weeks.

"That's great, Honey!"

"Yeah, but he knows nothing about you. I'm nervous."

"Don't worry. It'll be okay. I'll book him a room at the Silver Cloud. What time is he arriving?"

"6:30."

"Okay. Do this. You meet him at the airport; take your time bringing him to Daniel's Broiler near our hotel. I'll meet you there say, 8 pm, and will have a reservation. He's coming to get time with his Mom and that's what he'll get, plus a little more if that works for you."

"I know I'm being a mush but don't want him hurt or disappointed or whatever."

"Don't worry, Sweetheart. He called you for a reason and I'm sure it relates to the both of you having resolved Neil's murder and its impact in your lives. He wants, maybe needs, obviously, to see and be with you."

"Okay, if you say so. You're my love and all I want is for him to accept and love you."

"He's a grown man and he'll love you even more because you're taking care of yourself. We'll be okay, trust me. See you at Daniel's Broiler. They have great steaks and good wines, too. I love you."

"And I love you too," clicking off.

"Trust me" was a little bit of an exaggeration. I had no clue how our meeting would turn out, but at least I said something to give Patti confidence; as for me, my stomach was now in knots. How situations change so rapidly. I looked across to Conway and filled him in on what was happening, and called Daniel's Broiler asking for a booth for 8 pm, overlooking the water.

Spending time with Caitlin was, as usual, insightful. She had given us her opinion based on what little we had, and some directions for us to pursue. I decided to call it a day and suggested to Conway he do the same and go take care of his Mommy-to-be. I was planning to go to the hotel, shower, change, and confirm that a room had been reserved for our son, a suite if possible, overlooking Lake Union.

It was fluster time, something I haven't experienced for a while. What do I wear for meeting my fiancée's son, our son? Showered, I stood looking at the small closet and what we were able to bring along with us and decided to go casual. No choice. Light tan Docker pants, a plain blue button-down shirt, and a blue blazer. No tie and cordovan loafers with no tassels and dark brown socks. On with the English Leather and I was ready to go. Snowball wanted some attention, food and water, so she got just that. Then I had to brush her fur off my blazer. It wasn't far to walk, so that's what I did. Patti would have a car so we could return together later. The lights were glimmering across the lake from all the shoreline businesses. There was traffic but I didn't hear it, I was too preoccupied with what to say, how to greet him - and her. Can't plan this one, Kelly. Just let it be what it will be, I mused.

As I drew close to Daniel's, I saw Patti with a tall young man, her son Neil, and he's holding hands with a beautiful girl. Now I was confused.

"Hey Kelly, guess who surprised who? I want you to meet our son Neil and his fiancée Susan Webster," Patti said with a broad smile and excitement in her voice. Then in front of everyone, she reached up, putting her hands on my chest, and kissed me gently saying, "You're fine and I love you."

I went to shake Neil's hand, but he gave me a hug instead. I turned to Susan and she hugged me, too. The hugs were certainly unexpected. Then I just stood looking at them, admiring them and eager to hear about their lives, as well as to share ours. After all these weeks and the many conversations between them, I was meeting our son for the first time; Patti obviously knew him and what he was growing up to be like, but for me, it was my first impressive encounter with a son I would come to love so deeply.

"What a totally unexpected greeting. Welcome to Seattle," I said. "Your Mom and I have certainly been excited about you coming. And Susan, what a wonderful surprise."

"I know I didn't give you much warning," Neil responded.

"Doesn't matter. You both are here is what's important. Our reservation is waiting so let's go in and we can continue our conversations. We have a lot to share."

"And so do we," added Neil as he squeezed Susan's hand.

We began to walk in; the timing was great as my butterflies were trying to settle. Patti took my hand and looked up at me with her beautiful smile and glistening eyes. Her touch was warm and reassuring. Inside, we were seated with an exquisite view of Lake

Union. I slid into the booth next to Patti at the window; she was sitting across from Susan and I was across from Neil.

Once situated, we began to talk, you know, how was your flight, did you meet anyone interesting, how was traffic, all those superficial questions that keep people apart but gives them a feeling of communicating. Water, menus and some bread were delivered. We ordered a light appetizer to accompany our marvelous conversation; my weakness: artichoke hearts, spinach and parmesan cheese dip with colored chips. There was so much to be said we were almost stumbling over one another.

"A rather quick decision to fly up and see your Mom?" I asked.

"It was. We decided last night to come as our studies and commitments were giving us a brief break. So, we looked at each other and said, 'why not'. And here we are," he replied. "Surprising Mom with a call saying we were landing in a few hours seems to have been a round of surprises for all of us," began Neil.

"When your Mom called to tell me of your plans, she was in absolute panic mode; well I guess you can say I was as well, but I assured her you needed to see her and everything would be okay," I offered.

"Well you were right. With all the stuff about my Father's murderer, I felt I needed to see Mom for two reasons. First, to complete our conversations about Dad. Second, and probably at this point even more important, introducing Susan to her. To my surprise, Mom and you are now a thing too."

"Have you met Susan's parents yet?" I asked.

"Oh yes," Susan quickly responded. "He charmed them, and they readily feel in love with him."

"That's great, and your timing coming here is excellent. Your Mom and I had lots of intense conversations regarding your dad and his unsolved murder; the resolution, though, I knew opened old wounds."

"It may have done that, Kelly, but not knowing who did it or why was draining Mom and me more than we admitted until that evening, we talked, and talked."

"Yeah, I know about that night. Your Mom showed up at 3 in the morning knocking on my houseboat front door, letting it all spill out. Got her some blankets, coffee and food and by morning was able to send her home."

"Yeah, he was quite the gentleman. He even encouraged me to call in and take the day off, which I did," added Patti.

"Kelly, thank you for your instincts that led to the capture of my dad's murderer."

"It's a long story, but there were too many 'coincidences' in my case, coupled with what your dad was involved in, that I just couldn't believe were unrelated. I don't believe in coincidences; pursuing those instincts paid off," I added.

"More like a S.W.A.G.," injected Patti with a cute chuckle.

"What's a S.W.A.G?" asked Susan.

"Sweet, wild-ass guess," I responded. "It's my way of saying my instincts have no clue what or where we're going but we have to follow."

"Well, I'm impressed," remarked Neil, as we all chuckled.

"Mom told me about you at the airport. Of course, it's hard not to miss the ring she's wearing. This was after I surprised her, introducing her to her, your, soon-to-be daughter-in-law."

"Surprises tonight brings joy to our lives," I philosophized. "When did you and Susan get engaged?"

"I asked Susan formally a week ago. We've been together for three years, meeting initially in one of our classes. It was love at first sight. She's been so wonderfully supportive and helpful during those bleak days."

"Neil is being modest," inserted Susan. She has such an animated face, warm smile and a relaxed presence, it was obvious why Neil had fallen in love with her. "The venting of all those repressed emotions made our relationship stronger. I love him in so many ways I cannot begin to number."

Patti commented, "Seeing you at the airport, the tears of happiness I had suppressed, flowed. You are okay and obviously with Susan in your life, more than okay. What a wonderful surprise," looking into her son's eyes. "I was nervous about you coming so quickly without me preparing you for what Kelly and I have."

"You needn't be, Mom. I suspected you would eventually find someone. When did he ask you to marry him?"

"Romantically at Roche Harbor, north of here in the San Juan Islands, several weeks ago. We flew there on a float plane, one of those you'll see taking off on the lake (pointing out the window) and he surprised me with a week's holiday together. Mid-week, we were cuddling on our hotel deck and he slipped me the ring, only after telling me the week was the honeymoon we'd never had. We were high school sweethearts here in Seattle. When I was assigned back here I was excited, but had no clue Kelly and I would reignite our love."

"I didn't know you were high school sweethearts. But Mom, it looks good on you, in fact on the both of you."

"Yeah, we separated for some strange reasons after high school. But Kelly's case brought us together professionally and kindled the long-lost feelings we shared in high school."

Neil asked, "What are your plans?"

"None yet. A lot going on so we're taking our time. What are your plans?" she responded.

"I would like to be a June bride," began Susan, "but that may be pushing it with graduation coming up soon and my kid brother in the Navy. He's part of the Navy's carrier strike group stationed off the Korean Peninsula and being on a destroyer, not likely to be shipped back to the US while in dangerous waters. We've talked about a lot of options but haven't made any final plans."

Patti said, "Neil's dad and I got married right after graduation. We were off to work within weeks for an extensive 20-week training program with the Bureau. Our honeymoon was spent at Quantico, if that's exciting."

"Did you or dad get your yellow bricks?

Surprised by Neil's question, Patti asked, "How do you know about the yellow brick? And yes, we did, and I have them in a box somewhere."

"I read a little about agency training and found the yellow brick award for surviving the 6.1-mile physical endurance route designed by the Marines interesting. Where are you planning to live?" Neil responded.

She squeezed my hand under the table and rubbed her leg against mine. "Kelly bought a houseboat a decade ago and that's where we'll live. We'll show it to you, but currently it's being renovated, first time ever. We decided to make it our home with our stuff and our designs and colors. New roof, new siding, new furniture, a more open and airy feeling, its 2200 square feet currently with two bedrooms on the first floor; that's going to change. Living room, dining room and kitchen also on first floor. On the second level is a loft, open area being converted into a bedroom and bath, and a luscious deck overlooking Lake Union, overlooking what you see out this window. Beyond that, our only thoughts have been to attend your graduation. Kelly and I have been twenty-years in search of each other and now we found each other and do not intend to miss a single exciting day of our future together, or yours." Pausing, she continued "And you and Susan are welcome to come and stay with us anytime in the future."

"That would be cool, staying with you. I think I know what you mean, Mom. I've never seen you this happy and excited, even with Dad. I know you loved him as you love me, but Kelly, you've brought something absolutely terrific out of Mom and given her a new gleam in her eyes."

As he was saying those words to his Mom, she squeezed my hand again under the table. It was time to order as we had consumed the appetizer. Orders were taken and our conversations continued.

"Your Mom and I have arranged a suite overlooking the water for you in the same hotel where we're staying not far from the houseboat. Not knowing about you, Susan, being a part of his life, we made a good call. A suite with free breakfast, our gift for however long you wish to stay."

"As Kelly mentioned, I pounded on his houseboat front door when I needed a friend. Sat in his front room but could not remember anything about his place the next day. He just took care of me when I was a mess."

With teary eyes, Neil replied, "Yeah, I know and can see he loves you deeply, Mom. Susan held me that night so tight; she wasn't about to let loose. While we talked Mom, she was next to me the whole time and heard every word and saw every tear. I love her for being there when I needed her as you were for Mom, Kelly."

I saw him hesitate a moment, clasp Susan's hand and look me dead in the eyes.

"It's been difficult these past few years after my Dad's murder. More like anger, who would do this, why, and destroy lives, a family. Mom and Dad worked hard making a family in the business they were in. But after Dad's murder, I knew there would come another day when Mom and I would be moving on, beginning anew. For me, Susan crashed through my walls of anger and resentment and gave me hope and a more positive perspective on life. In other words, she helped me get my act together." He chuckled. "I also knew, Mom, that someday your life would change, and another man would be a part of our family. I just didn't know it was going to be Kelly, your high school sweetheart. But I'm glad it is."

He paused again, putting his hand up to stop his Mother from saying anything.

"Mom knows nothing, nor does Susan, of what's about to be said nor did I ask her permission," pausing, then said, "As I said, I knew this day would come and Mom would find another. Only I had no idea it would be this wonderful for the both of you. You both are deeply in love and it's visible. And I love my Mom for all she has been to and for me. Tonight, we are celebrating new beginnings, Mom, you and Kelly, Susan and I."

He paused again before continuing.

Patti and I shared a smile, squeezed hands under the table and I think finally relaxed. Meeting our son was a more powerful encounter than I had anticipated, a resolution to my own frustrations of not having gone after Patti or, until now, not being part of a family. My heart was pounding, my head swirling with joy, happiness, and wonder.

"Kelly, I see a lot of my Dad in you just in this very brief time together."

"That's what your Mother told me too," I injected. "I'm flattered."

"But you're now my Mom's fiancé and soon-to-be husband, making me your son as well. I'm scared to say this, and know, well, there hasn't been much time, but then again, rebuilding a family takes great care and bold moves. There's no timeline for this either."

"You sound like a skilled marriage counselor," I quipped. Neil smiled and laughed.

"Well I may be. Mom and Dad worked hard under a lot of duress to make our family work. Now I've grown up and Susan is part of my life, our lives, and you Kelly, are now with my Mom and part of my life. So, Kelly, enough of the bull and delays. I've done a lot of thinking about what I am about to say. (pausing) You're my new dad and it would be an honor to call you Dad, as in Mom and Dad."

Was that a lightning strike? Did I hear him correctly? He wants me to be his "Dad"? Whew! At first, Patti was simply stunned. I wasn't expecting that! Heck, we only formally met an hour earlier. Emotions climbed my throat. What he said, what he asked, took my breath away. Thought he would always call me Kelly, safe and distant from his own dad. Wow. I'm just a pushover as tears ran down my cheeks as well as Patti's, Neil's and Susan's. We all had to take a deep breath and pause. Breathe slowly.

"I'd be honored," catching my breath yet still crying with unexpected joy. "We've already been calling you our son; it's natural."

Susan and Patti reached across the table to hold hands. However, I got up, as did Neil, and hugged my new son. We were crying and smiling and laughing all at the same time. What entertainment for the rest of the dining room. What a fantastic miracle, mending a family torn apart by the brutal insanity of murder.

Tonight, Neil was home again. He had family. And so did I.

10

The past few hours had been a miracle. Unexpected joys, lives bonding. It wasn't planned and I knew it was late, but I called the Sergeant asking for the next day off, explaining what happened earlier in the evening when Neil and his fiancée flew in to surprise his Mother. Troy wasn't that surprised and had suspected there was more between Patti and me; I briefly told him we'd been high school sweethearts and found each other again. He chuckled and in a gruff voice told me to enjoy my day with the family. He paused before he hung up, then added, he wanted Patti to be told congratulations too. I think I heard him smile.

However, that didn't stop our killer from striking again.

Conway called early the next morning.

"We've had another shooting, again multiple murders."

"I assume the ME and Locklear are on the case?"

"They are. Apparently, the same MO. I'll do the preliminaries."

"Thanks."

"And I've made an appointment for us to visit with the Commanding Officer at Joint Base Lewis-McChord tomorrow. Enjoy your day with the family while you can."

"Thanks, Conway. Appreciate you covering."

Patti informed her office she wouldn't be in; if there was an emergency, to call. We agreed to meet for breakfast, then show the kids our houseboat, and some of the sites in Seattle including a ferry ride to Bainbridge and lunch on the Bainbridge marina.

The tour of our houseboat was somewhat of a shock with all the construction underway. We walked carefully through the mess showing Neil and Susan our soon-to-be new home.

"Mom and Dad, this is incredible. Never knew what a houseboat was like, but this is exciting," began Neil. "A bit torn up, but what a view!"

"It needed remodeling; been the same since I bought it. We decided it was time for 'out with the old and in with the new'," I said.

"We've put in what we like, remodeling the kitchen, adding a small hot tub, making it ours," added Patti.

After carefully navigating the construction and viewing the lake from the deck, not wanting to interfere with what the contractors were doing, we were off to the ferry.

The ferry takes a half-hour trip each way between downtown and Bainbridge. The 460-foot ferry, one of the largest in the fleet, can carry 202 cars and 2,499 passengers. The route is among the heaviest traveled; the entire fleet carries 23 million passengers annually, making twenty ports of call. It's an astounding feat, how twenty-four ferries connect so many communities across the Puget Sound. For tourists, like we are today, the Seattle ferries are a must-see attraction. For many residents, it's a daily compulsory ride between home and work and with time, probably lost its glamour.

Neil and Susan walked the ferry and stood on the forward bow, letting the wind whip through their hair. They were graduating from college but acting like kids, youthful, energetic, having fun, laughing, hugging and pointing at the sites. We walked from the ferry to Doc's on the Marina in Bainbridge, with its outdoor area overlooking the many anchored boats providing a wonderful setting, crisp air and warm sun and their usual fabulous food.

"Dad, when did you become a cop? What contributed to your decision?" asked Neil.

"It was fairly simple. My dad and uncle were cops, one with the City, the other with the Sheriff's office. Then in the Army I was made an MP because of my college major and my size. Enjoyed my stint with the Army but saw some nasty stuff. Wanted to make a difference, to contribute in some manner helping others like I tried to help the returning vets from overseas, so when I was discharged, decided to attend the police academy, and the rest is history."

"When did you become a detective?"

"About twelve years ago. Started in patrol, came up through the ranks, passed whatever exams I'd taken, qualified, and made homicide detective. One of the best moves in my life, though I have to admit, I'm not a big fan of dead bodies; lives are irrationally cut short, so finding the culprit is what drives me," I replied. "Helping those crushed by such insanity has been rewarding."

"You and Mom just came off that terrible case in which you found my father's killer. Weren't you frustrated and angry?"

"No question about frustration and anger. It began with four dead, a family, no leads initially and no reason for what happened. Two young teens, outstanding students and talented, one heading to Julliard School in New York, the other with an appointment to the Naval Academy, killed in their own beds, their own home. That drove me crazy and made me angry. The father had left a large amount of money in accounts to pay for their college educations. No beneficiaries except the kids; the principle was huge and was placed in a trust, so that now two scholarships in their names are given annually at their high school, for kids who want to go to college, but whose families don't have the resources."

"Wow, must have given you some sense of pride having their memory preserved," he said.

"It did. But the case itself was problematic, and I needed some outside help with the international money trafficking. Yes. I must admit my embarrassment, too. I knew your Mom was the new FBI head here, but I was scared to make contact and congratulate her. But as I told her, I followed her career over the years. Guess I still had that high school crush. When I contacted the FBI, which meant your Mom, it was the beginning. She captured two notorious international drug cartel criminals working right across the street from my office. Our department computer geek gave her tons of information, through which the FBI and Interpol are now slowly dismantling an international money laundering and drug smuggling web. You should be proud of your Mom's tenacity. She's a damn good cop. I also knew I had helped you and her to begin to heal when I identified your Dad's killer."

"We know and are grateful. I am proud of Mom and what she's been able to accomplish. But now the tough question. You and Mom knew each other in high school, you were sweethearts. What happened? You both went to college here but had no contact?" I guess Neil was trying to fill in the blanks.

"Well, I was stupid. We did part, but I still loved her. It goes back to how I was raised. Told not to feel this way or that, after a while I didn't know what to feel or when to feel. I was confused and let the best thing in my life escape; well almost." I looked at Patti. "After college I went into the Army as I said, came back into the police academy, married a woman who seemed to support me, but after a while she wasn't anything like when I married her. She didn't like me being a cop, upped and left. No kids, quick divorce; then I floundered for many years."

"And when Mom returned, all of your hesitancies came alive?"

"Oh yes. I was scared to see your Mom again. The first time

we met I had a ridiculously hard time. My professional needs were important, but my insides were doing flip flops. There was no question I wanted to be with her again."

"I was mushed too, the first time I saw Kelly again, but he didn't know or have any clue and I wasn't about to tell him it was love at first sight again," injected Patti.

"You both obviously got past those awkward moments and here we are."

"You have a very dedicated Mom who cares for you deeply, yeah, like most Moms would. But she's tried extra hard while your father was gone, to make family, and that takes effort and commitment and a special person," I offered.

"I know and I am grateful. She and my father set a high standard for our family and though dad was gone a lot, they worked well together and worked hard on making a family when times were tough. Maybe I'm too wise for my age, but I was raised by incredible parents."

Talk about being wise, perceptive and proud! All wrapped up in a man about to launch his own life and build a family. I'm so proud of him and how he not just loves his Mom but adores her, and rightfully so.

Asking his Mom, Neil continued. "And Mom, I know you and Dad were recruited by the FBI while in college. Why did you guys accept?"

"It's been so long." She paused to reflect. "Your father and I wanted a challenge in life and felt we could contribute serving as we did. We had degrees that were acceptable to the Bureau's needs, Neil's being accounting, and we ranked high in our class and were athletic. They took us, and unlike many of our student colleagues, we had jobs upon graduation."

"Did you and Dad feel you were making that contribution?"

Neil asked.

"Until you father was killed, I thought so. It took me some time to regain that sense of commitment, that focus needed to endure the lengthy investigations. Yeah, it's come back, and I have to say thanks to Kelly. But why all these questions?"

"Oh, I just thought I'd ask. We've never really talked about this except the night we cried, and I know little about Kelly, Dad, and what he does and why. And it gives Susan some background too about the family she's marrying into."

"Now that's the first time I've ever heard you avoid a direct question."

Neil smiled and looked at us with no comment and shrugged his shoulders.

After our return ferry ride, we returned to the hotel and told the kids to enjoy themselves for the evening. I was drained emotionally and needed some quiet time to reenergize; Patti felt the same way, so we got some wine and relaxed in the hot tub. The rest of our wonderful evening was spent in each other's arms.

Late the next day we were planning to see Patti's parents. They had a nice three-bedroom apartment with a deck at Judson Park, a retirement community overlooking the nearby Des Moines marina. We told them we would come to their condo, scoop them up and take them to dinner at their favorite restaurant, Anthony's Homeport Restaurant, at the marina a few blocks from where they live, to spend time with their grandson.

And we told them there were a couple of other surprises as well.

11

With another murder having occurred, I had to excuse myself the next day to return to the office but would rejoin them for dinner with her parents. Patti had extended her time off to be with the kids, which I knew they would all enjoy.

"Bring me up to date, Conway. What happened?"

"He struck the day before yesterday again. Same MO. One shot to the head, no shells, three dead homeless men this time. This encampment was not too far from the other site along the Mountain to Sound Greenway Trail."

"Anybody hear or see anything?"

"Struck out. The last two sites were hidden, and the killer had to stalk them, had to reconnoiter his getting in and out without being seen. There's always someone unexpected that sees something. Not this time."

Twelve dead. I know the Sergeant isn't happy, nor is the Chief. The media's having a hey-day with stories of a serial killer. So much for accuracy or keeping the lid on this mess.

The front desk called and let Conway and me know that three individuals were in the lobby angrily demanding to see us and would not leave until they did. They were advocates for the homeless, apparently the same ones pounding on the Chief's door for results. We looked at each other and agreed to see what we could do to deflect some of the heat the Chief was getting. As we began to leave the office, I opened the bottom drawer of my desk and pulled out an 8x8 jigsaw puzzle box, one that usually holds 500 pieces.

With a quizzical look on his face, Conway asked, "What's with the box?"

"It's a teaching tool."

"For whom and what about?"

"Many years ago, a friend of mine was a teacher-trainer. Her challenge was to get her students to think literally 'outside the box.' She devised a way to get them to visualize, for example, what they could use in the classroom as a substitute teacher with an hour's notice to prepare."

"That would panic me; hours' notice, strange setting, and strange kids!"

"And it should if you had no idea what you could do to engage the students. For example, based on a plastic hamburger meal she bought at Toys"R"Us she helped them understand how they could take that hamburger, for a history class, do the history of the hamburger or Ray Kroc, founder of McDonalds; for a chemistry class, list and evaluate the measurements and ingredients in a burger with fries; or for an English class, write about the marketing concepts that made McDonald's, or any other fast food restaurant chain, successful."

"Sounds interesting. Did it work?"

"She said it did; she kept the plastic meal on her desk, not only to remind herself to think outside the box but to encourage students and anyone who asked what it meant. So, let's give them a demonstration of thinking 'outside the box.'"

"Is it a plastic hamburger in that box?" Conway asked.

"No. But it's just as creative."

We gathered in a small conference room on the main floor. There were no greetings as we walked in, no introduction and they didn't even wait for us to be seated. They really had no clue who they were even talking too; in fact, we could have been disoriented candidates for jury duty. They glared at us and immediately launched, rather blasted, their uninformed opinions at us. We took our seats and gave them our attention and said not a word but let them dig their hole. In loud, obnoxious voices, they were off to a good start.

"Don't know who you are, and couldn't care less, but assume you're the one supposedly handling the homeless murders. Well, it's about time you got out of your sacred offices and did some work. Hope you didn't have a hard time finding this room. Damn it, don't you guys care? What the hell's going on? You're not even trying to find who's killing the homeless in our community. That's what we pay you for as taxpayers. They're humans to be respected, not dismissed as trash or worse. And don't give me any lame excuse you're working on it, for it doesn't seem that's the case," was the first angry volley. The woman wore jeans, sandals, a T-shirt that had "save the homeless" on its front, had her hair in a ponytail, and was in her early 30s.

"We're tired of your institutional pabulum excuses," began the man, about early 50s, wearing jeans, a blue T-shirt and a thin, insulated vest. "Homeless are being killed and you haven't done anything to find their killer! The newspapers and news channels are recycling the same old news, the only thing changing is the growing number of dead. It's obvious you don't care, and these murders are not a high priority. What does it take to get you off your seats and out of your offices and show some results in identifying the killer and protecting our homeless?" was the second insulting volley. "You're in homicide and that's supposed to be your job. It's criminal what you're not doing!"

Conway and I agreed to meet with these "advocates" if that's how you'd describe them. On the elevator down, we'd agreed to let them vent their frustrations first, then take control and bring the conversation around to some constructive dialogue, if that was even possible. It wasn't looking promising.

"We've been asking your Chief what's going on and no answers have been forthcoming. The stonewalling must stop! We want results, answers! Now! And we don't want your vague 'we're working on it' either!" was the third contemptuous volley, somewhat a repeat of the first one.

Uninformed 'group think'; it's dangerous. It seemed like they were through. Conway and I allowed for a quiet pause before we began.

"Ladies and gentlemen, we thank you for coming in and expressing your opinions. My name is Homicide Detective John Francis Kelly, and this is my partner, Homicide Detective Bob Conway. Yes, though you only assumed it, we are the homicide detectives assigned to the case, the murders of homeless men."

"At least you admit who you are," one of them grumbled, as she wrote our names on a piece of paper. "That's a miracle; since you're not doing anything; thought you would want to remain anonymous."

They stared, no expressions. I can imagine what was running through their minds, something like "now we know their names, got them in our cross hair and can hold them accountable. What a bunch of incompetents." Well, were they in for a surprise!

"We understand your frustrations," I opened.

"I don't think you do," interrupted the male do-gooder.

Ignoring his obnoxiousness, I continued, "And your frustrations are no different than ours. Our job is to find a killer or killers. At this point we have truly little to work with. No one has seen or heard anything."

"Then what are you doing to find someone? Sitting around eating donuts and drinking coffee?" was the arrogant retort from one of the women, probably in her late thirties, early forties.

"Not really," responded Conway. "Our office coffee is not that good," trying to be humorous.

Placing my puzzle box on the table in front of the three, I began my demonstration.

"Before you is a box; you'll note it says 500 pieces on the outside. Obviously, a jigsaw puzzle. Would one of you please open the box and lay on the table what's inside."

The man, in his fifties, balding with a short beard, reached for the box, with a rather tormented and contemptuous look, opened it and poured out the hand full of pieces. It must be difficult to maintain those appearances, such unhappiness in his life.

He snorted, "We're not into playing games and anyway, this one is short a few pieces."

"Nor are we. Please bear with me and I'll explain," I responded.

"What's this, then, all about?" he snorted again in a crass, curt and arrogant tone of voice.

"Okay, what does the box say? I asked.

"500 pieces!" he retorted.

"And what did you lay on the table?"

"About 30 pieces."

"Now I want you to solve the puzzle."

"There's no way in hell I can," mouthed the man, with a cocky tone. "Are you joking?"

"Most of the pieces are missing," said the woman dressed like a hippie, quizzically.

"This is ridiculous! Nothing better than to play with puzzles on the taxpayer's dollar! You guys are a work of art!" said the third member of this so-called delegation.

"Most of the pieces are missing, and that's my point. Listen, I've asked you to solve a puzzle where most of the pieces are missing. The same situation exists with our investigation. Let me explain and in the process, set the record straight regarding your ill-informed, if not, uninformed statements."

"But we don't see results? Nor do we need your fancy puzzle stuff," one of the angry women stated arrogantly. "We're seeking results or your badges!"

"Well, threats won't answer your concerns, nor will not listening. I said let me explain. If you wish to be combative, we're not going to get anywhere, and you will not learn what's going on in finding an evasive killer. Your option?"

Giving them a couple of seconds and not seeing anyone wanting to rant or rave anymore, but with piercing eyes and contempt visible on their faces, they moved uncomfortably in their seats. I proceeded.

"A murder investigation is like my puzzle. We need to find all the pieces that relate to the total picture to capture a killer. For example, we have few pieces to work with. The targets are homeless, killed at night, in locations that are obscure, hidden and randomly spread around the city. There's no visible pattern to those sites. We don't know why the homeless are being targeted. We're not sure how or when their hiding spots are located or whether the killer just walks up and shoots. We don't know if the killer is a male or female or more than one person working together. We have no motive and no suspects. And no one's seen or heard anything."

I paused to let what I'm saying sink in if that was possible. They didn't budge. One had their arms folded across their chest, a great defensive nonverbal cue for not being open to what's being said or explained. His loss. So, I charged ahead.

"If the homeless, who've reported finding some of these murder sites, aren't willing to identify themselves and offer us an opportunity to interview them, we have nothing. They fade into the shadows. We have one composite (passing the photo across the table) of a man who asked a woman walking her dog to report a murder scene near her home. He disappeared, no name, no questions. She gave our sketch artist enough to reconstruct what you see here. But we have no name, no clue who he is or where he hangs out, or why he was near that particular site."

"What do you want us to do with it?" was another snotty response.

"Show it around. If anyone can identify him, we need to talk to him. He's not a suspect but a possible witness that may have additional information that can help us. Often when we interview people, we're able to get them to recall something they forgot or overlooked. It's those tiny pieces that solve the puzzle,"

Conway then injected, "Why do you think we don't care or don't think we're doing anything?" He decided to go toe-to-toe.

"Not much is being released from the Chief's office," said one of the ladies. "We don't know what you're doing or even if you want to do anything. People ignore and dismiss the homeless as less than a full member of our society."

Conway dug in. "And you can continue thinking that or step back and realize you may be mistaken. We don't care who the victims are, they are victims and unjustly deprived of their life by someone. We are commissioned to find a killer, regardless of who their victims might be. But when you have as little as we do, we're working overtime to find a reason, figure out the killer's next move and often pray for a break that will help stop the insanity."

"We're not suggesting …"

I interrupted, "Oh yes you are. Conway and I are public servants sworn to protect our community and I can assure you our colleagues, including the Chief, are committed to finding this ruthless predator. We have but three things we know about these killings and I repeat, it involves the homeless, no visible motive, and the killings are committed at night in secluded areas at random locations around the city."

One do-gooder chirped up, "The newspapers say the homeless are killed with one shot and no shells are recovered."

"And you are correct. Now add to that what I said about the homeless, their locations and no observable pattern, and we still have nothing." The matter of the military weapon was not for public consumption.

"Now," I began again, "You have vented your frustrations and hopefully you can see ours. What might you do to be helpful in finding a killer?"

The gentleman in this group of three strong advocates chirped up. "We'll admit we might have been hasty in condemning the department for inaction."

"You were and are. Rather than ask questions, you made insulting accusations which don't build trust or respect. We're glad you came to learn and become informed. But we still don't have a killer. If the homeless community is upset about what's happening, don't pound on our doors. Have them begin to police their own camps, watch for suspicious activities, monitor who is living where and if they are safe, provide their own protection and report to us anything that is suspicious, particularly someone they don't know stalking around looking at where they live. Get word into their communication channels we have a serial killer on the loose. That will help us and potentially frustrate the killer if he is stalking and finding resistance or groups protecting one another. We've already been in touch with the missions and *Real Change*. We're hoping someone who may have seen something will come forward and help us."

They didn't say much more, not even an apology for being ill-informed and argumentative.

"Conway and I wish to thank you for coming, to express your concerns and to learn what we are doing to solve a very nasty series of murders. We must excuse ourselves to return to the investigation."

With that, we scooped up the puzzle pieces and departed the room leaving the "do-gooders" sitting quietly at the table. The group was wrong in all their assumptions, as many can be. They weren't ready to become front line observers either, and whether they had access to the homeless networks was unclear. They were leaving with new information, and, even if they didn't recognize it, a polite and graceful yet pointed reprimand.

"Kelly, I love that visual. I didn't know you had that?"

"Haven't had to use it before, but today seemed to be appropriate for its inaugural use. A visual tool sometimes works betters than just words."

"I bet Troy and even the Chief would love to see how to use it. The group seemed to get a clue of the challenge we're facing," Conway observed.

"I don't want to be that optimistic. They were pretty revved up and I'm not sure how open they were to hear anything outside of their own predisposed ideas. At least we've said what we can, and with that, pointed out their own ignorance."

12

His throbbing headaches no one understands and are severe and increasing in intensity. He was nineteen when he volunteered, well sort of, but now he feels ancient.

He remembers the many nights sneaking into villages, called staging areas, behind the invisible line separating them from the enemy, and having to execute those he encountered. It's what he was trained to do and do efficiently. Echoes in his head, some the dying gasp of those he killed, others the dying last words from one of his buddies, while other voices were reminding him what he had to do. He was no longer in combat but, based on his dreams, flashbacks, and voices rattling around his head, he'd disagree; he was reliving the dark every day.

Such duty bound yet disruptive years, the impact magnifying itself daily; he doesn't sleep, paces and gets easily agitated and spooked. He's barely able to hold onto his greeter's job, pure façade as he doesn't care, but needs the money for rent, food, gas, and ammunition.

At night he's a vicious marauder, dressing in a black hoody, black pants, and a black facial mask, cleaning his weapon, attaching a silencer, and then launching his stealth operations. The ugly, worthless, smelly drug-outs walking the street act as if there is no war going on. He strategically identifies them, and reconnoiters where they're dug in, how difficult it is to assault their encampment and can he escape without being seen or caught in enemy fire. He'd been caught there once and did not wish to repeat that fiasco. Each successful mission means someone dies and he prefers it not be him.

They say he suffers from PTSD. Now cure it. They can't. They've put him on a bunch of medications, antidepressants, and other kinds of useless gum drops, and in a weekly PTSD therapy session. It's just a bunch of bull, flapping mouths, little relief for what's dancing in his head. No one can feel what's inside him. No one was where he was or did what he did. Yet his group leader, a naïve female psychologist wearing a white coat, asks questions, says she understands, and wants us to express our feelings. The sessions feel like brain washing but there's no rinse and spin cycle. She doesn't know nothing but is trying to cater to those of us who've seen the dredges and brutality of life; not even in the Army anymore, and still can't get away from it. Orders to conduct deadly missions continue to be issued. No one told him when he joined that he would suffer for the rest of his life with the continuous loop of indescribable pain and brutal visions of combat. Aspirin doesn't help. The drugs he takes don't help. But night ventures put him back in his groove, like he trained; doing what for him comes naturally: killing the enemy!

13

Getting back on track with our investigation following our encounter with the three stooges, Conway made an appointment with the Commanding Officer at Lewis-McChord, now a joint command between the former U.S. Army base Fort Lewis and U.S. Air Force base McChord. That's their official status, but for those of us locals, we've called it Fort Lewis for decades and isn't something you can easily change.

Fort Lewis is 42 miles south of Seattle, its main entrance off Interstate 5. This joint base was ten years in the making. So many other bases on the West Coast were combined or closed, which had a negative impact on their surrounding local economy. For Lewis-McChord, their union had little negative impact on the surrounding areas and employment; quite the contrary. The base has been a stepping off point for military actions in Desert Storm, Iraq and Afghanistan, deploying ground troops, mechanized units and specialty units.

We had requested an hour with the Commanding Officer, advising his staff the meeting was to address the recent murders in Seattle.

Brigadier General Scott Hansen stood 6'2", a West Point Graduate, wore a perfectly pressed khaki uniform with colorful campaign ribbons, 5 rows of them, over his left breast pocket, a name tag over the right pocket, and a bright silver star on each shoulder. As we were escorted into his office, he welcomed us with his Midwest accent. We introduced ourselves showing our ID, shook hands; he motioned us to sit down in front of his desk. Flanking his desk were three flags, the American flag, the Army flag, and his personal flag, a large silver star on a red background signifying a one-star General. His walls were adorned with photos and plaques. We thanked him for his time and proceeded with our request.

"General, we have twelve murders of homeless men in Seattle. You no doubt have seen the news reports. Our reason for being here is based on our Forensic Psychologist's profile of the possible killer based on recovered slugs from the victims, said to be from a military hand weapon."

"Yes, I've seen those stories. Not sure what the Army can do, or how we are involved, but you have my attention."

"Thank you, Sir. The news reports give the basics: one shot to the head, no shells left behind, no sound, and no one has seen or heard anything. We have no clue why the killer has targeted homeless male victims; but where they've been killed, he's had to stalk them, find his way in and out without being seen. He knows what he is doing and is very skilled. What we've kept from the media is the type of weapon used; as I began with, based on the analysis of the slugs removed from the victims, the weapon's been identified as a military Sig Sauer Mark 25 9mm with a silencer. Based on the kind of weapon and what I just described as his killing habits, our Forensic Psychologist believes the killer to be mentally ill, delusionary, isolated and unpredictable, with a possible military connection."

Conway added, "Our Forensic Psychologist suggests a professionally trained killer with possibly Special Forces type training. We have no clue whether the killer is currently in the military or discharged, but likely the latter. She felt he might have been involved in what is called 'black ops' and now suffers from PTSD."

I continued, "We're reaching but with the profile, it seems to suggest a former soldier well trained and skilled with the weapon he uses. She feels he or she is sick and may not even know what they're doing or why. He or she may be obsessed or caught in the grips of what they had been trained to do while on active duty."

"Sounds like she thought it through quite reasonably," began the General. "The Army is trying its best to identify soldiers nearing the end of their commitment who may need additional help prior to discharge. During their enlistment, soldiers understand their obligations and live in a regimented atmosphere. Those sent into combat encounter situations we try to prepare them for; but whatever happens, it's not enough. Some handle the cruelty of killing well while others, it's a shock that ripples through their body, mind and spirit. If they remain in the Army, they have structure that appears to support them and make it easier to process the settings they've been in. But when they leave, they no longer have that affirming structure. Thus, we have a program through which all who are about to be discharged participate. It's an attempt to reorient them again to civilian life. It's through those classes we try to determine if there are soldiers who need more counseling assistance than others. Ultimately, once discharged, we recognize their physical or mental health relies on the services of the Veterans Administration."

"I need to ask about units such as Special Forces, Delta, or SEAL, and whether you have them here today."

"We have many brigades; and we've had such units as you mention in the past but no longer. The SEALs are a Navy unit and have never been located at this post; their training facilities are in San Diego, specifically Coronado. The Army moved the training of its other specialty units back east to more appropriate bases, consolidating training commands. However, we've discharged many here at Lewis-McChord, some with those kinds of backgrounds you mentioned."

"Would you have any idea if those discharged from such units are still in the area?" I asked.

"Not off hand; some soldiers are sent here for their last

assignment, others to receive medical assistance from Madigan Hospital, and others to muster out of the service. Each one has an exit DD214 which gives us a lot of information about their enlistment. Such information includes their full name, date of birth, social security and military ID numbers, rank or ratings, decorations, any accrued leave where payment may be sent plus their original hometown."

"General, I'm familiar with the DD214 as I served years ago as an Army MP, in fact, here at Fort Lewis. Haven't looked at mine in a long time. The information you describe, is it readily available, something we can access and scan?" I asked.

"They're considered 'confidential'. We usually don't reveal that information without authorization from higher up. However, current circumstances might warrant other consideration."

He saw my face drop with disappointment.

"Notwithstanding formal procedures," he began, "getting clearance through chain of command and the Pentagon might require excessive delay and unnecessary red tape. I gather your investigation doesn't have that luxury. You need answers, and I'll work it out with my superiors. How many did you say have been killed?"

"Twelve. If it wasn't for our profiler, we wouldn't even be here as she's the only one giving us a sense of direction."

"And her analysis appears thoughtful. As Commanding Officer, I think I can help. I'll direct our personnel office to glean specific information off those discharged DD214 with Special Forces training and provide you with a list of and a thumbnail sketch of each veteran discharged who seems to have remained in the area. Can't give you their DD214 but it should be enough to work with."

"That would be of enormous help," I responded, wanting to jump up and shake his hand.

"What kind of specific information might be useful? Can't give you everything," he asked.

"Name and obviously a local address or even original address, any medical information, combat zone where they served, social security number, date of discharge."

"How many years' worth of information do you think you'll need?" he asked.

"That's a good question. Though the murders have been recent, we have no clue who is doing them or for how long he, or she, has been planning this. Maybe, at least two years? We have no clue if there was a delay time between discharge and the beginning of the killings."

"Two years of information. It may be a lot but I'm assuming you'll have someone who can sort, or whatever you do, to narrow down your possibilities. It'll take a few days for us to compile the data."

"That's most appreciated. Our Forensic Psychologist has suggested the possibility of someone with post-traumatic stress. We have no clue how to interpret that regarding the mental state of whoever the killer is. Your thumbnail sketches will be cross checked by our departmental computer guru with information we obtain from the VA about veterans in therapy for PTSD. Once data is processed and matches are confirmed, our Forensic Psychologist with work with the VA clinical staff to see if there's any way we can identify a person or persons of interest. We know this is a gamble, but we've got to begin somewhere."

"Sounds like you have a plan for what you want to do," said General Hansen.

"We're aware it could be someone discharged longer than 2 or 3 years ago and if that's the case, we're back to square one. For the moment, however, you and the VA are our best hope."

"Good. As I mentioned before, we have Resilience Classes for those leaving the service but never know if they work or not. Connect with Madigan, American Lakes or the Seattle VA hospital, they'll have what you're looking for. It just bothers me it could be one of our soldiers who's unable to readjust."

"We understand your concerns too. For us, the VA is next on our list."

We thanked him for his cooperation, gave him our cards, shook hands and departed.

"What're your thoughts?" asked Conway as we walked to our car.

"More helpful than I expected. I think he sensed the severity of what we're up against. Whatever he gives us will give us something to work with. Meanwhile, let's head to the Seattle VA and visit with its Administrator."

14

The distance may be 42 miles back to Seattle; but getting through the traffic backup around the Tacoma Dome and all the highway construction usually takes extra time. It's a boring drive, 3 to 4 lanes in each direction, car, trucks and buses bumper to bumper going 60 miles an hour or faster, in a marked 55 mph zone with unmarked state patrol cars watching for those speeding their way beyond posted signs to their destinations. Interstate 5 passes on the west side of South Center Mall, no longer called that except by residents. It's a geographic landmark where Interstate 405 meets with Interstate 5. More stores, restaurants and movie theatres than you can imagine, squeezed into a multiple level building and acres of land, with parking lots and parking structures. The mall is mobbed, a place to spend money, acquire stuff, walk long corridors. It's a place, a happening, a hangout for social interaction. I avoid it.

The exit to the VA Hospital is north of the mall about 8 miles, exit at South Albro, left up Swift and 15th Street, right onto Columbian Way and left at the signal into the VA campus. The hospital is in the Beacon Hill district and recently underwent some expansion and remodeling. We parked at the curb leaving a "police business" placard on the dash and our grill lights flashing, and walked to the front welcome desk; we asked for the name and location of the Administrator's office and advised them of our car parked in front of the hospital. The volunteers, wearing green vests with the VA logo and pins from their military service, rolled their eyes – we didn't understand why - gave us the information and directions. We'd soon find out.

The corridors are alive with veterans, some in wheelchairs others with canes or crutches, escorted by their wives or significant others. So many broken bodies limping along, heading for their clinical appointments where waiting rooms are crowded. Young men looking old, older men looking ancient. World War II, Korea, Vietnam, Iraq, and Afghanistan emblazoned on baseball caps, proud but tired, struggling with their health issues.

We found the administrator's office. Introducing ourselves to his secretary and showing her our credentials, "We're here to see Dr. Horace Rumpp if he's available, please."

"Do you have an appointment?" asked his secretary with a slight smile. The name plate on her desk said Dorthea Jones. Her workstation was incredibly neat and well organized and she was impeccably dressed, both no doubt contributing to her success as the hospital Administrator's right hand.

"No. We're investigating several murders which may involve a veteran and this hospital."

Without another word, she called the Administrator's office. He said he did not want to see us without an appointment. We asked Dorthea if he had someone in the office, or an appointment soon to arrive, and she responded negatively. Conway and I looked at each other, asked Dorthea to put us on his calendar as an appointment. She then knocked on the door, leaned in to announce to the Administrator, his next appointment had arrived, and with a smile, turned and ushered us into his office. We'd asked Dorthea to hold his calls.

He was a bit taken back when we walked in. He was checking his computer for our appointment, then exclaimed, "I had no appointment with you for today until now. What's going on! You boys aren't welcome! I don't like you just barging into my office." There were no introductions or a "welcome, how can I help you?" type conversation. He remained seated and glared at us.

"We don't have time for delaying formalities, Doctor. We asked Dorthea to put us on your calendar as an appointment.

We know you have no one in your office, nor did you have any appointments on the books, until we arrived. So, let's dispense with your lame objections. We're homicide detectives with the Seattle Police Department looking for a killer who may well be a veteran and connected to this hospital. We're looking for your help and cooperation."

"Ya'll have balls just barging into my office, which I don't appreciate," he said contemptuously with a definitive southern drawl and a glaring expression. "Ya'll barging in doesn't set well for me to help you boys."

We're off to a terrific start. Certainly not a southern welcome, or even gentlemanly.

"We told your secretary to place us on your calendar as an appointment, since that is what you want. And we know this is a rather unexpected visit, but as I said, we are pressed for time and looking for some help and answers. We have twelve dead, no doubt you've read about them in the newspaper."

"So, boys, what's it about?" again said with more of a cocky southern tone, as if we weren't his equal. "You barge in, disrespect my office, then ask for help. Ya'll have balls!"

"First, we're not 'boys' and would appreciate being called 'detective.'"

"You correctin' me, boy? I'll call you what I want, when I want, got that! And I do what I want whether you like it or not."

Ignoring his arrogant retort, I proceeded. "What's not been told to the press is the identification of the murder weapon. Everyone knows the victims were shot, obviously by a handgun. But it's not public that it's a military weapon using a silencer. Our Forensic Psychologist profiled the killer as having a professionally-trained military background and possibly suffering from severe PTSD."

"Now boys, sounds like you got a problem, but whatcha want

me to do?" again said defensively with a belittling tone.

"We'd like your help, like the Commanding Officer of Joint Base Lewis-McChord, who is providing us data on soldiers discharged over the past 2 years, through his command, with Special Forces type training."

"Well, goody for him." Belligerently spoken with his annoying drawl.

"He suggested Madigan, American Lake and the Seattle VA may have therapy groups or individual counselors helping those with PTSD," I politely responded, although I wanted to slap his arrogant face. "We're looking to visit with your clinical staff who treat these PTSD patients to see if they can give some insights into potential persons of interest."

"Now, boys, let me set you straight. We have clinics that schedule group and individual therapy sessions for vets referred by their primary care doctors. In some cases, our Primary Care staff refer them into a star program, which is one-on-one short-term help. These group and individual referrals are confidential except to those in the group who know one another. I'm not at liberty to give you or anyone that kind of information. Got it?"

Restraining myself, I again stated our situation, which he was apparently ignoring.

"Twelve dead. More likely unless we can stop this killer. We think the killer has a military background, is severely ill, and may be or have been enrolled in one of your PTSD therapy groups. We're trying to expedite our investigation to prevent any more needless deaths. We need your help!"

Then he decided to play what he thought was his trump card, and obnoxiously said, which sounded even more demeaning in his drawl, "Boys, (he paused) you just don't listen do you. I ain't giving you or anyone that kind of information. We'd need a federal warrant to release names or allow you to speak with anyone here in this hospital along with the approval of DC. Otherwise, you're blowing it up your ying-yang. Got it? And even if I could help you, I wouldn't, not after barging into my office."

I pursued the matter one more time. "If the murders hadn't taken place just in Seattle, we wouldn't be here. We need access to names, to compare with what we get from Lewis-McCord to narrow down potential persons of interest."

"As I said boys, and in case you don't hear me right, again, no warrant, no information. It's classified. And we're a federal institution, not bound to comply with any of your requests." He sat glaring at us, determined to be the ass he was sitting on. "Now get out!!" he yelled.

We left our cards and departed, leaving cards with his secretary, too.

We were angry he wanted to play games for no apparent reason, other than wanting to be in control? Well, I can play too, and will. I have the upper hand, not him. My call to Patti will rock his sacred world. Knowing she was enjoying her day with our son, however, I opted to delay the request until she technically returned to the office the next day.

"What the hell was that all about, Kelly?" asked Conway.

"Can't believe he's so outrageously arrogant and rude as the hospital's Administrator. Totally unprofessional and uncooperative. He's so pompous and demeaning. And what's his attitude doing here in Seattle? Whoever transferred him here made a big mistake. I wonder how his secretary tolerates it. I'm sure he belittles her, too. Certainly not a southern gentleman nor a nice person. He may be a doctor; but I wonder where he got his degree, more importantly how and why they picked him to be an administrator of such a large regional medical facility. Regardless of whatever regulations he wants to hide behind, unlike the General, he didn't seem to care or want to cooperate at any level. It'll be interesting to see what Lewis-McChord produces; we'll get the VA information too, regardless of what he says," said with a smile.

"You mean you'll ask for help from your incredible and talented wife?"

"You've got it. Not today but maybe tomorrow. It's business so I will keep it away from our personal time."

"Must be a difficult line to walk?" remarked Conway.

"Yes and no. There are times we share, which is a way we support one another. With our son and his fiancée here, I'll leave my request until she returns to the office. That'll give me a chance to brief Troy. Okay, we have the irons in the fire and now need to give Sherlock a heads up as to what is coming in his direction."

Randy Sherlock is the department's computer/IT techie. Brilliant, he loves challenges and was a master at digging out hidden stuff in our last case. He's tall and lanky with hair that doesn't want to cooperate, the Einstein look. Something about being a genius and uncombed hair. He's so much into technology, we frequently get concerned about him coming up for air, water and food; we take him out for meals to reenergize him. Until a few weeks back he hadn't had a girlfriend. Though he mentioned a date one night, we've not heard another word and don't wish to disturb his delicate world. When he does his magic, we don't ask how he does it either and find that's usually a wise call. This job, with major data, will require an algorithm sorting, collating and narrowing down names to a workable list. He's our "go to" man.

"And what do you think we'll find with the VA information?" Conway asked.

"Vets suffering from PTSD, assigned to a therapy group," I responded. "I'm hoping Sherlock can correlate the Lewis-McChord information with the VA information and find names the clinical staff can review and discuss with Caitlin, about abnormal and irrational behaviors that might suggest a 'person of interest' where we can interview."

"Changing subject, did you see the front desk personnel roll their eyes when they gave us Rumpp's name?" commented Conway.

"Yeah. I think I know what you're thinking. As an MD, he may or may not be a proctologist, but he's sitting on his butt not wanting to do much of anything, and arrogant at that. My sense is he's not well liked nor easy to work with. I wonder what's the huge chip on his shoulder; he certainly needs better training in his bedside manners. His southern behavior is out of date and not welcomed here in the Pacific Northwest," I replied, smiling.

When we got back, I told Conway I was leaving early to take Patti, Neil and Susan to meet Neil's grandparents in Des Moines for dinner. They were being given three surprises, Neil's unexpected visit, his engagement, and an opportunity to meet their daughter's fiancé.

First, I had to check on Snowball in our hotel room, change my clothes and then gather up everyone.

15

He called in sick again, in fact, a regular habit. Had no intentions of sitting through worthless group sessions where other vets shared their feelings, making up stuff while the clinician was trying to get him to go deeper. Brain washing is all it is. You can't go deeper than the stuff he saw and did. His head always hurts, with the annoying throbbing, like the oversized drum being pulled on a cart in a circus parade. He's running low on sleep; the movie theater in his head has not closed its doors during the night. The visions are real.

His small apartment, located within a long walking distance of where he works, wasn't much, but for him it was a haven, a place where he can get away from the world and all its crappy noises. He had enough already reverberating in his head. When he did sleep, he soaked his bed and t-shirt in sweat. His appetite was dwindling as he neared going on patrol.

His land reconnaissance was dangerous, exposing him to needless threats. He has no aerial support or drones giving him vital information, apart from the use of Google maps, an imperfect aerial view of the city, its roads, buildings, neighborhoods, lakes, piers and parks. He needs infrared to detect the presence of warm bodies. It sure would make his missions easier. Now, he's going into new and uncharted territory.

He was on extra high alert as he slipped behind enemy lines. Invisible, dressed in black, the search began. Two targets found sleeping behind a grocery store. They'd shut down for the night huddled behind the dumpster and garbage boxes. He simply slipped in behind the store, completed his mission and exited.

16

The office coffee was nothing but black water, so I suggested to Conway we get lattes at the corner coffee shop. We were both tired and frustrated. The killings kept coming; it would be a week, maybe less, before the Army got us their list. Patti had been advised of the need for a federal warrant to gain access to veteran information at the Seattle VA. That was being processed and would be in our hands later in the day, tomorrow at the latest. She was stunned at the lack of professionalism, cooperation and how rudely we'd been treated.

Back in the office, we were greeted by our Sergeant.

"Kelly, Conway. In my office, now!" commanded our Sergeant. "What the hell have you got that shows we're solving these homeless murders? The Chief's upset."

"Yeah we figured. Here's what's going on. First, we have a profile for our killer from Dr. Ward at the University. She felt the identified military weapon used was a strong route to follow. As a result, we visited with the Commanding Officer at Lewis-McChord and it'll take 5-days or less to get thumbnail sketches on soldiers discharged the past two years with Special Forces training. The CO really went beyond what we had anticipated and is circumventing Army protocol to get us their information. We then went to the VA hospital at the General's suggestion, to ask for access to group or individual therapy sessions with vets suffering from PTSD, and names of their clinicians. Stone-walled! An arrogant administrator who wants a federal warrant. That's in process as we talk."

"Any closer to a solution?"

"Beyond our current efforts, no. I wish we were. We find it

interesting that with the locations of where the homeless are killed, no one has seen anything suspicious or out of the ordinary. We believe these locations are being stalked, so the killer is getting a rhythm of the comings and goings. That, to me, is military. We feel when we get the data and Sherlock's able to cross-index names, we'll find 'persons of interest', assuming the killer is still involved with a therapy group and among those we identify."

"We'll be asking Dr. Ward to help us with interviews of the VA clinicians in order to get their insights to any and all names Sherlock is able to cross-index," added Conway.

"What about those clowns you entertained downstairs?"

"They were so misinformed, ill-informed and uninformed. We didn't cut them any slack. We let them know we do care about our citizens regardless of who they are. We made it clear we were working hard to solve a puzzle and suggested they go back and get the homeless network to come alive using their own resources to protect one another or to report anything unusual. They didn't even apologize for their brazen arrogance and belittling behavior."

"Likely to return?"

"Your guess is as good as mine, but for the moment, no. We may have taken some heat off the Chief, but they think they're do-gooders and want to be combative rather than problem solvers."

"Sergeant, you should have seen Kelly's tool for giving them a visual about solving our case."

"And what might that be?" Troy asked as he look quizzically at me.

"Simple, you cannot solve a jigsaw puzzle without all the pieces. I had one of them open a 500-piece puzzle box with only a handful of pieces in it and asked them to solve the puzzle."

"Did it work?"

"They weren't overjoyed with my instructional genius, but I think they got the point. Learning is not what they wanted, however."

"It sounds like you're doing what you can. As soon as we have something even minute, let me know. The Chief is rattled with the pounding of the press on these killings."

"What's interesting is we've not heard from anyone in the city about someone's suspicious behaviors or prowlers near their businesses. Usually we would have a gaggle of leads to sort through but right now there's none; it's so unusual. This guy is good, and dangerous. He's invisible and knows what he's doing. Dr. Ward thought a lot might be subconscious; regardless, he's unpredictable," I added.

"Stay with it. Keep me posted and let me know if there's any difficulties getting that warrant."

17

"Kelly, there's a message for us to call CSI."

"Put it on speaker," then said, "What's up, Tucker?"

"Two more dead," were his first words. "Same MO, but this time in the White Center district. Found this morning behind a dumpster by a shop owner."

"Beyond two dead, anything different?" I asked.

"The location is certainly outside the general downtown area where the other killings took place. He may be stretching his reach, diversifying, I don't know. Just unusual."

"Okay, I'll let Troy know, as we just left his office and neither he nor the Chief are happy, and this will not add to their celebratory spirits."

"Good luck. Don't envy your job."

"Now what do we do?" Conway asked.

"Let the Sergeant know."

The day was slowly deteriorating. Early morning, I'd asked the FBI for a federal warrant to get the Seattle VA to release what we needed; Patti had agreed and said they'd advise the VA's DC office what was going on. Now we have two more murder victims, an arrogant hospital administrator forcing us to play an undesirable game, which he'll lose, and waiting on information from Lewis-McChord. Pressure from the top was increasing; and the community was outraged, thinking we weren't doing anything. When you don't know what you're looking for, how can you find it?

We touched base with our friendly Forensic Psychologist

letting her know of recent developments and what we are getting from the Army.

"No," she began. "I don't see the killer making a major shift, maybe a minor one. He's still targeting homeless men. The only difference is he's moved to the other side of the Duwamish River, to another precinct."

"As we told the Sergeant, no one seems to hear or see anything and now a shift in his location of the homeless," I sort of sputtered out.

"We're dealing with an irrational person, so we have to expect this. Up and until now, his targets are spread all over the city. If he's trying to keep us, or as he sees us as - the enemy - off balance, he's doing a rather good job, but I can't answer the 'why' at this point," she offered.

"We did take your advice about checking into a military connection and have visited with the Commanding Officer at Lewis-McChord. The VA was not quite so cooperative, demanding a federal warrant. As we speak, that is being prepared and will be served later."

"What's the Army providing?"

"They're giving us thumbnail sketches on discharged soldiers with Special Forces training. Their discharge DD214 carries a lot of information including name, rank, serial number, date discharged and local address at time of discharge. When we get the VA information, we're having Sherlock compare that with whatever we can get from the VA."

"Sounds great and I like your plan," she responded. "I think you're on track even if you're not sure. If I can be of help with the VA hospital information or clinicians, let me know."

"Would you be willing to interview those clinicians? They

might respond better to you than two gold shields."

"Give me a call and we'll see what can be arranged."

We felt a little more encouraged after our call.

18

"Hi, pretty one," recognizing her number. "What's up?"

"Looks like we're in this together again."

"Yeah, and I do like that, a lot."

"I've got your warrant from the federal district court and advised the VA in DC through our offices about your encounter. The warrant orders the VA, namely Seattle VA, to cough up the names of all individuals in group or individual therapy for PTSD and allows the Seattle PD and its personnel to interview the clinicians. Is that what you needed?"

"Perfect. Dr. Ward who is on contract with the Seattle PD, a Forensic Psychologist with the University, has agreed, well sort of, to assist with interviews of the VA clinical staff. She's a bit concerned about HIPAA (Health Insurance Portability and Accountability Act) requirements but will work with the medical clinicians on accessing what is classified as 'confidential' information and what we may need in assessing the volatility of a veteran suffering from PTSD."

"Sounds good. When do you want me to get this over to you?"

"Actually, I'd like you to serve it with Conway and me. That will take the air out of the pompous, arrogant, demeaning Administrator who is simply playing his controlling CYA game. It's a federal warrant and you're a federal agent. It might just upset his predisposed southern redneck attitude toward Conway and me. On top of that, I want to watch him squirm when you cook his goose."

"Sure. I'm game. When?"

"Come by and pick Conway and me up in 30 minutes? We'll show off our muscle."

I rode with Patti and two other agents she brought along, while Conway rode with three agents in the second SUV. We were a caravan of two black SUVs with dark tinted windows, blue and red flashing lights hidden under the front grill, and low out the back tinted window. We drove up to the entrance of the hospital and were surprised when met at the sidewalk by the VA police department. Getting out, we were greeted with attitude.

"You can't park here. This is a restricted area," the Sergeant stated.

"Well," began Patti. "We are federal officers with the FBI, on official business, and we will be parking here with one of my agents standing by the vehicles."

"No can do," the Sergeant continued. "We've been told by the Administrator we are not to allow you on the property, so you're going to have to move along."

Now both of his hands were resting on his waist, one on top of his weapon. Meanwhile, two of the agents in the caravan had quietly shifted to the rear flank of the Sergeant and his partner.

I decided to smart mouth, which drew a nudge from Patti. "Sergeant, I do not see a 'no visitors allowed' sign at the entrance to the hospital complex."

Ignoring my comment, Patti didn't waste any time getting started, attitude or not.

"Sergeant, my name is FBI Special Agent in Charge of the FBI Hancock. I have all the authority I need by presenting you my credentials, and warning, should you continue to pursue this discussion, I'll have no other choice but to arrest both of you on obstruction of justice and interfering with a federal investigation. Is that clear?"

A little stunned at her firm and aggressive statement, the Sergeant was visibly shaken and not sure how to respond.

"Sorry Ma'am, I have orders," he tried to spit out.

"And I am serving a federal warrant on the Administrator, which, should he not comply with, will cost him his job and an undetermined amount of time in federal prison," she replied. "Let me suggest you come with us to the Administrator's office and watch us deliver this federal warrant mandating cooperation with a murder investigation."

It was the moment of truth for the Sergeant. He could continue to object, with Patti prepared to arrest him. Or he could agree to accompany us to the Administrator's office while we served the warrant and get the information we needed.

"Sergeant, meet the team. Agents Hayden, Rodriguez, Lawson, and Chin are to your left and Agent Madera to your right. Alongside me are Seattle PD Homicide Detectives Kelly and Conway."

Each of us gave the Sergeant a nod.

"I'm leaving Agent Madera with the cars. They should be safe where they are. Now, would you like to lead us to your Administrator?" she firmly stated.

The Sergeant and his colleague did not say a word, but nodded their heads acknowledging her invitation and led the way.

The Administrator's secretary was surprised to see all of us walk into her office. I signaled her not to announce our presence, but determined that he was in his office and without another appointment. I wondered if anyone ever wanted an appointment with him. I asked her to hold his calls and to join us along with their own police personnel.

The Administrator was not happy to see us; in fact, he was on his feet and about to say something when I cut him off with a hand signal. We didn't wait to be introduced, just walked in, or barged in, depending on whose perspective. We were putting him in the proverbial hot seat, in front of his own police personnel and his assistant. Patti didn't waste a moment firing it up.

"Dr. Rumpp, my name is Special Agent in Charge Hancock with the FBI Office here in Seattle. I'm serving you with a special federal warrant ordering you to turn over the items as listed and allow Seattle PD personnel to interview your clinical staff," handing the document across his desk. She had her badge looped out of her suit breast pocket in clear view for the Administrator.

He slid it toward himself without reading it and said in his slow, contemptuous southern drawl, "I don't like ya'll barging in again. I'd told you that before! And Sergeant, I ordered you to not allow them on our property."

The Sergeant did not reply, which was the wisest and only move he could make. He was silent and showed no acknowledgement of the statement.

"I don't care what you do or do not like. The Sergeant and his staff understand the FBI has authority when it comes to federal facilities. Now, did you hear what I just said?" she pursued.

"I ain't deaf if that's what ya'll mean. I don't do anything unless it's cleared with my supervisor in DC."

Interrupting him, Patti said, "You don't need to clear this with anyone. DC already knows. This warrant has been issued by the Federal District Court and orders you, doesn't make a nice request, but orders you to comply. Failure to comply will be contempt of court and obstruction of justice leading to your immediate arrest and relief from your duties here at the hospital. The FBI is not messing around. We have a killer loose in our City and we need information the VA has on PTSD victims. The Commanding Officer at Lewis-McChord is cooperating without a warrant. The two homicide detectives here, were quite clear with you earlier as to the urgency. Now what's your choice?" She was dead serious and direct; her face showed her determination. There were no smiles. That's my Patti.

She asked Conway to have the other agents join us. When they entered, they had their badges hanging out of their suit breast pockets too. It was a definite show of force, and a very crowded office.

"We're waiting. Give us access or go to jail. Your choice? If you ignore the warrant, you pass go and don't collect $200, but go directly to jail, not local, federal. I'm waiting, and impatient."

Facial expressions and the growing color on his face showed he was livid to be shoved around, especially by a woman. He wasn't anxious to do much of anything, but decided to look at the warrant and called his secretary. She stepped forward from where she had been watching the drama unfold. He rose from his desk, all 250 pounds of blustering arrogance. He was about to speak at Patti, but she cut him off.

"Dr. Rumpp, don't go there. I don't understand your attitude, your belligerence, or your reluctance to cooperate with a federal warrant. Your delaying tactics are inexcusable. You asked, if not demanded, a federal warrant and we've delivered that to you. You are looking at what you wanted, what you demanded. The VA computerizes its clinical information, names of veterans and all their related medical issues and care. Don't mess with us about needing time to get that information. We're asking for the past two years' worth of individual and group therapy sessions for vets suffering from PTSD. I think you and your secretary can pull it together while we wait. Otherwise, we're going to be here a long time until we get what has been ordered to be turned over," said Patti. No slack. This man's arrogance was being challenged head on and he was losing. You could see he was steaming, as sweat began to drip down his forehead. He no longer had the control he wanted. And he was giving Patti his contemptuous look, leaning toward her with his two fists on his desk, ready to pounce; no woman's telling me what to do? Well, buddy, get used to it. It's happening!

But he persisted.

"Little lady, whatcha thinking of barging into my office with a warrant is going to accomplish?"

"Dr. Rumpp, first, my name is Special Agent in Charge Hancock. I'm with the Federal Bureau of Investigation and I can assure you I will make your life difficult. Second, your rudeness and belligerence and contempt are no excuse for ignoring the federal warrant lying on your desk. You either begin to give us the information requested or you're under arrest. Clear?"

She paused, and Rumpp turned red and started to blubber something out of his mouth. She simply held up her hand again and said, "Now, we want the full names, addresses and contact information for all clients in group or individual therapy. A simple list of names will not do. It's spelled out in the warrant. And we need the same for all your clinical staff; each will be contacted and interviewed by a Seattle PD staff psychologist." Patti had taken the lead and it was working. It was a federal employee being confronted by a federal agent and she was not giving him an inch. He sat back down, not graciously either. The chair moaned and bowed under his weight. I was waiting for it to break and for him to fall on the floor. That would have been dramatic.

We waited. We were all standing facing him, waiting.

He continued to be in slow motion. He was angry about being pushed into a corner, by a woman no less. He fiddled with the warrant paper, then asked, in a strained voice, his secretary to assist with compiling the information requested for the clinical staff handling the PTSD therapy sessions. She nodded and returned to her desk, her empire, smiling, though I might have heard a chuckle too. She knew what was going on and was enjoying it.

We waited and waited for the Administrator. He finally began to type on his keyboard; he said nothing but went straight to work, well sort of. He knew the clock was ticking. He wasn't in any hurry to give these northern boys, and this damn cocky, prissy female, the information any faster than necessary.

A half-hour, then an hour passed. We rounded up chairs for all of us to sit down. Conway offered to come up with some coffee and water. Recognizing it was late afternoon, we suggested the secretary order up dinners, including one for Agent Madera with the cars, should this marathon take longer than necessary. He began to object, and Agent Hancock simply raised her hand and he remained silent. His fingers slowly, and I mean slowly, continued across his keyboard. Finally, the printers woke up and began to print a page, then two pages. It became silent. Then it awoke printing several pages. We were apparently getting unedited versions of lists with names, addresses and contact information, nothing organized. "I ain't helping them any more than I have to" seemed to be his attitude, regardless of what the warrant said and demanded. We looked at each other and rolled our eyes. We knew their system was far more efficient than what he was doing with it. His contempt in facial and body cues was apparent. He was fuming, red faced, with sweat running down his forehead. More fuel was about to be poured on his embers.

"You know, Doctor, you knew this was coming. You even ordered your in-house police to be on the alert for our return and what you ordered them to do was illegal. We have murders to solve and someone within one of these groups may be the perpetrator. Your attitude is disgusting, and this waiting totally unnecessary. In fact, all this stonewalling and your despicable attitude will be reported to the VA, as I said, who were advised we'd be here today seeking this information with a warrant due to your lack of initial cooperation. You can probably count the days you still have this job, no thanks to anyone but yourself," stated Patti. She wasn't letting this turkey off the hook, no wiggle room. His goose was cooked, well, more like his turkey.

The first results were handed to Patti. She looked over the pages and handed them to me. Conway and I took separate pages and saw they were lists of therapy groups for vets with PTSD, who were in those groups, their names, addresses and contact information. It even listed the name of the group leader. Thirty minutes later another set of pages were handed to Patti, again more group therapy sessions. The secretary returned and, almost embarrassed, handed Patti more pages. We looked at them and found these listing all the clinical staff handling the PTSD therapy groups including their addresses, cell numbers and last names. An hour later we were handed more individual and group therapy groups. Dr. Rumpp stopped grazing on his keyboard, his face still red, sweat more profusely dripping down his forehead. He was glaring.

"Ya'll have what you want." belligerently said. "Now get out!!" he yelled, spitting saliva at the same time.

"Modern technology, Dr. Rumpp," I said. "Can you put all this data on a memory stick for us?"

You could slice the tension in the air. He damn near exploded, then did. "Get out!!" he yelled, pounding his fists on his desk.

We all rose, turned and exited. The secretary led the way out of his office. The door was closed behind her and you could hear him scream "You sonavabitch!" He wasn't a happy camper and it'd taken nearly four hours to get the information which might have only taken 30 minutes if his attitude had been cooperative. Patti leaned back into his office and said, "Thank you." The secretary smiled at us when we left. She was gloating and gave each of us a high five; we'd burnt his you-know-what.

Their police presence simply faded away down a corridor of the hospital, no doubt embarrassed by the Administrator's order and their observation of him in action.

Conway surprised all of us when he said to Patti, "If you need some backup for your report to the VA regarding their administrator's behavior, surprise, I recorded and filmed parts. of his explosive rants."

"You did what?" she exclaimed. "Incredible and wonderful. If you can forward a copy to me, I'll include it in my report as an addendum. Thank you, Conway, for doing that."

Returning downtown, I asked Conway to duplicate the lists, get the clinical staff names to Dr. Ward and arrange a morning meeting with Sherlock. I asked if he would contact Lewis-McChord and check on their progress, and to give me a complete set of what we had just received and keep a copy for himself. I also suggested if it was appropriate, the next time we visited with Troy, we might want to share it with him too so he could see and get a feel for what we had encountered at the VA.

I had another obligation; I was leaving early for a family commitment before our kids returned to college. I then suggested to Conway, he may want to spend time with Mommy-to-be.

Patti had returned to her office to file a report with her DC office and the VA as to how this situation was resolved. Maybe that wasn't the appropriate word, but we got what we had come for. Knowing her, she was recommending the local administrator be relieved of his duties because of his arrogance, belligerence and intentional dragging of his feet even with a federal warrant in front of him, and his demeaning behaviors toward federal and local law enforcement officers. And she would prove it too. He tried to play a game, but when you're up against the SAC here in Seattle, you'll lose. I'm also sure she will tell him he was a poor placement, dragging his southern redneck attitude to the Pacific Northwest. She never cuts anyone slack if it's warranted; in this case, it is.

"Give Troy a call and let him know we have the VA information," I requested of Conway. Thanking him, I checked out.

19

A shower and some clean clothes were needed. I knew Patti would be along any time and we had a dinner date with our kids. We had dinner reservations in the restaurant at the top of the Space Needle, Seattle's 605-foot icon from the 1962 World's Fair. The restaurant rotates so you literally get a 360-degree view of Seattle and the Sound. Renovations are planned for the Space Needle, but we were just getting in before things changed. We decided rather than drive, we'd pile into a cab.

Patti got back to our hotel about a half-hour later and we took a shower together, resisting the urge to bag the dinner and become entangled for the night. That'll come later.

"We need to ask Neil about his graduation. He hasn't said much, and I assume Susan is graduating at the same time," I asked.

"Agree, we need to attend."

"What do you make of all his questions the other day?"

"Not sure; I just think he's gleaning more information about us and our careers. Probably blocked it out with his dad's death, and, of course, he knows nothing about your background," she replied.

"Well, he's done some homework, knowing about the grueling fitness course and your yellow brick," I added.

"Yeah, he's smart. But I wonder why he needed to know now. The yellow bricks use to sit among some of our books on the shelves in our den. Maybe that's what triggered his curiosity."

We dressed and met Neil and Susan in the lobby. Waiting for the cab, they began to tell us of their exploration during the day to the Museum of Flight, a special place celebrating flight, space, heroes, and planes. Built by Boeing, it's an amazingly busy museum with simulators, short clips on aircraft and space, and displays of military and commercial aircraft, along with a supersonic spy plane and Air Force One from the Eisenhower era.

The cab ride was short, and the conversation a bit awkward; 3 stuffed in the back and one in the front. We arrived at the Space Needle and took its outside elevator up to the restaurant. The observation deck is above the restaurant, offering awesome views of Seattle, the Sound, and the Olympic and Cascade Mountains, with plans to expand that visitor experience.

"What a spectacular view," remarked Neil gazing out the window once we were seated. "It's awesome!"

"It's beautiful isn't it. We're lucky tonight, with such clear weather. Now you can see the reason we love living here," I said.

After we reviewed the menus and ordered an appetizer, I squeezed Patti's hand under the table.

"Son, when's your graduation? You haven't said much."

"It's coming up fast, early part of June."

"Your Mom and I would like to attend this significant moment in your lives."

"Both Susan and I are graduating and will walk. It's being held at the RIMAC field on campus. There's plenty of space and I'll get an invitation, parking passes and directions."

"I haven't even asked what's your major and yours, too, Susan."

"I majored in Computer Science with two minors, Business Administration and accounting. Susan majored in Pre-Law with a minor in Business Administration. You can guess in what classes we met," said with a proud smile as he winked at her.

"Any job prospects?"

"As a matter of fact, yes. I've got a job with a government

agency. Susan will be entering law school."

"It must be nice to have your degree and a job as you walk out the stadium."

Patti chirped in, "What'll you be doing and is it in San Diego or Southern California?"

"Not really, Mom."

"So?"

Neil looked at Susan and they both smiled. "We'll be flying to the east coast to live, work and go to school."

"Come on Neil. You're being evasive again. Not like you," added Patti scowling.

"Having fun, Mom. We are like father and mother. I've been recruited by your company and will fly to Quantico for training, beginning a few weeks after graduation."

Patti was stunned, and then began to cry and smile at the same time. She was squeezing my hand and then got up, walked around and hugged and kissed Neil. She then hugged and kissed Susan.

"I'm surprised but so thrilled for you. Now Dad and I understand your many questions the other night."

"Susan will attend law school at Georgetown University while I'm at Quantico. When I get time off, which is probably nil, I'll buzz over to spend time with her."

"Have you decided any particular field of law, Susan?" I asked.

"Not particularly, but with Neil becoming an agent, I've thought about litigation, like in a prosecutor's office. I know, too, the Bureau has lawyers on board, and they may want me along with Neil."

"How do your parents feel about law school in the east?" Patti asked.

"They're thrilled I'm pursuing a career like my dad's. That's what makes what we're doing so special."

"So, we know you're graduating within a few weeks. What about getting married?" Patti pursued.

"Neil told you I want to be a June bride, but my kid brother's in the Navy. My family is small with just my parents and an uncle and aunt and their families."

"This has been a trip of surprises. First, I arrive unexpectedly and surprise you with Susan. Now you learn I'm following in your footsteps and Susan in her dad's footsteps."

"Did you seek out this job, better yet, career?" Patti asked Neil.

"No. My plans were to find a corporation I would enjoy working for and build my career. Susan and I thought with her law degree, we'd make an awesome corporate team. Now we'll just be awesome," grinning broadly from ear to ear.

"And?" Patti urged.

"Mom, they came after me. They knew all about me, and they knew about you and dad. One day, I received a call to meet a recruiter on campus and the rest is history. I was a little surprised. I didn't ask or apply. I was called. We met him; Susan went along. When we got there, two agents were present, asking questions and then offering the opportunity. They knew me before I opened my mouth."

"How did you react?" Patti asked.

I just listened and absorbed this incredible story.

"At first I wasn't sure how to react. In part, I thought them brash to invade my background and dad's death. But because they were the FBI, I knew from your work, they can find everything about anyone without much effort. They had done their homework and knew what they wanted."

"Did you immediately accept or take the proverbial 'time to think it over'?"

"I'd watched you and dad and your careers, how much you cared about it and how much you felt you were making a difference in people's lives. Then, Dad, I asked you about your background with your dad and uncle as role models and it confirmed the decision I made. We took a couple of days to reflect on their offer and called them to meet with us again."

"Did they hand you the contract?"

"Not at first. They asked if I had questions, and I said no. They coyly asked if I had talked with you, and I said no. They told me their offer was special, as they were wavering the fact I was 22 not 23, and had no work experience. They must have felt I was a good investment, as they slid the contract across and asked me what I wanted to do. I took the paper and signed it."

"Wow. After our sobbing conversations about your dad and the murderer, I thought the last thing you'd want to do is become an agent. You were not really happy when he was gone."

"Yeah, Mom, but you both built a warm home for me to express those feelings and to watch you and dad struggle with being family when he was gone so much."

"That's why your decision surprises me."

"It's a good decision, and now you and Dad will have to attend a second graduation at Quantico."

"That's a deal," she smiled. Her face was radiant, and she was so proud of her son, our son, and what he has made of his life, considering his dad's murder.

Quantico. Never been there, so this will be an excursion for me but memories for Patti. Now we were watching the glittering world below revolve, changing perspective. We finished dinner and at the base of the Space Needle, hugged and kissed our kids. They were going to walk through the Seattle Center, look for the dancing water fountain, while we headed back to the hotel.

Having returned to our room, she said "I'm proud of what he's decided to do with his life, what they've planned together."

"He's your, our son, and has demonstrated incredible resilience. He's made a good choice selecting Susan, too."

"Aren't they adorable. She's a sharp and feisty one and will keep him on his toes."

"They both have good heads on their shoulders and will make their life together work. He'll graduate before her and I'm sure they've discussed his assignment and its effect on finishing law school. But I'll project within five years, maybe six, we'll be grandparents," I mused.

"You may be right. I find it interesting the Bureau gave me those awards and then waivered Neil's entrance requirements. I'm honored on the one hand, surprised and appreciative on the other."

"Like his Mother, he'll make a talented agent."

We hugged and cuddled. We both were exhausted this evening, but it was a good exhaustion.

20

The sounds of weapons popping, screams from those dying, visions of death, bloodied, lifeless, and deformed bodies, the gruesome smells and then deadly silence; unwanted images haunting him day and night.

"Duck! Incoming! Take cover!!" Dreams, but real, startling him awake in a cold sweat. Though prescribed, the drugs he's been given provide little relief from the all-too-real mental pictures. The theatre in his mind is always rerunning violent newsreels.

He's crawled in the dark of night into villages where his job, and those with him, was to sneak into homes and kill the enemy. Many were gathered with family or other soldiers, so their orders were clear, eliminate everyone, quietly and thoroughly. Were they the enemy or innocent villagers? That wasn't for him to decide. His orders were clear: eliminate anyone and everyone. He carried those orders out without question, detached, ruthless, almost robotically.

Because of their black ops, his unit was set apart from the main group, almost like they had leprosy. They had their own village within the compound, part of but set apart from, no fraternizing with the other soldiers. None of the others were to know who they were or what they did or where they went at night. They were invisible. They worked nights, slept days. They talked little, even among themselves, especially about any of their nighttime activities, yet depended on each other for support and protection. Each had the other's back. A deadly daily routine: eat, sleep, get their orders when to move out and to where, disassemble, clean, and reassemble their weapons and wait. They would follow their orders; heavy duty trucks would move them from camp to a staging area and from there, they walked, most time many miles.

When he joined Delta Forces, he was trained as a professional soldier. When given his special assignment, he thrived on the demands and expectations: specialized weapons training, physical and mental fine tuning, hand-to-hand combat and use of a hand weapon with a silencer, one shot, dead. Honing his skills as a lethal trained sniper, he was able to hide, more like disappear, by controlling his breathing, focusing his thoughts and remaining motionless for hours, if needed. He was a professional killer, a killing machine. No emotions. No reactions to killing. Do as instructed and it was done. No questions asked.

Afternoon's briefing about their night's operation heightened tensions. No paper, just verbal commands, and instructions. Maps and sketches had to be memorized as they were not useful after dark. The nights held many unknowns: who they might unexpectedly encounter; who wasn't where they should be; walking distances, avoiding visual detection and those stinking IEDs; sneaking into an encampment or village and killing those there; load up, move out and onto another mission. They just kept coming, mission after mission, orders after orders, killings after killings, the oozing of lives into red puddles. Each day the same boring routine he could do in his sleep. Each night the same conditioned tension between life and death.

Home, back in the good old U.S of A, some tell him "thank you for your service", but so trite and meaningless compared to what he'd seen, heard and done. He's still over there, still reliving the numbness of killing and watching red blood flow from head wounds, brains splattered on beds and walls. One shot, you're dead. He was deadly at what he did. He wasn't sure what was gained, but after a long and exhausting two years in hell, out of a six-year commitment, he thought he'd fulfilled his duty for his country.

21

I wasn't late or particularly early back into the office. Staying in a hotel bed, even with my sweetheart, wasn't the same as my own bed. Then again, the new one should arrive within a couple of days at our houseboat. It was something Patti and I jumped on, laid on, and, well, wished we could have. With a latte in hand, I was ready to tackle another day of looking for that proverbial needle in the haystack.

"Hey, Conway! Have you had a chance to browse the lists the VA provided?"

"The clinical staff names had all the information Caitlin needed and were sent to her. She said she'll begin interviewing by phone and letting them know what we were working on related to these murders. This would give them time to think about their patients. She said she'll tell them we're waiting for the Lewis-McChord names to cross-reference with the VA names. If something materializes, she'd get in touch with them again seeking further information."

"Well, at least that process is underway. Heard anything from Lewis-McCord?"

"They're progressing and think maybe tomorrow. They'll FedEx the package to our office. But you know, I've been thinking, which can be dangerous."

"Thinking about what? A name for the baby?" I asked.

"No funny guy. Our case."

Sherlock walked in. "Hey guys, what goes?"

"We have another stumper," Conway began. "Kelly and I have been to Lewis-McCord and the VA, and are receiving data on discharged soldiers with Special Forces training and vets who might be in therapy for PTSD."

"Whoa, back up a minute. What's this all about?"

"You're right. Forgot we haven't brought you up to date on these homeless murders."

"Yeah, saw that in the papers. Wasn't sure if you were working the case."

"We are. Here's what we have to date, in a manner of speaking. Each murder has been planned, one bullet to the head, no shells left behind. Done in the early morning hours, no one has seen or heard anything. The killer stalks his targets, so knows what he's doing. Dr. Ward, the Forensic Psychologist at U-Dub (a fond reference to nearby University of Washington), has done a profile for us of the killer. It's based on having identified the slugs from the victims as from a military weapon Sig Sauer Mark 25 9mm with a silencer. The press does not have that information. When she was told how each homeless was killed and some hidden in their sleeping bags, the one-shot to the head and the Mark 25 suggested a professionally-trained killer, likely a product of Special Forces training, a sniper or someone like that. We're getting two sets of data, one already in hand and the other coming likely tomorrow. This is where you come in."

"What kinds of data?"

"Sherlock, I have serious respect for you when it comes to piles of data requiring one of your algorithms to sort into something logical," I said. "We're giving you a copy of the PTSD group and individual therapy sessions held by the Seattle VA. You know what it is?" He nodded affirmation. "Dr. Ward thinks the killer might be a vet suffering from PTSD. Lewis-McCord is sending us data on discharged vets with special training. Cross-checking the lists, we're hoping you can narrow down the data to potential persons of interest, living locally, vets who have issues."

"What are you doing with it?"

"Once we get matching names, we'll pass them to Dr. Ward, who's working with the VA's clinical psychologists. She'll ask them for greater detail on each individual to see if the clinicians have more insights to offer, concerns to express, or simply a red flag for one reason or another. If so, we'll take those names and begin a more targeted investigation, more than likely face-to-face interviews; in some cases, we may wish to have a person of interest put under surveillance to see what they do and where they go, particularly at night. We hope this process will give us something more than what we have now, which is nothing."

"What do you mean red flag?"

"Names on paper may not reflect other more severe issues or concerns as seen by the clinicians."

"Like what?" Sherlock pursued.

"Anger issues, threats, mental imbalances or whatever other condition the clinicians reveal to Dr. Ward," I added.

"Sounds complicated. I didn't know you had a military connection to work with. Makes some sense. How did the Army and VA feel about this?" asked Sherlock.

"The Commanding Officer at Lewis-McCord was cooperative. Ready to get the information extrapolated from their database to us. As I said, it's due here sometime tomorrow. The VA was a circus. We had to get a federal warrant before their administrator, a Dr. Rumpp, would cooperate. Then again, you would've loved seeing Patti at work, federal agent toe-to-toe with belligerent federal employee who wanted a warrant and thought he could push back. She did a command performance and gave him two options: give us the information as requested in the warrant or go to jail. She won!"

"Yeah, I would have loved seeing that." Pausing. "His name

is what?"

"You heard it right," said with a big smile. "So, your mission, should you accept, is to combine the data and look for common names. We've got a needle in a haystack and are hoping this produces something."

Sherlock took the first group of data and retreated, smiling as he knew he could do it with ease.

22

"Okay, Conway, let's go. It's better than sitting here waiting for moss to grow."

White Center is a small residential-retail area near the south side of Seattle's boundaries, butting up against Burien. In fact, like many metropolitan areas, you don't even know when you're in one city verses another. We decided to use our precinct office in White Center as our beginning point.

Visiting with the officers on duty, we got a feel for the area and the business behind where the bodies were found. Economically, this was a very moderate-to-low income area, very diversified ethnically and, unfortunately, residence for several gangs. New low-income housing was recently built to the east of its downtown, with parks and green areas. Where the victims were found was behind a grocery store; the dumpster might well have been their source for dinner. We asked if they knew of any security cameras in the area and they indicated there were.

"Behind the grocery store and its dumpster is an ideal hiding area; how did our killer know that?" Conway asked.

"Who knows?" was the officer's response. "If they've lived in this area, for any period, no doubt they knew about its location, among others. The homeless are creative in finding shelter and food."

"It begs the question as to how our killer found their site; someone must have seen something," I remarked.

"Unfortunately, Kelly, our interviews revealed nothing. Not many are awake at those hours."

The officer then provided us the name and location of the grocery store and suggested, as we had planned, we visit with its owner. The owner, Mr. Nguyen, is Vietnamese and a meticulous businessman and very cooperative; after the usual introductory formalities, he showed us his security system.

"I have two cameras, one inside my store, the other one showing the back area. The back camera is set up under the roof in a spot not so easy to see. But it sees whoever is trying to get into the dumpster or back door," said Mr. Nguyen.

"What about your rotation of these tapes?" I asked.

"I rotate tapes every week on Sundays and retain tapes for a month."

Asking him to pull up the tape for the date we needed was redundant as he'd already began his search on his desk computer.

"What are we looking at?" I asked.

"The camera is at an angle to the back door and has a broad field of vision. Entering, you actually walk underneath the camera and that might be why the killer didn't realize he was being photographed."

Mr. Nguyen began to run the tape for the night in question, beginning just after dark. He said the camera had a motion sensor, otherwise it's idle. When activated it notes the time and date. He was on fast forward, looking for when the camera was activated.

"Okay," he said, "we've got the two homeless guys entering our view and obviously going to the dumpster. The freshest foods are on top, disposed of just before we close, though we discard throughout the day. They found something and are walking behind the dumpster. At that point, they're out of sight."

"It's a great cover and probably one where they felt safe," remarked Conway.

I said to Mr. Nguyen, "Will your system return to idle and pick up again with another motion?"

"Yes. It's now in hibernation until there's other motion. Because it's an outside camera, we made it this way to preserve tape. Often, we find little happening during the night, unless someone visits our dumpster."

"So, the next time your camera comes alive, someone or something has caused the camera to activate."

"Yes," he responded paying close attention to his screen. Then it began to track.

"What's happening?" I asked.

"Someone just entered the camera's view. Note we have a time stamp on the film, so this activity is taking place at 1:59am."

We watched as a dark figure in a hoody entered the screen and cautiously moved to the dumpster and paused. All we could see was his or her back.

"Can you go back and slow motion the film, please," I asked.

He reversed the tape and began again, in slow motion, with the person walking up to the dumpster, pausing, then stepping around, still visible, with raised arms, pointing something behind the dumpster. He bent over and briefly disappeared then retreated quickly; as he turned, not realizing he was on candid camera, we saw his face, in a manner of speaking. He was wearing night goggles like those used in the military. It covered his face, along with a ski mask, but gave us insight into how he's able to see so clearly in the dark.

"Can you print a photograph of his face?" I asked. "In fact, may we have several copies and the tape?"

With a touch of a button, the printer to his left shot out several pieces of paper. It had captured the image. It wasn't much for CSI, or any of us, but our first break, if you want to call it that. Mr. Nguyen then made a copy of the tape and handed it to us. We thanked him and left. We had our first break, so to speak; no firm identity but we now know how our killer is able to negotiate his maneuvers.

"What do you think we got?" Conway asked as we were leaving.

"We have a visual confirmation of the killing, date and time. When the figure bent over, he probably retrieved the shells. The gun was not visible, and the taping system has no sound. It wouldn't have mattered, anyway, as he uses a silencer. The face is covered," pausing, I then added, "We have the killer on tape but no way to identify him. However, we know he wears night vision goggles and shows no limp."

"The Sergeant isn't going to be thrilled with what little we've got," Conway observed.

"He may not be, but it's our first so called break. We have what happened on tape. I'm hoping CSI can help with some physical features like height and weight. Maybe they can tell something about his face or, for that matter, whether it's a he or she."

23

"Agent Hancock, we've got a visual of our killer wearing night goggles and that's about it."

"Agent? Funny man."

"Well I could call you Patti, or, more appropriately, Honey. Just don't want to embarrass you."

"Don't worry about me. Honey is fantastic and crazy nice. Now you said you have a visual. You should be happy, but I gather from the tone, not so."

"Yeah, something along those lines. He made a mistake and didn't realize he was on camera. The camera covered the back of the building. He's wearing night vision goggles and was dressed in black. CSI has the film too. Not much to show but we're taking a closer look."

"Get me a copy of what you have when you can, and I'll see if we can help. The goggles would seem to confirm your suspicions of a military background, otherwise, doesn't sound like much to work with."

"Thanks, it's worth a try. Will have Tucker get a copy to you. We're on our way to see the Sergeant and show him what we have, more like don't have. Will chat later. Oh, by the way, Honey, remind me what are we doing tonight with the kids?"

"Hum, getting forgetful, at such a young age." Pausing, you could hear her smile, too. "Yea, well. Too much on my plate," I responded.

"It's their last night, so I've made reservations for 7pm at Salty's on Alki. The view of the city's lights and skyline will be a nice going-away gift. They'll meet us there, as they have overnight reservations near the airport for their early morning flight."

"Sounds great. Meet you at the hotel, and I won't get lost either," I said smiling, with a chuckle.

Conway and I had made an appointment with the Sergeant. We were surprised when we arrived and found the Chief as well. She's been an incredible leader, demanding our best, striving toward excellence, encouraging and supporting us when faced with difficult situations. Her credentials are impeccable, including decorations for valor. She's a tough administrator, straight shooter and adamant about following procedures and exhibiting ethical behaviors. I like her Irish accent, too, as there's some Irish, well, more Cornish, in my background.

"Greetings Chief, Sergeant." She nodded but said nothing.

"Any progress?" the Sergeant pointedly asked. We'd come prepared.

"The last two victims were found behind a dumpster in White Center. We visited with the store owner and found he has an external security camera. The location of the camera was not readily apparent but covered the store's back entrance and dumpster area. We got a photograph of who we think is the killer (handing them the photograph) and have asked CSI to assist. They can probably give us some physical features since the night goggle obscure his or her face. The time stamp on the footage coincides with the time of death determined by the ME. The night goggles suggest our killer has a military background and that may account for his accuracy with the killings. Second, the list of VA clinical staff has been sent to Dr. Ward, our consulting Forensic Psychologist. She feels whoever is doing the killings is suffering from PTSD and is irrational and dangerous. She agreed to interview the clinicians and see what might shake loose, someone of note from either individual or group therapy. We're waiting for the list of discharges, individuals with specialty training, from Lewis-McChord for Sherlock to correlate with the VA lists. The Army said we should have their lists tomorrow. Getting the Army's information was considerably easier than having to dealing with a red neck, southern VA administrator who demanded a warrant for access to the group and clinical staff information. Sherlock has the VA stuff and will be ready for the other."

"What more can you do?" asked the Chief.

"Chief, the White Center tape is our first visual. We have our killer on tape. All the other homeless sites were just as hidden, but there were no security cameras near any of them and no one we've interviewed heard or saw anything. We think he reconnoiters his targets and, in this recent case, knew the guys were behind the dumpster. He messed up and missed the camera. That being the case, someone must have seen someone or something, maybe a car, unusual or out of place but no one has come forth. Our precinct officers came up with nothing from their interviews. Dr. Ward's initial profile is pretty much on the money; she recognizes he's kept his targets as homeless but is cautious about him changing to a broader audience. CSI is looking at the tape for other physical features that might help our search such as size, weight, male or female. We know now for sure our killer is not crippled, limping, using crutches or a cane. And, Chief, we had the opportunity to visit with the three stooges plaguing your office for answers and wanting to vent about us not doing our job. When Conway and I were through with them, we'd educated them that their public servants were on duty, paying attention to who's being murdered without consideration of color, walk of life etc., and asked them to be useful in getting the message to the homeless community to protect themselves. Don't know if it helped but we think the uninformed left better informed, at least I hope so."

"Kelly, you know the department's under fire. I can see you're doing your best. Is there anything more you think can be done?" asked the Chief.

"Both Conway and I have looked at these murders from several angles and don't believe we've missed anything to date. The killer is cunning, an expert with his weapon, and, as Dr. Ward believes, former military, based on the slugs identified, well trained and no doubt mentally ill. I think, at this moment, we're on the right track and hopefully persons of interest will emerge from these clinical interviews. Dr. Ward is the one who has given us a trail to follow. Obviously, we need time, time to correlate and sort the data we are being given, time for Dr. Ward to interview the clinicians, and time for us to interview the identified persons of interest. Frankly, I don't know what that means for a timeline but am estimating very roughly, at least two more weeks before we begin to narrow down our options, or find we have nothing."

"I'm hoping that for my next press conference, you'll have something of substance for me to use. Right now, you need the space to flush out your perpetrator."

"We appreciate that, Chief. He or she may be hiding, but we think we're closing in. We'll find whoever it is."

24

Driving to Salty's took about 20 minutes. We left early and figured if we arrived early, we'd sit in the bar and wait for the kids.

"You've not said much," she asked.

"Had a bit of a surprise after we talked. Our meeting with the Sergeant also included the Chief. Surprise!"

"Had to be. What did she want?"

"Actually, she listened and responded positively. I think she just wanted to be sure we were doing what we could. The White Center break, if you can call it that, helped in our briefing as it's current with a visual, even if you couldn't see much or recognize a face. The goggles were helpful."

"Did you let them know we were helping?"

"With the Chief present, I thought it best not to. I did say the VA wanted a warrant before they would cough up names, but that said, neither the Sergeant nor the Chief asked about the warrant. The Sergeant would understand since he is in the loop on our relationship. I didn't want her to get into protocols again."

"Probably wise," she responded.

"Not much more can be done than what's already in the works. It's a matter of waiting to see what breaks from interviews or, maybe, a mistake on the part of the killer."

"Tonight, it's our last time with our kids. Let's enjoy our time and not talk shop."

"That's okay with me." Pausing. "Our son has distinguished

himself and you should be bubbling with pride."

"I am. I had no clue he might join the FBI after all the other stuff, but he's really taken my breath away, including sharing Susan with us. I'm getting a fantastic husband (squeezing my hand), I have a son to be so proud of and now a daughter-in-law who is so precious, smart and beautiful."

"Yep, Neil knows how to pick them."

We pulled in and the valet took our car. Up the two short flights of squeaky, worn wooden steps, we entered a very noisy scene and checked in regarding our reservation. Another surprise: Neil and Susan were already seated.

Walking up to their table, "Okay, what's this costing us tonight? How much did you bribe the front desk for this wonderful corner view of the water and skyline? And you're aware that bribery is illegal," she said. Smiling, they got up and we all hugged and kissed and then took our seats. We gave the kids the best view of the skyline. We wanted them to have memories.

"You guys look fantastic. What have you been up to and where are you staying tonight?" I asked.

"We got a room across from the airport with a shuttle. We took our luggage and already checked in at the Hilton."

"And your flight?" asked Patti.

"Early. Too early for me but the least expensive option. Fortunately, only one stop and no change of planes. Will take a few hours, arriving just before noon."

"You know, you've been a wonderful surprise for me and your Mom. I'm so overwhelmed by your love and acceptance and love you both so dearly. I'm blest with you now as a part of my life along with your Mom. And I wish you both so much happiness and success in your careers and life together."

"Thanks, Dad. Our trip has been an exhilarating ride, sharing Susan with you, the thrill of my new career, and seeing Mom's engagement ring. I'm glad you are a part of our lives too."

It was a wonderful few hour of talking, laughing and crying, with hugs and kisses as we departed. Patti had a son to be proud of, who was able to navigate his father's murder. In fact, both had provided each other the reassurances they needed; they now know the who and why of Neil's murder and can move on as they have already done. As for me, the emotions and feelings are all mixed up and so wonderfully hard to describe. One day alone, next engaged to the love of my life, and now a son and daughter-in-law. Then the surprise of all surprises, "may I call you Dad?" Wow!

The kids had gone back to their hotel and we returned to ours; we were unencumbered, except for Snowball. Such a patient cat. We crawled into our hot tub. The glasses of wine, the hot water, and jets tickling our bodies, well, that wasn't the only tickling.

"They're gone. What do you think, Kelly?"

Smiling. "We got winners, two of them."

"Is that all you can say?"

"No, I can say your eyes are beautiful, you smile is seductive and your body is craving mine." There was some splashing and we were in each other's arms, kissing, caressing and cuddling. It was going to be another night short on sleep.

25

Arriving with a latte in my hand, there wasn't even time to sit down before the phone rang on my desk. It was from CSI. Tucker must have a hidden camera that tells him when I come in.

"Good morning, Kelly," Tucker began.

"Same to you as well. What's up?" I responded.

"We can't tell who the figure in your photo is, whether black or white," began Tucker, our CSI Team Leader. "We can't get access to the face or eyes and found he or she wears gloves. The hoody worn covered the back of the neck. He sure hides himself. Though the footage is in black and white, his outfit is dark, like what is worn in combat. He has on heavy boots. We agree, using the night vision goggles pretty much explains how it is easy for him to access what we had seen as almost inaccessible. We looked at his or her walk and since it was such a short clip, we're not sure if male or female. It's a smooth walk showing no signs of a limp or other difficulty with motor skills. We've determined height about 5'11 to 6-feet, weight less than 220. The weight might suggest a male but not necessarily."

"Anything else?" I asked.

"When he pointed his hands behind the dumpster, you can see them barely jerk from the movement of the weapon being fired, twice. Obviously, when he bent down, he was no doubt retrieving his spent shells."

"Good stuff, Tucker; much appreciated. We'll pass this information along to Dr. Ward as well. The motor skill issue may reduce the number of persons of interest."

"I'm just sorry we couldn't glean more off the film. Great break, in a manner of speaking, but lousy results," Tucker mused.

"It's fine and you did what you can. Thanks," clicking off.

"Good news and bad news," as I looked at Conway.

"Bad news first, please."

"CSI cannot ID the suspect."

"Here we go again," Conway said with a smile.

"Yeah, just kidding but they can't. They can't be sure if male or female; the goggles and his dark outfit including the hoody obscure any chance to determine skin color. Military type boots but as the film is in black and white, nothing else distinguishes itself. They said they could see two jerks of his arms behind the dumpster, probably the shooting of his victims. And they estimate the killer to be around 220 pounds and 5'11"-6'."

"That's a start, I guess."

"And I also forgot, CSI did not see any limp or motor skill difficulties, so it confirms what we reported to the Chief and Sarge. What little we have should give Dr. Ward some criteria for sorting out who might be a person of interest."

"What do you mean by that?" quizzed Conway.

"Simply, someone with a limp or artificial limb may have noticeable motor skill challenges. Tucker say the walk was smooth with no observable limp."

The front desk called; there was a package for us. It had Lewis-McChord as the return address. Good timing. Conway went to retrieve it.

It was a strange feeling I was having, anxiety over what we might find; better, who we might find among all the data being massaged. We're looking for a killer and are looking at names, brave men and women who served with honor, now in a battle to regain balance in their personal lives after seeing and participating in such gruesome combat situations. Frankly, I'm glad I was an MP, and saw these brave souls returning and finding themselves aliens in a strange land, struggling. It makes you wonder why one goes over the edge with all the help being offered.

"Here's our donation from the Army. How do you want to handle this data?" asked Conway.

"Let's get copies made. Get a set to Sherlock ASAP. Give Dr. Ward a call and let her know, as well, we have the Army's data. I'll call the Sergeant. We'll have to rely on Sherlock to sort through the data. Once he identifies any names appearing on both lists, we'll have him get those to Dr. Ward."

Duplicating took a little bit of time. Conway got copies to Sherlock and notified Dr. Ward while I called the Sergeant. Had to leave him a voicemail, essentially saying we had the Army's originals on our desk and were impressed with what they had gleaned for us from the DD214s.

It had been many years since I was in the Army and haven't looked at my own DD214. I vaguely remember all kinds of information and codes representing my years as an MP. Now the Army was sharing a shortened version of what others had accomplished during their enlistment.

After a few hours of reading, we needed air and food. The walk to the food court in the Columbia Center, located across the street from our department, gave us a chance to stretch our legs and smell fresh air. We were gone not quite an hour, returned finding the Sergeant wanting to see us.

"What've you got, Kelly?" he barked.

"Got my message I see. We have the data from the Army and

it's impressive. Good thumbnail sketches of vets. Sherlock has a copy and we let Dr. Ward know Sherlock is working on correlating the data."

"So, what's next and how soon will you have results?" he grumbled.

Conway offered, "We have the data where it can do some good, in Sherlock's hands. He said he's already loaded the VA information into an algorithm and was simply waiting for the Army's. As soon as he can sort stuff, we'll have something to work with."

"How long is this expected to take?" asked the Sergeant with a sour expression.

"We're not sure, but it's in process as we speak. It's far more than we had yesterday. As soon as we have names that appear on both lists, Dr. Ward will interview their therapists and when someone is red flagged, we go to work with interviewing or setting up surveillance."

"Sounds like a reasonable plan. The Chief wants an update, so I'll give her what you're doing. Any thoughts about timelines?"

"Not really. We're doing the best we can. Gave you both my estimate earlier and from what I see, we're on track."

"I can live with that. Now, did the FBI identify the photograph?"

"No. The night vision goggles blocked any attempt at facial recognition. We now know, at least, how he was able to get in and out without tripping. Some of those sites were dark and buried."

Then I looked at him with a quizzical glance.

"Kelly, give me a break. Patti is your girlfriend and the SAC. And I think you were wise not to mention it to the Chief, though you baited the matter with that reference of a warrant. Fortunately for you, the Chief did not pursue it."

"Appreciate that. I'm hoping something does materialize.

CSI gave us some physical features based on viewing the tape, but couldn't identify firmly if male or female, white or black. The goggles obscured too much. They gave us a possible height, weight range and said there was no limp or motor skill difficulties, confirming what I told you and the Chief earlier. This no doubt will eliminate someone with a physical disability from a pool of persons of interest."

"Stay with it, you guys. I feel you're closing whatever the gap is between knowing and not knowing who the killer might be."

With that, the Sergeant dismissed us and placed a call to the Chief.

Skimming hundreds of capsule profiles of discharged vets was not an exciting endeavor. The afternoon was slow, except the boot dropped again. Something may have changed; we called to confer with Dr. Ward.

"He's struck again," I said.

"Give me the details."

"First, it may have been evening hours not dead of night. That is a significant change unless these victims were targeted by a wannabe. The location is puzzling too. Backside of the Chinese Garden at South Seattle College. The campus still has evening classes."

South Seattle College lies on a plateau overlooking the Duwamish area; it's in the Delridge area south of the West Seattle Bridge. One of three colleges in the Seattle College District, it's known for its culinary training program and outstanding academic programs. It's a college campus without dorms. On its north end, years in the making, a special Chinese Garden was developed with its sister city as part of the larger Arboretum; not only are these an attraction for visitors, they're an integral part of the college's Landscape Horticulture Program, a living laboratory for their students.

"Who found the victims?"

"One of the students walking with his girlfriend."

"Has the ME confirmed time of death? It may not have happened today but last night."

"Have not got his feedback yet. I'll check and get back to you. I'm just concerned if it happened during the day hours, what it means, what's likely happening in the head of the perpetrator?"

"I know and would join you in that concern. Let me know what the ME says, and we'll go from there."

"Sherlock should have our correlated results shortly that will help you. Names!"

"That'll be appreciated, Kelly. Have begun to establish rapport with the clinical staff. Need to go." She clicked off.

I called Dr. Charlie Bain, our talented and overworked ME.

"Any information on those homeless victims from South Seattle College?"

"They're dead," chuckling a little. "Seriously though, same MO, one shot to the head. Forensics has the slugs. They've been dead at least twenty-eight to thirty-six hours, meaning they were killed last night, not this evening."

"Well that's one positive, in a manner of speaking. Dr. Ward and I were hoping he hadn't changed his MO."

"I don't blame you. Have you got any other clues yet?"

"Not specifically. We have the killer on film from a security camera he missed where he killed those two homeless hidden behind the dumpster at the grocery store in White Center. CSI gave us some possible characteristics and features and ruled out other issues; he was wearing night vision goggles which explains how he's able to get in and out without being seen."

"That's more than you've had!"

"Yeah, but still not much. Sherlock's working the discharge data received from the Army and the VA therapy group data, looking for that proverbial needle in a haystack."

"Sounds like a lot of irons in the fire. I don't envy the tediousness of this case but sounds like you're onto something with his use of night goggles and his apparent dark attire. Good luck." We clicked off.

I made a quick call to Dr. Ward and left a voice message. Then I brought Conway up to date on the findings and put a call in to the Sergeant.

"Again, Kelly? You must enjoy breaking up the exciting humdrum of my job."

"Don't want you to get to bored."

"Thanks!"

"The victims at South Seattle College were, according to the ME, killed between twenty-eight and thirty-six hours ago, so the MO is the same. I was concerned he had changed his MO. He hasn't."

"And progress on your lists?"

"Sherlock is getting close. Once we get his crosschecked data, I'm confident something will be revealed. That last step is up to Dr. Ward."

"I hope so. If this is poker, I'm losing my shirt," said in a cynical tone. "And I don't like losing!"

"Nor do we," I affirmed.

26

Conway and I brought in lattes from the corner coffee shop and began to dig into the stacks of papers on our desks. Sherlock bounced in with an unusual smile on his face.

"Hi guys."

"Did you find our killer?" I asked.

He sat down in the guest's chair in our office, smiled and leaned back with his hands behind his head. "No, but I found something else."

"Well, don't keep us waiting, what is it?"

"It's not an 'it' but a 'her' and she's incredible."

"Well, I'll be. When has all this happened?" I replied.

"Remember when I asked you for time off one evening some weeks back? That was our first of many dates. She's into computers as well, and runs a little shop fixing other people's messes."

"How did you meet?" Conway chirped in.

"There's a local computer club for geeks like me, where we exchange ideas and information, get caught up on systems type stuff, programs and the latest patches. She was there one night and that's the beginning, or the ending depending on perspective. We dated once, then twice, three, four, five and six times and then had some serious discussions about life in general; then she got down to basics, like what about her, and us, and where did I stand. Dumb me, I had to ask what we're talking about."

"And the final resolution?" Conway continued.

"You know me and how focused I get with a case and frankly

pay little attention to my needs let alone anything else. You've taken me out to eat to be sure I'm not starving to death."

"And?"

"We decided to move in together to see if it works. We're roommates and with her in my life, I'm learning some new things, will be making some adjustments and who knows what else."

I asked, "Do you love her?"

"I have a hard time expressing my feelings unless in digital code. Girls were never keen on me. Never had a prom date. Spent my time on computers, but now I must learn how to relate. I've let the computers do the talking, but now it's different. Clarice and I have had some incredible conversations, late night ones, in which we're able to express feelings. We're fond of each other, care about each other and believe we're in love."

"Clarice? Her last name?" I asked.

"Johns. Clarice Johns. She's like me. Never really had boyfriends, like I haven't had girlfriends; we started talking and it just clicked. She's an only child, her parents divorced. Not a good scene from what she tells me. Unlike me, she went to school for the certifications she needed to open her business. Now she's working on her bachelor's degree online in computer science. She got this idea of opening a neighborhood repair shop for those needing computer assistance and updates; she added a little coffee area and free Wi-Fi. The business has taken off. When I'm not here, I'm there."

"Well, I think the two of you are off to a good start," I commented. "It takes time to develop trust in giving yourself to another. Love is amazing and exciting," I added. "Congratulations, Sherlock. You deserve this in your life, and we are thrilled," as we shook his hand and patted his shoulder; I thought it couldn't happen to a more deserving person.

"When will we get a chance to meet her?" Conway asked.

"Soon."

Then it was time to get back to the business of finding our killer.

"How's your algorithm thing doing with all the data we piled on you?" I barged ahead.

"Lots of stuff, that's for sure. My computer is holding up with the task I've given it and we should have some initial results," pausing, "Well, I'm not sure when," pausing again, playing us, "How would you like the first results now? Surprise!"

Surprise it was. Guess I hadn't noticed the file folder he carried in as he took us in a direction we hadn't expected.

"What've you got?"

"You're getting thirty pages of correlated data, names that appear on both the VA and Army's lists. Maybe CSI can run background checks and come up with additional insights. I'm still entering what little data I have left, but this folder (he handed it to me) has the preliminary findings of those Dr. Ward may wish to explore with their therapists."

I could have kissed Sherlock but didn't want to upset Clarice or Patti. Conway took the folder and immediately went to the duplicating machine for copies, and sent copies to Dr. Ward, with a notation to 'call us.' It didn't take long.

"Kelly, Dr. Ward. Got Sherlock's information."

"Nice surprise. Sherlock's first deliveries, some thirty pages of vets with special training, discharged and living here locally, and in a VA therapy group."

"I love it and it's what I need for talking with the therapists. Just wanted to say thank you. Now I have a job to do," she clicked off.

Sherlock had meanwhile returned to his inner sanctum to crank out the last of the data. Conway and I took a few minutes to look over the data as well and decided a call to the Sergeant was in order.

"What have you got this time?" he asked in a ruffled voice. We had put him on speaker phone.

"We wanted you to know we have the first correlated data from Sherlock."

"Anything yet?" he growled.

"No, but it's more than we had minutes ago. Thought you should know the wheels are cranking. Once Dr. Ward and therapists identify red flags, they'll let us know and, as I said before, we go into action."

"Keep me posted." He clicked off. The Sergeant often wants results before we've had a chance to massage the information. He's under pressure from topside, and that we understood. So many deaths and yet no clue who's doing it or why. Even we're frustrated yet doing our best to piece this amazing jigsaw puzzle together.

I recognized my next incoming caller ID.

"Those night vision goggles obscured any possibilities of even the remotest of facial recognition. Bottom line: we have nothing. We ran the physical features but came up with too many to even think the data is useful."

"So, what you're saying is we have nothing to add to who the killer might be?" I asked.

"Yep, nada. Wish we could have given you something but this time the obscuring of the features provided nothing to work with. Sorry," she replied.

"I guess I owe you, even if you found nothing?"

"Oh yes, and ever so much. I'll collect later tonight."

27

"On another note," continued Patti, "can you set up a special gathering of the Seattle PD? I'd like to come over with a plaque of appreciation signed by our Director for the support Seattle PD gave us during the take down of the Colombian drug cartel."

"Can do. Want our Chief there?"

"For sure. We're bringing over an exceptionally large, flat, specially decorated celebration cake for the occasion."

"I hear something more at play and what might my sweet little precious one be up to?"

"We've established the protocol for the FBI and the Seattle PD, you and I, to work together when needed. I want to personally announce our engagement formally to the Chief, your Assistant Chief and Sergeant."

"Sneaky you, but I love it and you. Think our Sergeant already knows."

The Chief of Police agreed on a two o'clock time for the ceremony. The Sergeant agreed and invited officers and staff for the special presentation. The Chief agreed to meet with Patti and me before the ceremony in her office.

Taking the lead, I introduced Patti to Assistant Chief Plummer who oversees our Investigative Division. Patti had previously met the Chief of Police and Sergeant Troy. The hand shaking and pleasantries were slightly awkward. Then Patti took the lead.

"Chief, thank you for your quick response in hosting this 'thank you' ceremony. But that's not why I wanted to meet with you and the others before the ceremony. This is rather unusual. You know I grew up in Seattle and attended high school with Kelly. I left the area after college graduation and became an agent along with my husband. He was killed several years ago; a little over a year ago, I was assigned to Seattle. It was an unexpected assignment, but coming home, to where I grew up, was a wonderful breath of fresh air. What you may not know, but may have suspicions about, is that Kelly and I were high school sweethearts. When I returned and he asked to visit with the FBI, with your permission, regarding the case we're celebrating a successful end to today, we reconnected, not immediately, but eventually we courted again and rekindled our love." She paused, and I stepped in, taking her hand.

"A few weeks back, I asked Patti to marry me. Yeah, the big guy finally takes that big step. I'd like to introduce my high school sweetheart and fiancée, Patti Hancock."

There were smiles, hand clapping and handshakes and, in fact, some unexpected hugs.

"Congratulations. I've suspected something was happening. Just so much FBI in our recent cases, but now I see why. Unavoidable. Thank you, Patti," said the Chief, "and you can feel free to call me Carol."

"We have a presentation for you, Chief, and it comes from our Director who wishes he could be here but is tied up with Congressional Hearings. I'm the lucky one to say thank you to you and your department. Kelly and I just wanted you to know about us before the ceremony. There is no intention of distracting from what we wish to do and that's to say an enormous thank you," Patti smiled, looking at the Chief, Assistant Chief and our Sergeant.

The Sergeant looked at me with a slight grin; he had guessed, and he was right.

The Chief then said, "Then let's get this show on the road." With that we left her office to where the officers, staff and news representatives were gathered. The Chief led the way, followed by the FBI SAC.

As we entered, the room went silent. The Chief did not waste any time and immediately stepped up to the microphone.

"Ladies and Gentlemen," she began. She was standing before the crowd in her blue uniform and all her decorations and stars. The exceptionally large, flat, decorated celebration cake sat on a table in front of the podium with the word "Congratulations" in blue on white icing between the logos for the FBI and SPD. "Welcome to a special event for the Seattle PD and its partner, the Federal Bureau of Investigation. Without further delay, I wish to introduce Seattle FBI Special Agent in Charge Patti Hancock."

She turned to Patti and had her step forward; her shield was displayed from her left suit breast pocket. Flanked by the Chief and Sergeant, also in his dress uniform, along with the Assistant Chief for the Violent Crime Section, Patti made her presentation.

"Chief Flanigan, Assistant Chief Plummer, Sergeant Troy and members of the Seattle Police Department, it's my pleasure to stand before you today. It's been many years for me away from my hometown, and to be back has been a wonderful experience. Today I have a unique role

as the Director of the FBI is unable to be here. You know, bureaucracy, testifying before a Congressional Committee. So, the Director asked me to express, on behalf of the Federal Bureau of Investigation, our appreciation for your support in helping to capture two of the most-wanted international drug criminals in the world. Eduardo Delgado and Carlos Ramirez are in a Federal penitentiary awaiting their punishment. It was a case Homicide Detectives Kelly and Conway were working. The murder of a local family began a whole sequence of events leading to the internal collapse of their drug smuggling web; the cartel made some bad decisions and tumbled their own international operations. We were asked to assist. The persistence of Detectives Kelly and Conway connected the murders here in Seattle with the murder of my agent-husband several years earlier in Southern California. That resolution was welcomed by me and the FBI."

Pausing, she continued.

"On behalf of the FBI, Chief Flanigan, I wish to present you and the Seattle Police Department with a commendation authorized and signed by our Director. You made it happen and we are grateful. Washington DC knows what you did and wants you to know how important it is to them, and to our team here. Along with the Director, I present this plaque as a small token of our deep appreciation for the professional partnership."

Turning to the Chief and handing her the commendation and copper engraving on a mahogany plaque containing the FBI logo and inscriptions, they shook hands and stood together for press photos. The applause was loud and long; maybe it was just the ceilings were too low for all this frivolity. Then Patti began again, part of a surprise.

"Chief Flanigan, the FBI has taken the liberty to issue special commendations to accompany the departmental recognition. Chief, Assistant Chief Plummer, Sergeant Troy, Homicide Detective John Francis Kelly and Homicide Detective Robert Conway; the FBI wishes to recognize each of you for your support, tenacity, and enormous courage in toppling a notorious international drug cartel. We also wish to recognize Randy Sherlock and his incredible computer talents that helped unravel the convoluted networks for drug smuggling and money laundering. Our international partner, Interpol, and our overseas offices have taken the information you've provided and are, at this minute, boarding ships, closing ports, and arresting individuals tied to this enormous drug smuggling and money laundering network. Congratulations."

The Chief stepped back to the podium. "The City of Seattle

and the Seattle Police Department wish to thank the FBI team for your tenacity not only in getting your own killers but in helping us get ours. Thank you."

With a sly grin on her face, the Chief looked at Patti and me.

There was applause, cameras flashing and some whistles in the background. The Chief then said "Our ceremony is concluded. Let's celebrate."

There was lots of handshaking with "thanks" or "congratulations" depending on who was greeting whom. The mutually supportive role of a federal agency and the local police department was appropriately saluted and now celebrated with cake and soft drinks. The officers, staff and command staff stood around enjoying their moments away from the heavy duties awaiting them at their desks. Jurisdictional issues, who's in charge, who'll take credit, at this moment were a thing of the past. A new dawn was upon us as federal and local law enforcement worked together for the betterment of the community.

For me, the commendation was appreciated, but in no way diminished the hours it took to find a killer. The one lingering regret was the unnecessary deaths of two talented teens whose lives were taken, and society robbed of their contributions. At least there's a memorial scholarship, in their memory, at West Seattle High.

While Patti was working the crowd, I spotted the Chief and Sergeant talking and wandered over to them.

"Thanks, Chief. I appreciate your support and understanding."

"I think it's wonderful and you both deserve the happiness you've longed for," she added. "Any plans yet?"

"We're remodeling my houseboat to make it ours. We just spent a few days with her son and his fiancée. Beyond that, no date's been set. Neil is graduating from college in a few weeks and stunned Patti and me by announcing he was following his Mom and

Dad's career in the FBI, so we're looking at attending his Quantico graduation, too. We'll keep you informed. Thanks, Sergeant, for your support too." They smiled and shook my hand.

"You're one hellava cop, Kelly. Go and enjoy some cake," the Chief said. "Later you can tell me about our current evasive serial killer."

I wandered over to Randy Sherlock, standing alone and away from the crowd.

"You really are the master, Randy. Your talents broke that case wide open," I remarked.

"Just doing what I do best," he quietly replied.

"Well, I know you're uncomfortable in crowds, but know you are very much a valued colleague and friend. This is for you as much as it is for anyone else."

"I know, and thanks, Kelly. You sure are one good cop to work with and I appreciate you too.

28

Then came our anticipated challenge. No more speculating; we were looking for and hopefully going to find our perpetrator. The drama was unfolding, oh so slowly.

"Kelly, this is Dr. Ward. Of the subject profiles you've sent me, which we appreciate, we've identified eight who their clinicians, three of them, describe as passive-aggressive, bi-polar, and angry. They're sitting on their emotions or dismissing the group activity as unnecessary and intrusive. Some of the time they explode with emotions claiming no one understands them. Whatever, the clinicians have gut feelings these eight are playing a variety of mind games."

"They certainly were prepared to respond quickly to your request. You said from three groups? Eight candidates and three therapists, right?" asking to confirm her statement. "Did they sense any one of them to be more dangerous than the others?" I asked.

"Not totally. They're not even sure these could be our killers or would want to kill, though they've killed in the past; just very mixed up, isolated, angry vets."

"Can someone diagnosed with PTSD become violent or a threat to themselves?"

"All of the above. PTSD is in their heads; it's the protective reaction to severe traumas, observation of unsettling actions, and a reaction to something in which they participated. The traumas are outside their own framework, what they grew up with. They don't have the structure emotionally and psychologically to handle and process what they've seen or done, when placed back into civilian life. They aren't prepared," she added.

"Simply, the hidden victims of war," I added. "What I don't understand is why whoever it is, has targeted the homeless?"

"That's an ongoing, unanswered question, Kelly. It might be one of many reasons. It may relate to the former setting in which he was a military operative. It might not have any relationship to what he's done. We don't have that explanation and may never know."

"Send me those names and profiles. We'll take it from here and begin our investigations and interviews. Before I forget, we need the names of the psychologists who have identified these eight. We're putting them under a protective shield should our killer decide to turn on his therapist. You may want to let them know, too."

"Smart move, Kelly. Hadn't thought of that but agree; the one who flagged four of the names is Dr. Leslie Stephens. She oversees all the clinical groups and their therapists. She's one smart cookie too." She clicked off.

While we talked, the profiles appeared in my inbox. I decided to forward those names to CSI requesting background checks. Then I called the Sergeant.

"Sergeant, you'll be happy to know we've just received our first eight persons of interest from Dr. Ward."

"Finally!" he exploded.

"She's got names from three therapy groups, one therapist forwarding four names, each clinician suggesting these are persons of extreme interest because of their erratic behaviors. Little more standing out, currently, than their suspicions and concerns. We've asked CSI for additional background and will review each case, and determine our next steps regarding interviews, surveillance or both."

"Sounds like you have a plan and I am grateful to hear of this progress. I'll let the Chief know we're into some serious review and sorting of candidates for 'killer of the month' nomination."

His sarcasm obviously reflected his frustrations.

Where previously we had been frustrated for lack of leads, Conway and I now had our work cut out for us. What we had requested was now on our desks. In the quiet of our office, we began to read the synthesis profiles for eight vets, each one suffering from PTSD, in therapy, and of concern to their therapists.

> Sgt. Travis Sledge, 6'1", discharged 18 months ago, 8 years in Army, Delta Force. Wounded in Iraq but doesn't talk about where or how. Awarded Purple Heart. Single. Comes from a farm community in Western Nebraska, currently lives in Kent. Bold, obnoxious behaviors, struggles with issues in group therapy. No arrest records. Two traffic tickets and one DUI warning.

> Staff Sgt. Brett Noble, 5'-10", discharged a year ago. 8 years in Army. Delta Force, head wound in Iraq from an IED. Awarded Purple Heart and Bronze Star for meritorious combat duties. No details regarding where or how decorations were earned. Married, lives near Des Moines, two kids. Full disability with the VA, participates weekly in a PTSD therapy group, angry at the Army for a botched assignment. Works for the City of Des Moines. No arrest records. Born in Tacoma; attended Tacoma Community College before joining the Army. Parents live in Sequim, Washington. One of three children, two younger sisters in school.

> Staff Sgt. Benjamin Hassle, 6', discharged two years ago. 7 years in Army. Delta Force, Iraq and Afghanistan tours, head and groin wounds, Distinguished Service Award, Silver Star and Purple Heart. No details as to where or how decorations earned, Married, no kids. Works as security at front desk for Port of Seattle; lives

in Burien. No arrest records. Born and raised in Seattle. Attended Franklin High School. Parents divorced, mother in Lacey, father in Texas. No siblings. No longer in a therapy group; personal decision.

Staff Sgt. Anthony Franklin, 5'-11", discharged less than a year ago, 7 years in Army. Delta Force Iraq and Afghanistan, severely wounded during second tour; awarded Distinguished Service Cross, Silver Star, and Bronze Star for exemplary service and a Purple Heart for multiple injuries. How or where he earned the decorations are vague in his record. Single, attends VA therapy session, angry at life and feels nobody understands him. Attendance in his therapy group is erratic. Employed with a large retail store. No arrest records. Born in Shoreline. Parents divorced, mother lives in Kansas, father's whereabouts unknown. Ordered by Courts upon high school graduation into service over jail for bullying and getting repeatedly in trouble.

Sgt. Tracy Zimmerman, 5'-10", discharged 18 months ago. 6 years in service in Iraq and Afghanistan, multiple wounds, no physical disability, Bronze Star and Purple Heart. Where or how decorations earned unknown. Attends therapy sessions for severe PTSD. Bold, outspoken, aggressive, sometimes verbally explosive, angry at life. Threatened superiors while in service. Single, lives in Edmunds and works for the highway department. No arrest records.

Sgt. Norris Gamlem, 5'11", discharged 20 months ago. 8 years in the Army. Delta Force in Iraq and Afghanistan, multiple wounds including head, and left arm shattered; rebuilt. Leg with shrapnel in it, inoperable. Awarded Bronze Star and Purple Heart. No indications as to where or how decorations earned. Single. Lives in Burien. 100% disabled vet. Feels the Army owes him more for what happened to him. Having difficulty adjusting to life. Attends therapy group but has moments of irrational outbursts asking why no one understands. Other times sits with little to offer. Concerned there are other issues building inside. No arrest records. Born and raised in Seattle; attended Ballard High School.

Sgt. Orville Cushman, 5'-11", discharged 18 months ago. 7 years in Army. Delta Force, service in Iraq, severe wounds from an IED explosion; must go to VA monthly for tending of wounds and rehab. Awarded the Bronze Star and Purple Heart. Lives in Ballard, married with one kid. No arrest records. Attending North Seattle College working on degree in culinary arts. Tends to be quiet and withdrawn. Wondering if a ticking clock ready to explode or has exploded.

Sgt. Malcolm Fletcher, 5'11", discharged 18 months ago, 8 years in Army Special Forces, assigned overseas, operational background vague, multiple wounds, torso and extremities, including head wound requiring lengthy hospitalization and recuperation. Awarded Distinguished Service Cross, Silver Star, Purple Heart. 100% disabled. Lives in Capital Hill district. Divorced, one child. No arrest records. Attends therapy but alternates between silence and angry outbursts.

"Interestingly sad, such talented and decorated soldiers now suffering from their combat experiences," offered Conway.

"I agree. We have eight possibilities, all Sergeants, all wounded, awarded medals for their service and heroism, five singles, all attending or been in therapy, all live in or near the city. All seem angry, explosive, and frustrated. Not much to distinguish them as a possible killer, yet."

"They obviously saw and did some bad stuff that haunts them. In fact, their records don't even provide any insights into what they did or where," added Conway. "What's next?"

"My suggestion is we visit the one candidate who left his therapy group, SSgt. Hassle, and see why he's on this list."

"What do you want to do with the other seven?" Conway asked.

"We'll know after our first interview."

29

We called the Port of Seattle to get the work location of Sergeant Hassle. We drove over to Pier 69 and parked in front of the building, on Alaskan Way, placing our police pass on the dash and leaving our grill lights flashing. The sergeant was one of the security personnel checking visitors in at the front desk. There was another person on duty with him. Discretely we asked him aside flashing our shields and told him we wished to briefly visit with him. He told his colleague it was business and he'd be back shortly. We found a couple of chairs near the front windows. We were next to a fabulous glass-encased model of a container ship, one of those mega ships that carries 5000 containers.

"Sergeant Hassle, my name is Homicide Detective Kelly and my partner Homicide Detective Conway. We thank you for stepping aside for a few minutes to assist us in an investigation."

"What's this all about, Detectives?" he quickly asked.

"We've seen an abbreviation of your service record; quite impressive, especially your decorations. But you left your VA therapy group after a year. Your name was given to us, as a former PTSD patient we were asked to interview. Why did you opt to leave?"

"How the hell do you know all this about me?" he angrily responded. "That's privileged information. Don't get why that's important and why it would involve the Seattle PD."

"Please bear with us. We have been in consultation with your VA therapist as part of our investigation."

"So, you're homicide detectives. What does murder have to do with me? You can see I'm a top cop for the Port of Seattle," he bluntly stated.

"We're looking for your help and insights. Why did you leave your VA therapy group? Weren't you being treated for PTSD?" I continued.

"Don't know why you need to know," he stated. "Sounds like a ruse of some sort and I don't appreciate the breach of my privacy."

"I will affirm that our meeting is confidential," I responded.

"Yeah, just like my medical records. That sucks."

"Can we focus a little more on why we're here?"

"Yeah, okay." He paused. "I have PTSD and struggle with my life. Sessions became boring, though I did gain some insights into what I have. The reality is you're never cured. They trained me to kill but didn't train me how to live with it after all the killing."

"Your therapist felt you still have unresolved issues."

"Yeah, I guess I do, we all do, and will have for the rest of my life. Different situations and events will trigger recall and memories of things I did, saw and regret. Every day will be an ugly remembrance. Time served, rotten memories for life. Not what I would call a pleasant trade off."

"You were in combat?"

"Oh, yes. My duties took me and my platoon into dangerous territory day after day, hunting the enemy and wiping out their so-called staging areas. Suited up in all our gear, we'd walk miles clearing the path ahead. The tough stuff was when we had to go door-to-door and clear houses of their occupants or get into a firefight with hidden enemies."

"You were wounded and received several decorations?"

"All of us who serve, serve with honor. We do what we're ordered to do. Much of what I did was nasty, ugly. What I did and saw will always be with me. Cannot get the pictures out of my head.

Unresolved issues? You bet. At night I did more, a lot behind the enemy line, killing of individuals, told to kill not knowing if they were truly our enemy. They lived there and the logic seemed to be they were our enemies. Therapy was trying to give me tools to deal with those repeated visions and memories. Damn. I dream, at times, I'm back there where I no longer wish to be, but it's in my head, the awful memories. And I have to look at myself in the mirror each morning and admit I'm not such a nice guy."

"Sergeant, what were your specific responsibilities?" I asked.

"Behind the line at night, going into infested areas and quietly killing the enemy. During the day, more confrontations. I don't talk much more about it and that's why I get upset with the therapy sessions. They don't want to hear the truth, or acknowledge, in this case, that I was ordered to carry out some gruesome tasks."

"Can you share them with us?" I prodded.

"Let me put it this way. Regardless of how you see me, or what I am wearing as a security officer, regardless of the Army's decorations stuffed in a footlocker at home, I am not a nice guy. I killed at night; I killed ruthlessly. I killed without remorse; I did my duty, and for that I've got a headache, don't sleep well at night and can't have sex with my wife. I should be grateful? Maybe I should, as some of our heroes didn't come back. But I'm not there yet and may never be. Damn it, I can't piss without it hurting. No forgetting."

"How were you wounded?"

"Damn firefight with an unexpected patrol. We got hammered. Grenade nailed me good. Ticket home but not from the war!"

"Did your command figure out why there was an unexpected patrol?

"Not that I'm aware of. In fact, nothing was further said about our so-called behind-the-line classified operations. Even part of our own unit did not know what some of us did at night. We didn't talk about our nights in hell. But this unexpected encounter with the enemy, command must have been blind not to know where they were."

"How do you feel today about all that happened?" "As I said, it's a damn movie theater in my head, visions I cannot get rid of, sounds that echo, commands I hear and situations remembered, and I react to unexpected noises and sounds. I did a lot of ugly stuff as I've said, and those memories will always be with me."

"You're married with no children, working here with the Port of Seattle."

"Great job, a bit boring, but appreciated. Head of security and working the information desk. Guess my Army training qualified me for Head of Security. I have headaches from my head wound; doctors said it would decrease with time. I doubt it. Grenade got me in the groin so my wife and I are considering adopting children. Told you, every time I need to pee, it hurts. Decided I needed to move forward and felt my therapy group was holding me back. Too many war stories and looking backwards. I want a family, and to distance myself as far as possible from the ugly. Don't even want to be with other vets. Too depressing. I'm building my own life and a circle of meaningful friends in addition to our family."

"As a former Army MP, I appreciate your candidness and welcome home, Soldier."

"Thanks, but I'm still not sure what this is all about," he remarked.

"Wish we could be more specific too, but let's just say we've had a visit with a remarkable man," as we shook his hand. He wandered back to his duty station. We had heard his message. Frustration, bitterness and hurt, but not grounds for killing.

I felt before our investigations were over, Conway and I would hear more of these traumatic stories, the horrors of daily reliving their dark past.

"Kelly, you were in the Army. You must've encountered these guys. Are they all as bitter as this guy?"

"I'm not an expert on PTSD but, as an MP, I saw a lot of messed up guys acting out their frustrations, getting in trouble, some being arrested for assault or something else. Many getting drunk, thinking it would push away those memories. All it did was get them a night in the brig and a black mark on their record. We discharged our guys with the assumption they would re-enter society and their lives would be okay. That was a major miscalculation; our combat experienced guys each handle what they did and saw differently. But each will have the visual reruns and sounds bouncing through their heads until they die."

"I can't even imagine how much they suffer. So many put on a good front."

"Yeah. But these guys feel deeply that no one understands them, because they haven't been where they were or saw or did what they did, all in the name of duty. Vets will develop their own structures to help cope with their painful past. Some will affiliate with veteran's groups while others will wear baseball hats, vests, or jackets with their unit insignias on it. Still others will simply stuff it and try to live a normal life the best they can. Others seek help which may mean therapy groups and/or medications. Tragically, some will commit suicide, finding what they're harboring too much to handle. From Vietnam, we learned a lot of hard lessons from our returning soldiers. PTSD was out of control and at that time, little was known as to what it was or how to address it; our vets, men and women, suffered. I'm not sure we've progressed that much, and it may be that PTSD will always be a cancer tied to combat military duty."

"I feel so sorry for those that hurt, that struggle. Having not served, I cannot imagine the pain," commented Conway.

"The guys coming back from WWII and Korea were expected to meld into society, marry, build a family and work hard. Most stuffed what they saw, emotionally and physically shoving their war memories into a footlocker. They were not expected to do or be anything but veterans and to be thanked for their part. But not today. There are those same expectations, but our guys come home messed up, especially those doing what Sgt. Hassle spoke about. For them it's a living hell, they're home but the war is still with them. They try to be normal, whatever that means; some manage, others don't."

"Our other persons of interest will be suffering the same way or similarly to how Sgt. Hassle feels?" Conway asked.

"Yeah. They are today's victims and walking a very lonely path in life. Unless you've been there, they feel you can't understand what they went through or battle with now at home. Even I cannot fully relate to their pain. And frankly, most people don't know or care or wish to hear about the trauma a vet is suffering. Not an easy society to meld back into."

"That's so amazing. We train them to be professional killers and don't give them the care they need."

"It's a complex issue. Research just wasn't there, and now the VA is trying to address this massive, almost hidden, wound that cripples physically and emotionally so many. The Vietnam vets were not even 'welcomed home' amid the social turmoil of the 60s. They felt abandoned, ignored and neglected. That was adding insult to injury. Regrettably, many went from the service to the streets, got caught up in drugs and social indifference. It didn't work and they only became a casualty in another life-threatening battle. It's easier to treat a visible wound than to tackle the unseen."

"Kelly, you've never been this candid about your experiences with the Army. I know you didn't see combat."

"Don't be surprised. I saw this stuff happening. I don't talk about it but then again, I don't have horrible dreams or massive headaches or feel a need for drugs. I guess I was lucky. I sometimes reflect that our attitudes toward returning combat veterans is to simply ignore their issues and hope maybe those issues will go away. It doesn't work that way, and how or why we come to think that way, remains a mystery. We asked them, ordered them, to walk in harm's way; they did, and now they pay for it. I wish I could do more, but in reality, I know there are qualified medical and social service personnel trained to assist in whatever manner possible."

"Wow." He paused. "Well, I guess we need to see who we want to interview next?" asked Conway.

30

Dr. Ward arranged a meeting at the Seattle VA with Dr. Leslie Stephens. She was one of the group therapists handling vets with PTSD and coordinating all the therapy groups. From her conversation with Dr. Ward, she had flagged four persons of interest, Sergeants Hassle, Sledge, Franklin and Zimmerman. We wanted to know more about her reasons, since we had already interviewed one of her referrals and cleared him from any further consideration.

Dr. Ward introduced us to Dr. Stephens and offered a short profile of her medical portfolio, which brought us to this meeting.

Dr. Stephens, sharp dresser, 5'5" professional in her white clinical coat, with dark hair and a toned body, runs triathlons when not buried with her clinical work. She and her psychiatrist husband transferred to the Seattle VA, where he assumed oversight of the new Mental Health wing. She completed her Ph.D. at the Oregon Health and Science University in Portland, otherwise known as OHSU, doing her internship, residency and serving on staff at the Portland VA located across the street from OHSU. When they hired her in Seattle, she was given the leadership opportunity of coordinating the group therapists treating vets with PTSD. For the family it was a good move, with two teens at West Seattle High School, and their home in West Seattle with a water view of the "Three Tree" peninsula. Don't ask why it's called that; it just sticks a short way into the Sound.

"Dr. Ward speaks highly of you and we're glad you're willing to collaborate in our investigation," I began.

"Glad to try to assist. We have a lot going on, but I think

you need to know a little more about me before we continue our discussions of the others. It might help put our perspectives in context."

She wasn't wasting any time getting started, nor telling us about herself.

"First, I'm damn good at what I do. Not egotistical, but letting you know I know how good I am at what I do, and love. Second, I'm an Army vet, no Special Forces but sure felt like it during my 6 years. Third, I was in a war zone. Fourth, no one who goes into combat returns the same. They are forever changed whether they recognize it or not. Fifth, I was discharged through Lewis-McCord and went through their Resilience Classes. It's a conscious and subconscious challenge, how vets deal with change; it's an individual journey and often exceedingly difficult. After I returned home, I decided I had to try and help those who faithfully served and found themselves all messed up. I went back to school, and focused on vets and the traumas they suffer, the agony they experience, the isolation they feel, and the lack of tools to cope with their unexpected life changes."

"And that's why you became a psychologist?" I inserted.

"Right. I found it's the only way I can make a difference. I'd been where they'd been, I killed and saw the killing; I saw the unexpected impact and how the services are struggling to equip vets for their return to non-military life. We hurt when we come home and don't even know it. If you've been wounded, that's an observable trauma; it can be repaired but, there again, it takes years to heal, not just the wound but the violation of the human body. It's not that simple with the unseen wounds. I'll go even further and say it isn't simple with any wound period."

"I was an Army MP, not sent overseas but stationed where I had to address some of those residual behaviors, alcohol, assault and murder. My take was those returning were lost, fumbling with not knowing what they wanted to do or where to go, maybe even who they were any longer. They were getting out but scared; maybe more like being pushed out."

"You're right on that, Kelly. Seeing so many messed-up lives, I felt maybe, just maybe I could help them to, in some manner, regain a portion of their lives again. I find hospitals are unable to cope with PTSD. The VA is making a valiant effort but it's an overwhelming combat wound, misunderstood and misdiagnosed and only recently being seriously paid attention to. And it's something that takes a long-term commitment, by therapists as well as patients."

"Do you feel you've been successful?" asked Conway.

"Success is a difficult term to use when addressing a long-term remedy. I've seen vets come and go through our therapy programs; some I feel are better equipped than others to rebuild their lives. Those who are married have challenges and support. The spouse will likely not understand what he saw and participated in, yet she can be of enormous support simply being next to them, encouraging them, and holding them. Then again, there may be a spouse who's unable to handle it and walks away, leaving her combat injured spouse to flounder; or the vet himself screws up his family life not knowing what to do or how to handle his new role. Coming home may sound easy but the vets must make all kinds of unexpected adjustments. It's also been said those who stay at home also serve. That's so true. They're the ones, as a single parent, who handle the checkbook, mortgages or rent, grocery shopping, getting kids to school and home. They're making all the household decisions and then their spouse returns. Troubles in River City, unless the vets are coached and given tools, encouragement and support in understanding their new, literally, a new role being in the family they left behind."

"What about those without a spouse? Five referrals we have are single, including one divorced."

"They struggle. They have no visible support structure and may rely on the therapy group for that support. Others just resist being vulnerable, yet they are, and then try to go it on their own. Without the tools and resources, they will often fail and that's when you see them on the street. They, too, are wandering, trying to identify who they are in a world they've not been a part of for quite some time. We've tried to apply an outmoded expectation on our soldiers. My cousin, who fought on Iwo Jima, was expected to come home and be normal. Well, there is no normal after you've been to hell and back. We're trying to respond and can help if the vet recognizes he needs help and is willing to explore positive resources for rebuilding his life. I'm only one of many trying to help while the overwhelming tide keeps washing ashore the wounded."

"Are your colleagues as experienced, trained and insightful as you?" I asked.

"I wish I could say yes, but that's not the case. We have many psychologists who have received their degrees, one after another, without substantive experience. I've had the tough field experience I wouldn't recommend to anyone, but it gives me an edge. I was a soldier, one of them. My colleagues have great intentions and some are honestly doing their best to understand the vets suffering from PTSD. I counsel many of my colleagues, listening to their own frustrations and asking how to fix it. 'Fix it' is not an operative term. Many can be helped, but you can't 'fix' them. You give them tools and resources they can use to make their lives better; often life isn't the same as before they saw and experienced killing, in the raw, the disregard for human life, as politicians play their macho games. Pardon my political commentary. Some take the tools and make positive adjustments. Others take years for their lives to balance out. There's just no quick fix."

"From my experience as an Army MP, seeing so many of these cases arrive at then Fort Lewis, I can't but wonder what kind of support you get with all these emotionally draining encounters?" I asked.

"My husband, who I met at OHSU, is a psychiatrist. He heads the mental health wing here at the VA. We talk and often have marathon sessions sorting out issues and observations. He's my support, as are our two incredibly talented and active teens. Never a dull moment in our household. Now, I hope you understand my background and the context for my observations and decisions."

"As a matter of fact, we do. We came to ask questions and you've already helped us understand your frame of reference. You gave us four names, what we call 'persons of interest' from your groups. What made your referrals stand out from some of your other clients?"

"Good question, Kelly. I think Dr. Ward will enjoy part of my answer, too. We have nearly 50 therapy groups that meet each week, except weekends. Several meet twice a month. We limit them to twenty-five vets: male and female, Army, Navy, Air Force or Marines. Recent discharges or discharges having taken place within the past five years dominate those in the groups. Their Primary Care Physicians, and we have a crack team here at the Seattle VA, guide them into the program if there appears to be an emotional need. Some are automatically enrolled due to physical trauma, loss of a body part; psychological damage because of a crippling wound or being shot but not disabled; or abnormal behaviors. When you add up these numbers, we're handling about 1,200 plus vets a week. The need is so much greater." She continued.

"When Dr. Ward talked with me, we discussed criteria for anyone to be reviewed. I'm privy to a lot of personal information and in general my patients are working hard at recovery. The four I sent you, Sgt. Hassle, Sgt. Sledge, Sgt. Franklin, and Sgt. Zimmerman have issues. Whether they wish to admit them or acknowledge them or not, each is responding in their own manner to the therapy sessions I hold. For example, Sgt Hassle is bitter and angry. He's been this way for over a year and cannot seem to make a breakthrough. I can't take away his hurt, his damage, his frustrations. But he must come to grips with them and work out a life that'll be more meaningful. He was wounded in the crotch and is unable to have sex of any kind. He is mutilated and embarrassed about that and what it means with his wife. He quit out of frustration and I can only hope he's able to move forward in rebuilding his life."

"Interestingly, he was the first one we interviewed. No question he's angry, frustrated and bitter but he's decided to move on with his life, accepting his wound, though it hurts every day. He and his wife are considering adopting children, and he was emphatic about not listening to war stories but moving ahead with his own friends and family," I inserted.

"That's great. I sure would not have expected that, but he's motivated and that's part of what's needed for healing, for dealing with PTSD, and for moving forward. Sounds like he's on the right road."

"You gave us three other names, Sergeants Zimmerman, Sledge and Franklin. Are any of these likely a killer? Sgt. Hassle certainly wasn't."

"That's a hard one to call. Any one of us could kill, especially since we've already been there and done that. When you meet Sgt. Zimmerman, you'll find her carrying one hellava chip on her shoulder. She was wounded and is single. She saw some nasty stuff and has severe PTSD, doesn't want to talk much about it. She feels less of a woman because of her wounds, which are not debilitating, and only visible when she's undressed. Sgt. Sledge, as you can image, gets a lot of hassle for his last name. He's a loud, obnoxious, pushy and demeaning cowboy who flaunts his background. Rather than returning to Nebraska, he's chosen, for the moment, to live in Kent and come to therapy, but is a reluctant participant. Almost an oxymoron. Wounded, he's livid at the world, and isolated. I'm not sure if he has a job or not; if so, I've not heard him talk about it. Sgt. Franklin is not much better."

"How do you mean?" asked Conway.

"Like Zimmerman and Sledge, he's single. He attends sessions but misses them more frequently than not. He was Delta Force black ops. They may not have used that term but going behind the lines at night to carry out a mission is black ops, deadly and dangerous. In fact, many of our referrals were on those kinds of deadly missions. These types of classified missions are not something that is widely known or admitted to by the Army. Sgt. Franklin says I don't understand him, what he was ordered to do, and did. He's a terribly angry man, above normal anger in my opinion. Something else is at play but I don't know what it is. You can see his background was turbulent, the Army was the option he picked over jail at the end of high school. In the Army, he excelled. He has three major decorations and a Purple Heart; he was wounded saving his own squad. If not for him, as I understand it, his squad would have been wiped out. But in the group sessions he's moody, and when he's not, his outbursts seem disconnected with reality. Getting any kind of an understanding of where he's coming from has been elusive. Irrational, bitter, and irritable are a few simple terms to apply to what I see as an overly complex trauma. In my clinical opinion, he's depressed, not stable and, no doubt I may have to recommend he be hospitalized for assessment and treatment beyond the medications he's now prescribed."

"He's single. As you said, no one for support. Is that a complicating factor toward recovery?"

"I'd say yes, but not totally. He has a greeter's job and apparently does little else. He has nothing happening in his life that gives meaning, from what I'm able to assess. His irrational outbursts and accusations toward me as the therapist are not healthy, by any means, accusing me of brainwashing him. Frankly, he scares me as to what he could or might do."

"Could he kill?" I asked. There was a pause.

"That's pretty speculative. He's killed for the Army, been a trained professional and apparently excelled. Could Sgt. Franklin be your killer? I could even ask if Sledge or Zimmerman could be your killer? I'm not sure I can categorically say yes or no. It's a good question and I'd imagine if circumstances were right or something sparked a fuse, it's possible. They've all previously killed."

"That's a surprisingly good job of dancing." She responded with a smile. "What the press do not have is the weapon used, a military issued Mark 25 9mm with a silencer. The killer was just caught on a hidden camera and wears night vision goggles. Our CSI describe the figure to be around 220 pounds and between 5'11" – 6'. The other information about the killings is public knowledge. We're not sure why the killer targets the homeless; but because of how well they're hidden, we suspect the killer does reconnaissance to select his routes in and out."

"Your killer is a serial killer. I'm not sure any of our clients could be that. But again, I don't always know totally what's going on in their heads. In my many years working with vets, I've seen a lot, a lot of it tragic and disturbing. You sometimes want to hold them and say it's going to be alright. But it isn't. Some of my patients are passive, others aggressive. Some are silent, others vocal; other sit passively, while others act out. Listening and asking them questions is geared to getting them to look at themselves, acknowledge their life has changed and will not return to what it was, no matter how hard they try. Then to guide them, in developing alternatives, strategies that will help them on a new life journey, for themselves, their families and children and their new work environment. Sometimes I see encouraging results; most times I'm not sure."

"Dr. Ward told you we've put a security umbrella around you and the other therapists. We're not sure whether any of the persons identified might turn on you or the other counselors. We don't know, and it sounds like you aren't sure either. So, we're working on a premise the killer is unbalanced and irrational."

"The protection is appreciated, but as you can see, we don't have our last name on our clinical jacket, just first names. No one in the group knows me except as Dr. Leslie. Or any of our clinicians except by first name. We do this intentionally while other medical personnel use their full names. It's our way to protect our own privacy, and you can see why with the patients we work with. Even the front desk doesn't have our last names, just first names and the clinic location and times they meet."

"We appreciate your candidness. We're looking for that proverbial needle in a haystack; you and your colleagues have given us some people to look at. We're grateful for your time and insights. Thank you."

We left Dr. Stephens with a better insight into her reasons for identifying the four names. Her own combat experience gives her insights others might not have, thus I felt comfortable with her assessments and selections.

"We should visit our female person of interest, Sgt. Zimmerman. From what Dr. Stephens told us, she's vocal and angry, but I doubt she's our killer," Conway suggested.

"How can you draw such a presumptive conclusion?"

"Just an instinct, Kelly. Just an instinct."

We reviewed her profile.

Sgt. Tracy Zimmerman, 5'-10", discharged 18 months ago. 6 years in service in Iraq and Afghanistan, multiple wounds, no physical disability, Bronze Star and Purple Heart. Where or how decorations earned unknown. Attends therapy sessions for severe PTSD. Bold, outspoken, aggressive sometimes verbally explosive, angry at life. Threatened superiors while in service. Single, lives in Edmunds and works for the highway department. No arrest records.

It took some persuasion with WDOT (Washington Department

of Transportation) to locate where Sgt. Zimmerman worked and to allow her to meet with us. Arrangements were made to visit with her the next day.

31

I checked out. Being with Sgt. Hassle, talking with Conway about my own insights and experience and our lengthy meeting with Dr. Stephens emotionally exhausted me. Damn, the houseboat was not finished, so I couldn't retreat to my deck overlooking Lake Union. The hotel didn't have an outside garden or sitting area. What I wanted was fresh air and a glass of wine. Guess I was going to have to settle for the wine, the hot tub and recirculated air.

My tenure as an Army MP was uneventful, except having to deal with disorderly soldiers returning from combat. There I heard their stories, felt their pain and wondered why we hadn't given them training to cope with what they did and saw, emotionally and psychologically. I guess it's "don't talk about it or admit it exists, therefore it doesn't," well, until that cup runneth over. Dr. Ward was seeing through her interviews how the psychologists were handling their groups and, obviously, their gut instincts said it's only a stop gap action. For me, I don't have such vivid pictures dancing in my head, but again, I wasn't in the killing fields.

When I got back to our room, I figured crawling into the hot tub would relax me. I opened a bottle of French wine and climbed in. My timing was rather good as Patti came in with an arm full of food. The big question was whether we were hungry tonight. She was smart and put it in the small refrigerator. It was there if we wanted it.

She didn't take long to strip down and join me in the hot tub. Decompressing from our hectic day was important. We were sitting opposite each other; I adore her face, her nose and soft lips, her hair just on her shoulders, and her luscious body in general.

She broke the quiet. "I sense your day was a bit stressful?"

"Yeah, in an interesting way. A lot of conflicting emotions."

"Such as?"

"Long story, but Conway and I had to interview one of the persons of interest on the PTSD list, decorated Special Forces type working with the Port of Seattle. Bitter and hurt but not our killer. He got into how so many say 'thank you for your service', but have no clue what he did or what he lives with as a result of that service. He was wounded in the groin and bitter about that impact on his life and marriage. It snagged some of my own feelings."

"Tough stuff?"

"Yeah, and he'll never forget what he went through; the physical wound will be there every day of his life and remind him. He's struggling to regain a balance for his life. His therapist is one sharp cookie, however, who gave Conway and me additional insights. She is former Army, combat experience. She provided a lot of information on vets suffering PTSD, their battles, and insights into those she had referred to us. Some really damaged goods."

"Sounds like a solid day of investigation!"

"It was. What about your day? Any new activities occupying your time?"

"Not much. Ongoing our daily briefing on the cartel and dismantling of their network around the world. Still haven't got Delgado and Ramirez into court. Working on protecting our prosecutor and his family, and the integrity of the trial. Enough said. Now how overcharged are your hormones?"

We smiled, moved toward each other into a wet embrace, kissing and fondling each other. We both needed each other, and intimate touches were even more needed. Our bodies were like one. We enjoyed our glass of wine and decided it was bedtime even at this young hour of the evening. No food either.

After making love, catching a cat nap then making love again, it was near midnight when we laid in each other's arms and heard our stomachs growl. Guess that's the signal to feed that neglected part of our bodies.

The morning arrived way too soon.

For me, it was another person of interest. For her, the continuing saga, coordinating with Interpol, the dismantling of the cartel's drug smuggling and money laundering networks. Not an easy task, but one step at a time.

And for Sgt. Zimmerman, her day was just beginning.

32

Edmunds is just north of Seattle, home of Rick Steve's "Europe through the Back Door" travel agency, often seen on PBS, and a vibrant arts community. We arranged to meet Sgt. Zimmerman at a downtown restaurant, neutral ground in some ways. When we made the appointment, she was defensive and abrupt. We explained the circumstances the best we could in generic language and suggested it may be best her colleagues not know about our visit. She was suspicious, which we anticipated, and wary about meeting us; to keep her from totally coming unglued, we conceded we needed just to talk about her combat experiences and therapy sessions. She gulped on the phone and said, yeah, sure. We weren't sure she'd even show, but found her waiting for us.

"Thanks for meeting with us. We know a little ..."

"Oh, cut the crap. I know you're checking me out. For what I'm not exactly sure but will no doubt know soon."

"We are," I responded and decided not to cut her slack either. "You're among several person's identified by your group therapist as having PTSD, with whom we need to talk."

"So, what am I being talked to about?"

"We've got a summary of your career and want to clarify what's going on."

"Oh, bull! You're so damn evasive. I didn't come here to waste my time or play games. Someone says you need to talk to me. Why? Because I don't put up with bull? I don't! A lot of people don't like a female calling them for it. So, stuff it!"

"Okay, what do you do with your evenings?"

"Why? You want a date?" she sarcastically responded.

"No, we're asking how you spend your evenings? An easy question!" I responded.

"Not much. I'm shot up, so not at the top of any dating list," she again sarcastically responded. "So, why are you asking me about what I do at night?"

"You've seen the newspapers about a killer stalking the homeless. What you don't know is we're sure it's someone with a Special Forces background like yourself. We have no clue why he or she is doing it and why just the homeless. You've been a part of some ugly missions, back from situations you were not prepared to encounter, let alone endure. We can appreciate your pointed comments and attitude. We're trying to find out why your therapist thought we should visit with you. Truce?"

"Okay, maybe too defensive. But no one understands me or even cares about trying to. So now some counselor suggests I might be a killer! You must be kidding! And even if I was, you don't think I would just up and tell you?"

"Let me interrupt you. I'm a cop now but was an Army MP. I saw others like you come home messed up, a chip on your shoulders. I listened to their horrible stories, and I know they hurt in ways I can't even begin to understand. But I'm trying and listening again. I need to know you better than 6 lines on a piece of paper saying you served, was wounded, decorated and discharged and now suffer from PTSD."

She sat making no comment. The silence seemed like a long time, but she looked at me and said,. "Ask your questions and I'll see what I can do," more reasonably rather than defensively.

"What got you the Bronze Star?"

"My unit was assigned to go behind enemy lines, which

seemed to change every hour; we were charged with killing specific targets, another nice military term for humans. These were dirty night ops, sneaking out of our own camp and crossing into no man's land, watch where you stepped to avoid an IED. One night our unit had been successful in reaching its objective. But somehow, someway, they were alerted and waiting for us. The firefight was ugly and that's where I got wounded. Though wounded, I was able to drag one guy and carry another out of the firefight. Both had been critically wounded and the one I dragged didn't make it. We called in support to suppress their gun fire, allowing us to retreat into safer territory. (pausing) Sonofabitch, they were waiting for us! We walked into their crosshairs and got hurt. One dead, five of us wounded, and the others unscratched but like all of us, scared to death."

"Did you find out what happened, how they were waiting?"

"Not really. A few of us suspected someone inside our compound was secretly getting word to their neighbors about our operations. No one was really sure, so our command structure moved us to another location where our stealth ops handed the enemy the casualty numbers they wanted."

"You returned and were discharged and placed in a therapy group due to your wounds."

"Yeah, I mouth off too much and took on somebody with rank. They said it was therapy or a less-than-honorable discharge. I had a Bronze Star and they wanted to give me a less-than- honorable discharge? Bull! I took the therapy and the honorable discharge. Being in a hospital does things to your head, and I was totally pissed I got hurt because someone in the field screwed up and didn't see the trap."

"Sharp tongue, people aren't accustomed to?"

"Yeah, especially the military. No-one got rapped on the knuckles for screwing up. It would have been unnecessary if whoever had been doing their job. We got ambushed and no one was held accountable. That sucked! I got shipped out and patched up."

"You're in therapy and working. Has the therapy group sessions helped you with your feelings of not being understood?"

"Not really. I have a hole through my left breast with ugly stitches, shrapnel cuttings on my ass that cause pain when I sit, lay down or go to the toilet, bullet scars on my leg and a head that won't stop making sounds and running ugly memories. I'm no candidate for a beauty contest or a bikini. Great rest of my life for serving my country. Now can you see why I'm disillusioned. I can't get rid of the images or scars or pain."

"Let's go back to my original question. What do you do evenings and at night?"

"Sleep if I can. I stay away from booze and drugs. They don't help. Been there, done that. I have a boyfriend who tolerates seeing scars and a hole in my left breast. He's the first. Others just stared and that was the end of that. So, I'm single and deformed, thank you very much, U.S. Army."

"I wish I could be more optimistic and encouraging, but you know better than I what is walking around in your head and what your therapist is suggesting that may help you. I would hope your bitterness will eventually mellow out. I know each morning in the mirror, for the rest of your life, the memories will resurface."

"For a cop, you're not bad. At least you're not looking down at me, asking to see my deformed breast or asking me how this or that felt. I did my duty. I killed and was shot at and damn near killed. I'm using therapy to help me, not them, and to use whatever prescribed medications they recommend to reduce and endure my emotional swings and physical pain. I'd like to be optimistic but I'm not able at this point in time."

"Do you own a weapon?" I asked.

"No, and that's probably good. I'd shoot the sonavabitch who screwed up and got me damn near killed. He got away clean and I'm wounded and having to live with the memories of his screw-up the rest of my life."

"I wish for you it was otherwise. I wish you a better life as you continue to confront your traumas."

"Do you still think I'm your killer?" she blatantly asked with a sarcastic tone.

"If we did, you'd be under arrest and in cuffs. No; but we know you're angry and for some good reasons. Thank you for being honest with us." We picked up the tab and departed.

"Sure has a chip on her shoulder," began Conway, "I don't see her as our killer, however."

"She was pretty honest and explicit; can't blame her. She's going to be okay, but it will be a long time coming."

"Now we're down to six."

"Yeah and need to check with Dr. Ward if she's got others. We'll give her feedback on our visit as well."

33

Traffic wasn't that heavy back into Seattle. The day was cloudy, like many in the Pacific Northwest, but muggy warm. I decided we needed to stop at my houseboat to see how renovations were going. Conway said he'd like to see it as well, so a detour in our route was made, and very much a surprise was waiting for us.

We parked where we could find a spot and walked toward where it was berthed. "Look at it," I said. "The new siding's on, the roof's done, and I'm hoping the hot tub's in."

"Kelly!" I heard from behind me. "I was just about to call you. I just finished the final inspections and your house is ready to be lived in," said our interior decorator and renovation coordinator.

"You're ahead of schedule? From what I see, it looks fantastic, colorful and bright. Nice touch with the potted plants. What about the inside?"

"You'll be surprised! As I said, you can move back in. We're about a week ahead of schedule and wanted to surprise you. Everything you and your fiancée asked for has been done; it just waits for you." She led us down the pier, unlocked the front door, handed me the keys, and let us in. Wow! My heart was racing. A bottle of wine was sitting on the dining room table with two glasses, colorful napkins and a bouquet of freshly cut yellow roses and baby's breath flowers in the center. The front room looked warm, inviting, and magnificent; but I wanted to see the master bedroom, hot tub and then my upstairs haven, the deck. Conway followed me, wandering around while our coordinator waited patiently in the front room. Tonight was going to be a surprise for Patti! We're coming home.

I thanked the decorator and she said the final bill would be in the mail by Monday. Out of the advance I had given her, she'd paid for the hull inspection, the installation of new cement-board long lasting siding, a new aluminum/vinyl roof, new composite board for our decks outside the front room and master bedroom, and the upstairs deck with "deck correct" as a finishing, and most of the interior décor and furniture we had selected. Oh, is Patti going to be thrilled!

"Conway, I have a big favor to ask. Would you help me move our stuff from the hotel back into our new home?"

"Sure. I know Patti's going to be surprised!"

It took us but a little over an hour to gather up what was at the hotel and move it back into our new home. Snowball was a bit confused, but would have the afternoon to explore and become familiar with her new home. Her food, water, and cat box were placed back in their usual spots.

"Now it's my turn. I know she'll not object, but I'd like to have you and Cindy come over for dinner Saturday night if it works for you?"

"As far as I know, we're free. Cindy doesn't normally work on Saturdays. We can be here around 6:00," Conway replied. "It works for us."

"She's still working?"

"Oh yes. Looks terrific, feels terrific, and wants to keep working as long as she can. She'll take leave but return after that; her clients are happy she's having a baby and happy she's returning. Guess she has them spoiled."

Back downtown was another thing; we asked to visit with the Sergeant.

"Out of the eight 'persons of interest', Sergeant, we're down to six. I don't want to push my luck. We've already talked face-to-face with two of the decorated vets and they've been eliminated as a threat. Incredible stories and certainly a lot of bitterness and anger, but not our killers. Our time with the VA's lead therapist was also illuminating and gave us some insights into PTSD."

"What's next?"

"Of the remaining six, we'll interview the married ones first. My gut tells me we'll need to be more careful with those who are single, and we have 4 remaining in that category. My thought is the two remaining married vets will likewise pan out the same, leaving us the single vets. Dr. Stephens says those who are single have little support structures and my guess is our killer falls into that situation. We may wish to have the vets who are single put under surveillance, especially tracking their night movements, as a precaution."

"Let me know what you need and when," said the Sergeant.

"I think we should go with it now; Conway will get you their addresses."

"Works for me," responded Troy, "We'll have coverage begin this evening."

Conway and I returned to our office and looked over the remaining persons of interest. Six and maybe, just maybe, our killer is in the mix.

"Have to head home. Cindy and I are attending our first Lamaze class."

"Sounds good to me. Tell Cindy I said 'hi.'"

34

It was late in the afternoon and time to have some fun.

"I'm picking you up in thirty minutes if that works for you?"

"What's going on, Kelly?"

"A little surprise!"

"What about my car?"

"You can get it tomorrow," I told her and clicked off. Surprise!

After Conway and I removed all our stuff from the hotel room, I figured picking her up and taking her home would be a better surprise than having her meet me at the hotel. On top of that, wine and the new hot tub were waiting.

Conway and I did our last-minute stuff for the day and signed out. He was off to care for his pregnant wife and to let her know of our dinner plans. I figured that would be another time to surprise them as well.

"What do you have up your sleeve, Kelly," said as she got into the car. "This is so not you."

"Yeah, I know. But can't always be predictable."

"Well this is definitely in the category of unpredictability," she chuckled.

"Conway and I had another tough interview today. We made a detour coming back from Edmunds and I wanted to share what we found on our detour."

"Uh huh. Okay, enough of the BS. Why have you kidnapped me? You know you can get in trouble; I'm a federal officer and kidnapping is a felony."

Toying with her was fun. This wasn't going to last long, however, when we drove near the hotel and keep going. And so, it was.

"Okay, that's our hotel," she said.

"Operative term, was."

She looked at me and began to smile. "You've got to be kidding? Are we going home? What about our clothes?"

"Yes, my surprise part 1. We are going home. We found, by sheer accident this afternoon, it was done a week early. Conway and I dropped by and the decorator was about to call me when we walked up. Surprise part 2. He helped me move our clothes home and check out. Even Snowball is getting acquainted with her new surroundings. And surprise part 3, there is a bottle of wine on the table with two glasses and we have our own hot tub. Am I rescued from the charge of kidnapping a federal officer?"

She leaned over, kissed my cheek and took my right hand and squeezed, smiling with tears dripping down her cheek.

"Home. What I've wanted with you for twenty-plus years. We're going to our new home."

Laying her head on my right shoulder, she was trying not to interfere with my driving though her suggestive movements made me want to let go of the wheel and have fun. But that will wait.

As we walked down the pier, she caught sight of the new colors, giggled and jumped up and down clapping her hands. Then she threw her arms around my neck and gave me one of her seriously sensuous kisses. Wow! That was worth waiting for.

Opening the front door, she gasped. The new furniture, fresh carpet and paint gave the interior an awesome look. Flowers on the deck outside the front room window were in full bloom, chosen by our decorator. She ran her fingers along the new stainless steel kitchen appliances and marble countertops, looked and felt the padded wooden stools at the new kitchen bar, rubbed her hand over the surface of the birch dining room table, then walked into our master bedroom, and gazed out through the new expanded double insulated windows and sliding doors, past the deck decorated with flower pots. The hot tub and double sink bathroom brought a smile to her face; wandering upstairs, she found the new bedroom-bath and the modernized deck. Walking out on the deck, pressing her hands on the new rail with its clear glass panels, and smelling the fresh air, she turned and grabbed me, flung her arms around my neck, kissed me and held on tight. Whispering into my ear that it was "tub time, I'll get it started, you get the wine."

We didn't make it to the tub. We tested the new queen bed and view of the Lake from behind the sheer curtains. After a while, we quietly laid next to one another, her arms across my chest, her head cradled in my right arm pit, peacefully dozing.

When we regained consciousness, I told her we were hosting the Conways for dinner Saturday night and we needed another surprise for the soon-to-be threesome. She'd give it some thought.

It was early and we had truly had little sleep and hadn't eaten since yesterday afternoon. We were famished. We were both still naked under our plush warm robes, relaxing with coffee, eggs and toast.

The call on my cell shattered the quiet of our new home. Our frivolity was broken by the news of more killings. Two bodies near the intermodal tracks in Magnolia. Found by a railroad employee. Same MO. ME on the scene. Damn! Here we go again.

35

"What have you got on last night's victims?" I asked the ME. He's damn good at what he does, down to earth, straight shooter, and accurate. Bad pun.

"Sometimes I wonder, wonder who does this kind of thing and for what reasons? Oh, I know, I'm just blabbering. Murder is unpredictable, inexplicable, and insane." He paused. "Here is what I have. Same MO. One shot to the head. Slugs have been sent to forensics, but I think they'll be identical to the others. CSI found no shells. Bodies were nestled together behind some piles of junk near the tracks; death sometime between 1 and 3. These guys were well hidden."

Thanking him and clicking off, I asked myself when was this going to end? We have sixteen dead homeless men. I knew the answer, but I didn't like it. Then I called the Sergeant.

"Same old stuff, Troy. Same MO. Killed between one and three. The ME says they were very well hidden, so the killer had to know what or who he was looking for, knew where to find them too."

"Any tie between what you're working on and the killer?

"Not yet. Charlie has a theory the homeless are targeted because they're like the people killed in the killer's overseas assignment. Doesn't give us a killer but maybe some insane reason behind his selected targets. Regardless, he's messed up. Conway and I are going to interview the remaining married names on our list. Hopefully, we'll be able to eliminate them. We'll let you check in with the surveillance teams regarding their observations last night."

"Okay Kelly, follow your instincts. We also took your recommendation and have protective coverage for the therapists already in place."

"Thanks. We told Dr. Stephens we were giving her and her colleagues this coverage. She appreciated our efforts."

While I was talking with the Sergeant, Conway was calling the ME to ask if he had fingerprints or any identification on the victims. He would send us his findings.

Conway and I got the addresses for our other persons of interest and were out of the office as quickly as possible.

Sergeant Cushman was our next interviewee.

Sgt. Orville Cushman, 5'-11", discharged 18 months ago. 7 years in Army. Delta Force, service in Iraq, severe wounds from an IED explosion; must go to VA monthly for tending of wounds and rehab. Awarded the Bronze Star and Purple Heart. Lives in Ballard, married with one kid. No arrest records. Attending North Seattle College working on degree in culinary arts. Tends to be quiet and withdrawn. Wondering if a ticking clock ready to explode or has exploded.

Sgt. Orville Cushman was at home when we knocked on his front door; he was a bit surprised. We introduced ourselves and asked to visit with him and his wife.

"I'm not sure what this is all about, but I don't have any outstanding traffic tickets," said with an embarrassed smile. "I'm not able to drive yet. But you said homicide?"

Unless there was a conspiracy involving his wife, he was not our killer. But we proceeded with our inquiry anyway to clear him. Using crutches, he invited us into their front room, where we could comfortably sit. The crutches disqualify him from our investigation; I'm surprised he was referred to us. The man on camera in White Center didn't have crutches and it was doubtful he could negotiate the hidden sites along the interstate.

"No, we're not here for traffic tickets. We're working a disturbing case. For reasons we don't understand, your therapist flagged and suggested we talk with you. We've been working off a long list and you were on it."

Looking at his wife and taking her hand, he introduced us to her.

"I'd like to introduce my wife and incredible support, Kathleen. She's been with me on the long road to recovery."

"It's nice to know you've had her at your side."

"Not sure what you're looking for," he smiled.

"We're not sure either but would like to hear your story of what happened to you." I gently remarked.

"I can assure you, you don't go to war, into combat, kill the enemy, without changing. That's what they fail to tell you or prepare you for. They work you through boot camp and other maneuvers and assume that prepares you for what you will encounter emotionally. My body's taken a beating when an IED exploded. I'm lucky, but many others were not so lucky. Having to slowly learn to walk again with this one leg so shot up. At least I didn't lose it. I crawled through the night killing people I was told to kill, not really knowing who they were or whether they were any kind of a threat. I feel we dehumanize the other side and decide they are the enemy and therefore it's okay to kill. Some reports are about firefights or use of cruise missiles, and then they report the damage done in the area in military terms, which might, in plain English, be a school, neighborhood, hospital or whatever; then add there was 'collateral damage.' That's garbage. After a while, that stuff gets all mixed up in your head. And that's how it is with me. I honorably served my Country in the manner they ordered, but it messed with my own values and head. The damage to my body is one thing and will always be something I have to live with. But I also live with so many other memories and sounds, that my head is really not peaceful."

"Detectives, Orville has suffered in ways I cannot even imagine. I'm his wife, partner and lover and all I can do is support him, love him and hold him when he desperately needs it. He often awakens with nightmares. I hold him. He falls out of bed and gives order to duck. I hold him. His therapist could no longer understand him or what the hell he was reliving. He's become gentle. He's no killer. He's a loving father who worships his son and loves me deeply."

"She's right. Life is too short and we're working on building our life together. I did my duty. All that stuff, those decorations and other junk, are boxed in the garage attic. Unlike some, I don't hang memorabilia. I don't need anything more than my fragile body to remember, or the headaches and nightmares I have. Oh, how I would love to have one single peaceful night's sleep."

"Our forensic psychologist and the VA's senior medical doctor, overseeing the PTSD therapy groups, say those sessions are designed to assist you to navigate these traumas," I commented.

"Yeah, sometimes those sessions are helpful, other times questionable. I attend, and if possible, try to use ideas I hear that might work in my family. But I'm among the lucky ones with an incredible wife, who though she was not overseas with me, understands what I've brought home. For that, I am grateful beyond words. My head may hurt but my heart is filled with love, love for my wife, my family, and my being alive. Now how do I fit into your investigation?"

"Sergeant …"

"Please, no Sergeant. Orville is okay."

"Okay, Orville, it sounds like you're working on rebuilding your life and at this moment, we have no further questions of you. There's no need to bother you any further. As a former Army MP, I wish you well in the days ahead. Welcome home."

With that, we shook hands and departed.

He was reconciling his wounds and service time and would always have memories. But he had a support structure in his wife and child and was seeking peace in his life torn apart by war. He was no longer considered a person of interest.

Returning to our office there was a message from the ME.

"Kelly, I've identified fourteen of the sixteen homeless killed. Fingerprint were the best we could capture. I've forwarded the information to CSI to see if they can get us background and local family information, if there is any of the latter."

I mused how we were just adding to this growing scenario, but knowing who they are, if they are former military or just random victims, will help fill in some of the puzzle pieces and assist with whatever funeral arrangements are needed.

CSI was working overtime, knowing our case was frustrating. We received an email with the preliminary profiles on those homeless found dead. Fastest turn around I've seen but again, maybe this was the only gig in town to occupy their attention.

16 dead. Background on the latest two victims, pending.

3 had addresses out of state. Why they were here was unclear.

4 had addresses outside Seattle including Shelton, Montesano, Chehalis, and Spokane.

The other 7 victims were residents, well former residents, of Seattle or at least at one time lived here. Only two had a local address. Of the 7, five were veterans.

We emailed Fort Lewis to ask about the 5 victims who were vets. We sent all the names to Dr. Stephens at the VA seeing if any were under the care of the VA, and if so, who their therapists were and if by chance anyone was in the groups from which current persons of interest had been generated.

Again, not much more we could do at this point until we received the requested feedback.

36

Getting a weekend off is special, particularly while we still have a serial killer on the loose. Not much we could do pending receipt of, or verification of, information that was being processed. We figured we'd have some long days and possibly long weeks ahead, so we took the opportunity to ask and were surprised when it was granted.

Saturday evening, Patti and I decided to cook a chicken fettuccini Alfredo dish for the Conways, served with garlic bread, tossed salad with avocado, tomatoes, croissants, and poppy seed dressing. Simple but filling. The table was set with a baby patterned tablecloth and colorful napkins matching the colors in their baby's room. We figured the best gift for them was a $100 gift card to "Babies R Us." That way they can fill in their needs as they see fit. They'll need lots of disposable diapers for sure.

Conway knew where we lived, and the knock on the front door told us he hadn't gotten lost. After the greeting ritual of hugs and kisses, Patti accepted their unexpected housewarming gift, a wine rack, which we needed. More hugs and kisses.

"Come let me show you around," Patti said to Cindy.

While they were off and looking, I asked Bob, "Beer or wine?"

"Beer please," he responded. I poured myself a glass of wine and handed a cold beer to Conway and we retreated up to the new deck to enjoy our drinks and the fantastic view. It was a quiet evening on the Lake, though one noisy float plane was revving its engines for takeoff. You know when they're making their run for liftoff by the incredible engine noise. Once airborne, they ease back on the throttle and cruise lazily up the Sound to their exotic destinations in the San Juan Islands or Victoria, Canada.

"You really have a great home," commented Conway.

"Thanks. Our renovations turned out even better than we anticipated."

"Must have set you back financially a bit?"

"No, not really. The hull must be inspected every 2-3 years and was due. It looks good. The rest was just to remodel and rejuvenate an otherwise tired houseboat into a more vibrant living space. It was worth the expense."

"Wish we could remodel but for now, one room at a time. The rest of our house is good for a few more years. The baby will dictate the order of what needs to be done, such as junior bed, swing set and all those good things that keeps him occupied and happy."

"You said 'him'? Is that what you're expecting, a boy?" I asked.

"No. Just a generic term. We don't know if it's a boy or girl."

"Your lives are in for a major change, one you will enjoy, well maybe not at first with what they tell me are sleepless nights and endless feeding schedules. Patti will know more about that and the girls can compare notes."

"Yeah, resting up for that already," said with a smile and laugh.

"Did I tell you about the surprises our son Neil had for us when he visited?"

"Not exactly. I'm happy you took some time off to be with him."

"Yeah, thanks. Patti called in a panic to say he was arriving that evening. No mention of a fiancée, so when Patti met him, rather them, she was introduced to her soon-to-be daughter-in-law."

"That must have been a big surprise for the both of you."

"She then told Neil and Susan about me. Surprise in reverse.

He really was thrilled to see his mom in such good spirits and had noticed her engagement ring so wasn't that surprised after all. We all met for the first time on the street next to Daniel's Broiler and hugged."

"Patti rebuilding her life with you after all these years. You're damn lucky."

"I know. Neil's fiancée Susan has been with him three years and was with him the night Patti called to tell him his father's killer had been captured."

"How did he react?"

"They cried out their souls. Though their lives had been shattered, healing from that devastation was now possible. At dinner, Neal surprised both his mom and me when he asked if he could call me 'dad', like in Mom and Dad."

"And how did you respond to that unexpected question?"

"With tears. Don't repeat any of this in the office (smiling). I was stunned; I expected he would call me Kelly to differentiate me from his dad, but no, he wanted it to be Mom and Dad. I said I'd be honored."

"Their visit was filled with happy surprises."

"You haven't heard the final surprise. You know how you want your kids graduating from college to be able to find a good paying job? Well, both have. Susan is going to law school and Neil is working for the government."

"The government?" inquired Conway.

"Here's the grabber. Patti wanted to know what his plans were. He said he was following in his mom and dad's footsteps."

"That being?"

"He accepted and signed a contract to join the FBI. Stunned Patti! Tears flowed, then the hugs and excitement over what he was doing."

"Incredible."

"He'd actually been asking questions the previous few days about our careers and what I did, how I became a cop. There was, what you call, foreshadowing but neither Patti nor I caught on. Just thought he was getting information about my background, you know, filling in the blanks."

"And Patti?"

"She's so proud of Neil; we both are. He's building a new life; Susan's a sharp cookie, too. Her dad was a lawyer so they both were smiling about following in their parents' footsteps."

A sweet voice from below said dinner was on the table. Wandering downstairs, I realized how more open and airier the house is. The only thing missing from dinner was Italian music.

Dark settled in, so we adjourned into our new front room and imbibed more wine, except Cindy, who was carrying her ever-present water bottle. I asked Conway if he was okay and he assured me Cindy was also the designated driver. Our unexpected gift brought Cindy to tears again.

Since it was a weekend night, when they left, I told Patti that I'd do the dishes in the morning, and we enjoyed our overdue date in the hot tub. It needed to be christened since we hadn't made use of it the previous night, and there was no better time than our second night in our new home. Wine was poured into glasses and set next to the tub, hot water was filling it and we were undressing each other. Oh, how it only gets better seeing her trim body and realizing how much I missed her all these years. Sliding into the tub, we sat opposite each other, able to look at each other and talk; well, that too.

The curtain design in our bedroom allowed us to open the curtain while the sheer remained closed, just a push of a remote from the ease of our bed. From where we lay, we could see the lights along the other side of the Lake. It was romantic and so was she, well, I guess I was too. Why not? This was the life we had both dreamed of, and now it's a reality.

The morning snuck up on us again. We had been asleep several hours and our bodies were awakening with renewed urges and intimate needs.

37

After the weekend, Conway and I looked at the initial reports coming in from the officers tailing the four single persons of interests. No unusual activity. Normal day activities, whatever that meant. Three stayed at home, the other drove over to Alki and watched the weekend volleyball tournaments, mostly of young women in small tight bikinis. Nothing unusual to report about the nights.

Up next was our interview with Sergeant Noble; we arranged to meet him at the Des Moines City Hall. His profile read:

> *Staff Sgt. Brett Noble, 5'-10", discharged a year ago. 8 years in Army. Delta Force, head wound in Iraq from an IED. Awarded Purple Heart and Bronze Star for meritorious combat duties. No details regarding where or how decorations were earned. Married, lives near Des Moines, two kids. Full disability with the VA, participates weekly in a PTSD therapy group, angry at the Army for a botched assignment. Works for the City of Des Moines. No arrest records. Born in Tacoma; attended Tacoma Community College before joining the Army. Parents live in Sequim, Washington. One of three children, two younger sisters in school.*

At City Hall, we found a small conference room the receptionist said we could use for an hour. Sgt. Noble was given directions to meet us there.

"We know this is an inconvenience, but appreciate your supervisor giving you time to visit with us," I began.

"What's this all about, Detective?"

"We know you served overseas with a Delta Force unit and were awarded decorations for your wound."

"Glad to know you know all about me," sarcastically said.

"We need your help. Please bear with us. We need to know what you do at night?"

"Why at night?"

"Please, can we focus on the question. It will clarify itself in a few minutes," I responded.

"I'm not sure what will be clarified and I'm not sure why you're even having this conversation with me," he persisted.

"We're conducting a sensitive investigation and we're eliminating 'persons of interest' and you fall into that category."

"Categorized by whom?"

"I prefer not to say, but the person is fairly familiar with your combat history."

"Oh, her. She not the brightest light bulb I've met."

"Why do you say that?"

"She's okay but has no clue what I feel or experience daily. The therapy session is not likely to relieve my pain."

"We understand these therapy sessions are designed to assist you in coping with the unfamiliar world you've returned to."

"Yeah, that's what they say. Look, I was trained to kill and did it quietly and efficiently. I got caught in a mission that went wrong, seriously wrong. Came under a mortar barrage. Someone back at headquarters screwed up; seems like a norm rather than an exception. And now I have a head wound with shrapnel still lodged in my brain. It's inoperable without threatening to cause severe paralysis, maybe even death. I opted to live with it the best I can."

"You've got this head wound. You've got a family, two kids,

and you sound so calm."

"Look, it's not going to do me any good to get all angry and frustrated. In fact, that only makes my head hurt more. I'm reconciling myself to its reality, the shrapnel is there and I'm grateful to be alive. My wife and kids like that, too."

"How old are the kids?"

"Brett Jr. is turning 9 and Carolyn is nearing 5. My wife was pregnant with Carolyn just as I was sent overseas. When I came home, I had a daughter and a son. It makes me feel special inside, to recognize these gifts and their impact on my life, their love. When they hold me, it's hard to describe the warm feelings of love. Their warmth makes me melt on the spot. 'What's wrong daddy?' they ask. 'Nothing. Daddy's home and I love you so much,' I'd respond. They understand vaguely their daddy is hurt but we still rough house, well noticeably light rough housing. They are my salvation, along with my wife. She's a dream and handles the kids and home so effortlessly. I'm blest. From therapy, I got the tools I need to make my being home, work."

"I was an Army MP. And hopefully you won't mind me asking you this question. You speak of tools and support, yet you're not impressed with your therapist. I don't understand."

"It's easy. She wasn't there. I use the therapy group to glean what I can for myself. She does provide guidance and resources we can draw on. I am sure my life will get easier as time goes on, but I have metal in my skull that will always be there. What I do now at home has been one of the bigger adjustments, recognizing my wife must run the household and the kids, so I've taken a back seat. I am not macho but glad to support her."

"Is that one of the major adjustments for vets, returning home and realizing someone else has been handling all the details? I asked.

"Yes. It's a big issue. It's called 'adjusting to a new reality' in which you weren't present. Change occurred with the aging of the children, the wife acquiring skills to make a home. And now I return not sure of my role or where I fit in. Some vets get angry and resent the fact their world changed while they were away. It isn't the same and they cannot adjust comfortably. Conflict and dissention occur, stress and strained relationships occur and sometimes the rubber band stretches too far and breaks. I've learned to support my wife and not to expect the same family role as before. Maybe that will change, but my wife and I will work on it together. What we want is a warm and loving atmosphere in which our kids are raised."

"You have some wonderful insights into how PTSD affects you, how your service has changed your life and that of your family."

"You don't go into battle and return the same. You change. And most around you do not understand that change or understand why those of us, who were in combat, have such difficulty re-entering society. For me, I'm glad to be alive and being cared for by the VA."

"One last question. You're not the first vet we've interviewed claiming they were wounded because of a botched situation. How can this be, so many screwed up campaigns or missions?"

"That's how I describe walking into mortars we had no warning about or knew nothing of their existence in this one area. Whether brass was aware of them or not, I do not know. I just know we got hammered."

We never really got an answer to what he does evenings, but we doubt it was searching for someone to kill. We didn't need to prolong our interview. We said our 'thank you', wished him a happier life, and departed. Why the therapist had flagged him was unclear, but he wasn't angry, resentful or our killer. He was an incredible model for those returning, broken in body but not in spirit.

Cross another off our list.

"Have we heard anything back about the five local homeless victims and their families?" I asked.

"Not yet, but I'll gladly put in a call to CSI and see what they've got."

Staring at the data didn't encourage me. Sixteen horrific and unnecessary deaths. Homeless men. An MO suggesting someone with a military background, though anyone can buy a Sig Sauer Mark 25 at any gun shop. I looked at Conway and asked if CSI had gotten back to us on the stores that were selling the Sig Sauer Mark 25. He said no but would check on that as well. Of course, he might have brought it home with him, then again, maybe he didn't. Looking at Sergeants Gamlem, Franklin, Fletcher and Sledge's profiles, what was I missing? We're down to four and running out of "persons of interest." I suggested to Conway we interview Sgt Gamlem, then Fletcher next.

We examined his profile before we made our visit.

Sgt. Norris Gamlem, 5'11", discharged 20 months ago. 8 years in the Army. Delta Force in Iraq and Afghanistan, multiple wounds including head, and left arm shattered; rebuilt. Leg with shrapnel in it, inoperable. Awarded Bronze Star and Purple Heart. No indications as to where or how decorations earned. Single. Lives in Burien. 100% disabled vet. Feels the Army owes him more for what happened to him. Having difficulty adjusting to life. Attends therapy group but has moments of irrational outbursts asking why no one understands. Other times, sits with little to offer. Concerned there are other issues building inside. No arrest records. Born and raised in Seattle; attended Ballard High School.

We met the Sergeant at his residence. A bit surprised when we showed him our badges, he reluctantly invited us in. We explained that his therapist had referred his name to us and he was among a group of vets we were interviewing.

"We're interested in what you're doing with your time," I began. "We've got a situation and need to ascertain what you're doing evenings."

"Well, being vague is a good start," he said sarcastically. "Why the hell do you care?"

"Being evasive doesn't help us either. We need to know what you do evenings?"

"Nothing. I'm single. Have a head wound that's healing, shattered arm, can't concentrate. Girls are not flocking to be with me, if that's any help. Evenings? Can't get the crap I saw and did out of my head; I'm a good boy and go to therapy, for what it's worth, and I try to sleep. Sometimes I drive down to the water for solace, but that doesn't work all that well either. Is that enough of an explanation of what I do? Anyhow, why do you give a damn? No one else seems to care," he blurted.

"We're doing our job checking vets with PTSD. You were on our list for unclear reasons. Sorry to offend you, but as a former Army MP I've seen others like you return from nasty situations, and am trying to understand the pain you're in."

"Well I'll be damned. A do-gooder trying to say he understands me. No, you don't, and no one will."

"You're pretty angry!"

"You would be too if your body was cut up. I'm not a good patient for enduring pain. On a scale of 1-10, I rate a minus 3. So, the VA gives me meds to ease the pain. It doesn't work and being constantly in pain drains me, interferes with my attention span, and cripples my spirits."

"Are your therapy sessions helpful?" I asked.

"Not for pain relief. Get some good ideas for dealing with life, but little to relieve the pain the VA says will ultimately diminish."

"How did it happen?"

"What do you care about how it happened? I was in a firefight and I got shot up and caught in a partial explosion of an IED. My buddies were luckier and died."

"We're familiar with your service record," I calmly inserted.

"So, you know what it says. I did what I was told to do and damn if it didn't nearly get me killed and sure screwed up my life. Great memories."

"I know you're struggling and can appreciate the strength it takes to overcome what's happened to you."

"Glad someone does. But you're still not me and you still don't feel the pain I do. It's constant and when I walk, almost crippling. Purple Heart or not. Getting shot up is not fun and few understand unless they too have been wounded, and then it's different with each person. And no, I don't appreciate being ticketed for reckless driving when I'm learning how to drive again, only this time with a screwed-up arm and shrapnel in my leg. Pain is almost constant. Any other stupid questions?" He barked. "Take your badges and leave me alone. I don't need sympathy or anything else."

Conway and I did exactly that. We thanked him and left.

"Well that went south on us. You didn't mention anything about attending Ballard High?" commented Conway.

"He's explosive and bitter but I don't think our killer. He's in a lot of pain which, after a while, begins to interfere with concentration and mobility. Remember Locklear said he did not see a limp and apparently two hands held the gun when it was fired. His mobility or lack thereof says he is not our killer. And I think if I had mentioned Ballard, it would have interfered more with our interview than gleaning anything useful."

"Remove him from our list of potential persons of interest?"

"Moving on we need to visit with Sgt. Fletcher," I concluded.

38

Sergeant Fletcher's record was like all the others we'd seen, patriotic, did his job well, received recognition, and now lives a tough life after military service.

Sgt. Malcolm Fletcher, 5'11", discharged 18 months ago, 8 years in Army Special Forces, assigned overseas, operational background vague, multiple wounds, torso and extremities, including head wound requiring lengthy hospitalization and recuperation. Awarded Distinguished Service Cross, Silver Star, Purple Heart. 100% disabled. Lives in Capital Hill district. Divorced, one child. No arrest records. Attends therapy but alternates between silence and angry outbursts.

It took some time coming back to Capitol Hill from Burien. Traffic! Our conversation with Sgt. Gamlem wasn't pleasant, but none of these vets were living an ideal life. Their social skills were tainted by their wounds, anger, and struggle to readjust. They're all carrying a lot of baggage from their active duty time, and justifiably so. They killed other humans and must live with those gruesome realities.

Finding him at his residence, we introduced ourselves.

"What's this all about," he said.

"We got your name, among others, from the VA, where we understand you're in a PTSD therapy group."

"So what?" was his terse response.

"We're investigating a complicated case and need to find out about your recent activities, especially during the night. May we come in."

Stepping back, he allowed us to enter his sparsely decorated apartment. We hadn't even taken a seat and he was "off the blocks" with his questions.

"What is so complicated about your case? And you said you were homicide cops?"

"We've got a complicated case and need to know what you do at night?" I stated.

"Being in homicide, you must think I killed someone? You're kidding, I hope. Would like to kill my ex-wife, who walked out on me with a child that wasn't mine, cleaned out my bank accounts, and had the gall to sue for alimony and won."

"Is she still in the area?"

"No, thank god. She took off with some guy and is hiding in Texas or Montana, hell I don't know where or even care. I'm disabled but that didn't deter her getting the courts to cough up five hundred a month of my disability pay for her comfort. Gets taken automatically by the court and sent to her, so no, no idea where she lives or with whom."

"Have you spoken with an attorney about assistance with this matter? Maybe someone through the VFW or American Legion or Legal Aid can advocate for you," I inquired.

"No. Having to deal with her is a bitch, in fact, she is one. Not interested in resurrecting that stuff again."

"Let the legal professionals handle your case. I sense a cruel injustice and, as a former Army MP, suggest you get corrected the mistreatment you've experienced. Stand up for yourself like the way you did that brought you two significant decorations."

"Can't afford that legal stuff. Cheaper to leave her alone. And about those decorations, one was for getting shot up leaving blood all over the place. I'm hurting physically, my body and my head, and to have to wade back through the crap of dealing with my ex-wife is almost too much for me to handle."

"Sergeant, that is being naïve, and you know damn well you didn't go into a battle without a good lay of the land. The attorney can help push the issue of the child's father, with DNA testing. The attorney can ask the court to suspend your payments pending a DNA confirmation. The attorney can ask for the cessation of your payments, and maybe even ask for what you've paid to be returned. The attorney can do the work for you and shield you from your ex-wife. And if she's out-of-state, the attorney can handle all the necessary arrangements. Whatever, if you begin processes here, as this is your residence, the actions will most likely be completed here."

"It sounds too good to be true. I have no hope. No feeling that justice will be granted."

"Okay, I can understand that's how you feel. But there are sources to help vets like you, and I can assure you from my vantage point, a great disservice has been done to you, who faithfully served, sacrificed and was decorated for your bravery."

"So, what is it you wanted to see me about? Certainly not my divorce?"

While he talked, he was almost in constant motion, shifting how he sat, fidgeting with his hands, rubbing an arm or leg. It was obvious he was uncomfortable and not from our presence but from his pain and wounds.

"You're right," I began. "But knowing about your divorce is helpful. My partner and I are investigating a difficult case and your name was given to us by the VA, to visit with."

"I don't know why the VA would refer me to you. Just having a bitch of a time putting my life back in order after being in some major stuff."

"We understand that. But we need to know what you do with your evenings."

"I killed and killed. I saved a buddy, dragged others out, did stuff behind lines no human should have to, got shot up, hit in the head and shrapnel in other parts of my body, and yes, was thanked, decorated, kicked back into a world I don't recognize. Am I bitter? You bet! Then kicked in the teeth by an unfaithful wife and the naïve courts who sided with her. Evenings in the quiet of my apartment, I cannot silence the sounds or pictures of where I was and what I did. I cannot get out of my head how I've been betrayed, and no one cares."

"Let's start first with: we care. I've given you some steps that will help you regain your integrity and right a wrong. I wish I could, but cannot, take away your hurts. But, back to my questions, do you have a gun or any weapons?" I asked.

"No. It's not safe. I know how to use them but don't want them around. Too many dark memories."

"As an MP, I saw many like you return from war. I can only empathize with the internal battles you are waging. Yes, you are bitter, rightfully so. But personally, as one whose wife walked out on me too, I would encourage you to seek legal assistance and let them resolve what appears, clearly, as an injustice to you. I think it will be in your favor too and might help your perspective on life," I offered again.

He nodded but said nothing at first. Then, "You know, when I was young, I dreamt of being a soldier. When I trained, it was the fulfillment of a childhood dream. I wanted to be like those movie stars, heroic. Then I was sent into hell's hole, caught in a devastating firefight, wounded, sent home, repaired the best they said they could, told thank you, and then kicked out into a world protesting and arguing about where I had been and whether it was worth it. I don't know the politics behind being overseas, but I wanted just to come home, to a quiet home, and be like so many others, married with kids. It sure hasn't turn out that way. All I have for the moment are the memories that keep me awake at night and the damn alimony being deducted from my VA check."

"Sergeant, welcome home! You served and sacrificed. I hope your future will be brighter as you recover from your wounds and injustice. Please, take my advice about an attorney or legal aid. You should at least visit with one of the VA advocates next time you go to your therapy group. They are there to help vets like you and may be able to give you additional resources to consult. You've been unjustly treated and that needs to be corrected. Thank you for your time."

I did something rather unusual. I handed the Sergeant my card and told him to call me if he needed any further encouragement or guidance regarding his unjust divorce. Seeing his hurt made me hurt inside as well. Based on what he said, there's been an obvious injustice which wounds him as deeply as his physical wounds. Why a court would award an ex-wife alimony or childcare for a child that is not his, raises questions about the treatment of a returning combat veteran let alone the court system and an apparent bias against the male partner. I'm certain an attorney could challenge the court's decision to take part of his "disability pay" for alimony or childcare, and be successful in righting a wrong.

With that, Conway and I shook his hand and departed.

Bitter, angry, but not likely our killer.

39

Dr. Ward left a message: two other names were being emailed. One is a "person of interest" with a blacks ops background.

Sgt. Samson Bowles, 6", six-years Delta Force, Iraq and Afghanistan, Bronze Star, Distinguish Service Cross. Discharged 24 months ago. No wounds. Complains of headaches. Married, no children, employed by Boeing. No longer in a therapy group.

Dr. Ward wasn't sure if there was a coincidence or not but since she'd seen the last name before in our investigation, wondered if there might be a connection. The woman had not reunited with any known family, leaving questions as to what was at play.

Sgt. Monica Wright, 5'-10", Army 5-years, severely wounded in Afghanistan, Purple Heart, Discharged 6 months ago, medical, lost part of her leg, PTSD therapy group. Single, partial disability, in rehabilitation, lives alone in a rented room near the VA hospital. Has a relative in the area but wishes not to be reconnected.

Conway and I immediately took note of Sergeant Wright. Our instincts guided us to make a return visit with Bee Wright. I don't believe in coincidences, nor did Dr. Ward.

Conway and I found Bee walking her dog near her apartment building.

"Bee, we're glad to catch up with you. How's Macho?" smiling.

"He's doing okay. Nice to see you both again, too."

"We have a situation we need to clarify with you."

"Whatever I can do. Told you what I know and saw; whoever it is still hasn't stopped killing, has he?"

"You're right on that matter. Your composite of the witness was perfect and has been distributed in an effort to locate him. So far, nothing. We've been interviewing returning vets, discharged veterans who've returned from combat with either a physical, psychological or an emotional disability."

"Not sure I follow you completely."

Conway continued. "Bee, you've been a wonderful help. But the question we have may seem interesting, unusual or a bit personal. Kelly and I do not believe in coincidences and looking at a list of vets, a name appeared on our list and we were wondering if you know a Monica Wright?"

There was a pause. Her face went white, a nonverbal drop in her animation and she stumbled. I took her arm.

"She was my niece, killed in Afghanistan."

"Did the military notify you? Was her body brought back for burial?"

"No, her letters stopped, so I assumed she was killed." A pause. "Her parents died many years ago before she went into the Army. She came to live with me for a short time before she joined; seemed to find a home, friendships and purpose, and all that. She always was eager to demonstrate her ability to conquer any challenge and the Army became one of those challenges. She wanted to become a highly trained soldier. And she appeared to be reaching her goals. She shipped out; she wrote me regularly and then the letters just stopped. The last one said she was going on a dangerous mission and didn't think she'd return. By the time I got the letter she was no doubt dead."

"Can we find a place to sit?" walking toward a couple of benches near her apartment building. Macho hopped into her lap when she sat.

"We got some news for you about Monica."

"Oh dear!"

"No, quite the contrary," continued Conway. "She's alive and here in town."

Bee sat there in shock, and then the tears began to roll down her cheeks. She was hugging Macho and began to shake. Conway leaned over and placed his hand on her arm. She slowly regained her poise, and crying asked, "How do you know?"

We spent time telling her what little we knew, and it was our intention to locate her and try to visit her.

"We aren't sure why she didn't let you know she was alive but injured. With your permission, we'll let her know, when appropriate, you know she's home."

Bee agreed. We sat silently with her for a while to be sure she was going to be okay. We asked her not to do anything or try to attempt to locate Monica, as she has her reasons for not letting Bee know she's home, disabled. We explained more of the nature of PTSD, how it affects our troops and how her Monica was no doubt suffering a double blow, being caught up in dreadful combat and losing part of her body. She was working on both issues and, for those efforts, she showed determination.

As we were departing, Bee said, "I want to see her; I want her home," then began to cry again. We stayed with her as a silent comfort until we felt she'd be okay.

"We'll do our best to make it happen, but it all depends on Monica," was my affirmation.

40

I asked Conway, "Can you call Dr. Ward and have her arrange a visit with Monica. I think we'll have to finesse this. She doesn't want to go home and admit she's crippled."

Conway made the call as we drove back to the office. Dr. Ward told us the therapy group Monica was in would be meeting in a couple of hours, and she would meet us at the VA hospital. With that news, we altered our course and drove down to the hospital, asking Dr. Ward to meet us in the south cafeteria.

"Hi guys," was the soft voice of Dr. Caitlin Ward. "What do we have?" as she grabbed a chair to sit at our table.

"Hi yourself, and thanks for coming. (She nodded) You gave us two more names, one being Sgt. Monica Wright. You said her name was a coincidence as it had appeared elsewhere in our investigation. Why did you flag her?"

"The name was familiar from your reports. Decided to explore if there was any connection. Her therapist filled me in. She lost part of her leg and is deeply angry, angry their unit was caught off guard, angry that the Humvee she was in did not prevent an IED from tearing it apart. She sees herself as damaged goods, a female missing part of her leg and doesn't feel any male will want to be with her. She's working on the crippled part, the combat fatigue part, and a sense of guilt about not letting her family know."

"Has the therapist gotten anywhere with the family matter?"

"No, she just doesn't want to speak about it."

"She's missing part of her leg and still recuperating, so Monica's therapist may have been presented with an opportunity to help her heal. Her parents died of unknown causes, prior to her going into the Army. She lived with an Aunt here in town, who you know we met during our investigation. Bee Wright is her name and we just visited with her again. She thought her niece was dead as her letters had ceased, the last one saying she was going on a mission and didn't think she'd come back."

"Wow!" said Caitlin. "The description the therapist gave me about her frustrations and anger are complex and likely more than just PTSD. I'm suspecting there's enormous guilt and some embarrassment about her physical damage, and not wanting to see her Aunt."

"She may feel she failed too; according to her Aunt, she had bold goals about her accomplishments in the Army. I'm not a psychologist," I smiled at Caitlin, "but my instincts concur and think a reunion would not only be good, but cause Monica's defenses to literally melt. It might be healing beyond our imagination for both Bee and her."

"How do you want to handle this?" asked Dr. Ward.

"Well, I was really looking for your help on that matter. She'll be here shortly for her therapy class. Maybe you can arrange to have her therapist's help in getting her to meet you and then us, and in a private room, please not too small; we'll ask questions and share what's going on. Her Aunt wants her home unconditionally. She was shocked and cried when we told her Monica was alive and here. She wants to see her."

"Okay, let me go and see her therapist, and what I can do to have Monica join us. And can I get her Aunt's address too?"

We gave Caitlin the Aunt's information and assumed she would advise the therapist. She told us of a small conference room down the hall from where the therapy group would meet, and said she would meet us there.

Monica, about 5 foot 10, very trim and fit, was still on crutches. She was well dressed and had on long pants so you could not see her partially amputated leg, fortunately below the knee. We were told she was being fitted for a prosthesis but waiting for the swelling of the nub to recede. Regardless, she was extremely attractive, had a very animated face, and an Army-hard body.

"Okay, I agreed to meet you guys, and I know you're cops."

"Yes, we're guilty."

"What do you want with me?"

"We're conducting an investigation that has us checking lists of vets in therapy with PTSD. We asked Dr. Ward, who you've met, to help interview the therapists. Dr. Ward found your name of interest and asked your therapist about you."

"I'll beat you to their conclusion. No, I am not crazy. Yes, I have seen combat. Yes, I have a Purple Heart and only part of one leg. Yes, I feel lousy about all of this and don't think any guys will like a one-legged girlfriend."

"What we found interesting is you've said nothing to the therapist about family," I continued.

"Nothing to say," she responded.

Conway then led, "But you haven't mentioned your Aunt Bee who lives here in Seattle."

Her eyes went glassy and tears began to slowly run down her cheeks. "How do you know about her?"

"Long story but we'll make it short. You've read about the serial killer of homeless men. One of the sites where he killed was not far from your Aunt's apartment; a homeless man who found the dead bodies saw her walking her dog and asked her to call it in."

"Macho," she inserted.

"Yes. Asked her to call the police, disappeared, and we

responded. We interviewed her."

"She's my only living relative," sobbing. "I just didn't want her to see me in this condition until I can walk without crutches."

"We know. We suspected that after we talked with your Aunt two hours ago. She thought you were dead since you've haven't written her. She was in tears, but happy to know you're safe and here, and she said unconditionally she wants to see you and have you home. I think it would be good for her and enormously helpful to you."

She nodded in agreement, the tears still gushing down her face. She was trying to hold it together but was losing it, slowly. We slipped the box of Kleenex across the table for her to use.

"Monica," said Dr. Ward. "After having lunch with these officers and arranging for this meeting, I made other arrangements unbeknown to either of them. Can we take you to see your Aunt and go home?"

Pausing, behind her tears, she nodded.

"Are you ready to see her?"

Again, she nodded affirmatively.

"I'm so happy you have wanted to see and be with her. She doesn't care about your wound or rehabilitation. She just wants you home. So, I'm accelerating the process. Excuse me."

Dr. Ward left the room and a few minutes later re-entered with Bee and Macho in tow. The tears were streaming down Bee's face as she saw Monica. Monica rose and almost fell but was helped by Conway. She stumbled forward on her crutches into Bee's arms, both bawling and hugging. Even Macho was excited, jumping up at her for attention.

We left them alone. Caitlin had arranged for transportation to take them to where Monica lived, to pick up her personal things, and then take them home to where Bee lives. Monica was an incredibly attractive woman who wanted to be loved and accepted, and felt that wasn't likely to happen. What a positive new beginning was unfolding for them both.

"Talk about an emotional moment," began Conway. "I was hoping something like that would happen to those two beautiful women."

"Monica was just embarrassed for feeling less than the attractive woman she is. Now they will have plenty to talk and cry about, and maybe along the way, healing will take place in both their lives."

"That leaves us with Sgt. Bowles. I'll have CSI track down his residence and as he is married and working for Boeing, I suggest we visit him as well."

"He intrigues me too. No longer in therapy, so why did the therapist flag him?"

CSI got back to us that Sergeant Bowles and his wife live in Everett, where he works for Boeing at Paine Field. He manages their welcome center and oversees public tours of the Boeing facilities, and serves as their security chief. Given his work location and recognizing it was now late in the day, we slated the visit till morning. Depending on traffic, it might take us an hour or more via Interstate 5 to Boeing's location. With that, I decided to call it a day.

Patti got home soon after I did. The grill on our deck was already warming up to host four small tenderloin lamb chops, the artichokes sitting in bubbling hot water and potatoes in the oven. I was chopping the Romaine lettuce for our Caesar salad with parmesan cheese, croutons and the dressing we liked. I told her it would be a half-hour before I put the chops on, and she could shower and change. Dinner was not spoiled, but the quick shower together was very reinvigorating. Dressed in more casual clothes, the makings of a delightful dinner were laid on our new dining table; we sat across from one another, sipping the wine we loved. Our conversation focused on the joyful reunion of Monica and her Aunt Bee. Following dinner, dishes sat in the sink as we sat in the hot tub, our wine glasses on the edge of the tub and us in each other's arms. The soothing hot water, her warm and sensuous body rubbing again mine, provided all the distractions from the office I needed.

But what Conway, Caitlin and I were able to make happen that afternoon continued to warm my heart, as did holding the one I loved.

41

"Damn, he struck again last night," announced Conway as I walked in.

"Didn't any of our tails see anything?"

"Apparently not. Either he evaded them or he's not among the remaining persons of interest."

"Good analysis. I'm sure CSI and the ME will have updates for us when we return from Everett."

The drive to Everett was slow with heavy traffic, though not as bad as the crowded lanes flowing back into the City. We found the Boeing welcome center and Sergeant Bowles at the front counter. We carefully introduced ourselves and asked if he could be relieved, to visit with us for maybe a half hour. Showing us to a private office, he offered us coffee or water and asked us to please sit down and be comfortable.

Sgt. Samson Bowles, 6", Delta Force, Iraq and Afghanistan, Bronze Star, discharged 24 months ago, Married, no children, employed by Boeing. No longer in a therapy group.

"How can I help you?" began Sergeant Samson Bowles quizzically, 6-foot and dressed in a pressed Chief of Security uniform. His name plate said he was manager of the welcome center.

"Thanks for your time. To the point, we're investigating a complicated case involving vets with PTSD. In cross-checking some lists, although you no longer attend, your group therapists flagged your name for some unknown reason. We're here to follow up as to why she did."

With a sarcastic tone in his voice, he said "Oh, she's a gem. In my opinion, academic degrees and little practical understanding."

"What does that mean, Sergeant?"

"She tries hard but has no clue about us returning combat vets. Very patronizing."

"She wasn't helpful?

"I'm lucky, blest. I was Delta Force, eight years, saw some really bad stuff, even committed some bad stuff, not wounded, and decorated for what it's worth, then discharged. But I was told to attend a group therapy session under the VA to help with my transition back to private life."

"Has it helped?"

"That's what I meant, degrees and little more. No one who's not seen or been where I was is able to understand what I did or saw. The Army makes us killers. We killed people who were called our enemy, but we really had no clue if they were or not. We'd go out at night, do our thing and crawl back. Yeah, I was in a couple of vicious firefights, too. Saw some of my buddies blown away, half their heads missing, blood dripping down my uniform. Why was I so lucky?"

I simply smiled and nodded, suggesting I understood. He kept talking.

"She tries to help with questions and suggestions. She wants us to express our repressed feelings and frustrations. She wants us to share the anger or guilt we have, coming back alive with buddies left behind. And when some of us spoke vividly about our experiences, you could see her shudder and draw back. She had difficulty hearing the horrors we faced."

"Do you feel guilty coming home while your buddies didn't?" I asked.

"God has a purpose for each of us. I didn't know it then, but know now He was watching over me. He protected me and I came home. My therapist doesn't understand my conversion. She kept saying it's escapism from the harsh brutalities I experienced. Well, yes and no. You see, Jesus says for me to keep my eyes on Him; He's the one in charge, He's the one who knows better, He's the one who placed the stars in the heavens and amid all the evil on earth, gave us salvation from death and our sins through His Son's death on the cross. He's the one who loves me, any of us, unconditionally, and gives me hope. My head is full of ugly pictures and visions of what I experienced. Those will always be there as with any of us who've been to hell and back. But my focus is on Jesus, not the traumas I suffer, and she couldn't grasp that life changing truth for me."

"Are you still under any care with the VA?"

"I get my prescriptions which help, my physical annually. Beyond that, no. I have a great life. My wife is carrying our first born, due in five months. What more precious venture in life than giving life and nurturing it to its potential. I'm excited."

"I can only imagine."

"Not married?" he asked.

"No, but engaged to my high school sweetheart after many years floundering. Pardon me, though, but going back to your activities overseas, you describe what we've heard from others, the brutality, human destruction, stress and so much more. That certainly shifts the meaning of life after the service."

"The Army taught me to be a killer. Those memories, sounds and pictures will always bounce around in my head. The therapy group was to help me cope with these aftereffects of being in a war. But God has really been my salvation. He has given me a peace, a peace with myself and forgiveness for what I've done."

"And you left your therapy group?"

"Yes. As I said, the therapist did not understand what I have seen and done. Some useful ideas were shared but after a while I figured I was wasting my time traveling from Everett to Seattle for an hour session. So, I dropped out and don't regret it either."

"You're able to get along on your own without assistance? You have a support network locally?" I asked.

"Yep. As I said, good job, great friends, wonderful wife and a baby expected. I feel blest as I lean on God to guide my path, give me joy. I'm sure, too, that what I continue to hear, see, and have nightmares over, will wither with time."

"You have found a fabulous life. We appreciate your time Sergeant."

"The Sergeant stuff is behind me. It's Samson."

"We wish you and your wife much happiness then, Samson."

As we left, Conway said, "We can scratch another off our list."

"Yeah, he's no killer; he's found meaning and purpose for his life and really no visible desire to seek revenge; he's looking forward to their baby, like you and Cindy."

"Each day she grows bigger. She's energetic and happy and so beautiful, pregnant."

"Any names being tossed around yet?"

"Yeah, we're making a list for either a boy or a girl. Some names are family names. Others we like for no other reason than that."

"Prioritizing them?"

"She wants the boy to be a Junior, but I'm not sure. She wants the girl to be Jean, named for her younger sister who prematurely died in her youth. I'm okay with the girl's name."

"Feel embarrassed or uncomfortable with a Junior?"

"Not sure what it is. Not sure I want someone to bear the same first name as their dad."

"We did, that is Patti and Neil did with Neil Jr. and it's worked well. No issues. In fact, it may have helped Neil through all the traumas of his dad's death. Robert Conway, Junior. Sounds rather good to me."

42

We weren't back even ten minutes when the Sergeant called us in.

"You both know about last night again?" he asked.

"Yeah, we got the news just before we left to interview one of our 'persons of interest'."

"How'd that go?"

"He's not the killer. Happily married, expecting their first like Conway, lives in Everett and is Manager of the Boeing Welcome Center at Paine Field, and Chief of Security."

"Well, the Chief is asking about last night."

"We haven't seen the CSI or ME reports," I said. "Doubt if there's much difference from the other murders."

Conway then said. "Sarge, I suggested this morning there really is only one of several alternatives. Either the killer is not one of our 'persons of interest', and we only have two left to check, both being tailed; or it's someone we've not identified, or a bit embarrassing, one of our tails missed the person making a move. It can happen."

"What's your gut telling you?" asked the Sergeant.

"You know all the military stuff, their training. (pausing) CSI is running down whether any Sig Sauer Mark 25s have been sold within the last five years, where and to whom. The answer is probably quite a few. These are the two being watched." I handed him their profiles. "We've eliminated everyone else. Maybe our tails missed something."

Sgt. Travis Sledge, 6'1", discharged 18 months ago, 8 years in Army, Delta Force. Wounded in Iraq but doesn't talk about where or how. Awarded Purple Heart. Single. Comes from a farm community in Western Nebraska, currently lives in Kent. Bold, obnoxious behaviors, struggles with issues in group therapy. No arrest records. Two traffic tickets and one DUI warning.

Staff Sgt. Anthony Franklin, 5'-11", discharged a little over a year ago, 7 years in Army. Delta Force Iraq and Afghanistan, severely wounded during second tour; awarded Distinguished Service Cross, Silver Star, and Bronze Star for exemplary service and a Purple Heart for multiple injuries. How or where he earned the decorations are vague in his record. Single, attends VA therapy session, terribly angry at life and feels nobody understands him. Attendance in his therapy group is erratic. Employed with a large retail store. No arrest records. Born in Shoreline. Parents divorced, mother lives in Kansas, father's whereabouts unknown. Ordered by Courts upon high school graduation into service over jail for bullying and getting repeatedly in trouble.

"Franklin has quite a portfolio," commented Troy,

"We've interviewed all the other 'persons of interest' and found none of them suspicious in any manner. Some of their portfolios were similar. Most are struggling with their personal traumas, angry and frustrated, but none seem to want revenge or viciously act out their struggles. Some are pissed at what happened to them and at whoever may have screwed up causing the situation that cost them their physical trauma. Most recognized their nightmares will be with them the rest of their lives. We've cleared them. These two are the only remaining persons of interest unless we get more from Dr. Ward, like we did yesterday. Those were also dismissed after interviews."

"Are you going to interview them?" he asked.

"Likely," I responded.

"I'll let the Chief know the latest, what we've eliminated and are still doing. You're getting close?"

"Close to the end of interviewing but have no idea if we're nearing the end of our search for an elusive killer."

"Stay with it, Kelly," he closed, waving us out his door while he called the Chief.

The CSI and ME reports said two homeless men were each shot once in the head, no shells recovered. The encampment was hidden behind a commercial building on the edge of the University's Arboretum. Of course, that baits the question of when and how he finds these locations. The victims were dirty, hadn't showered for some time, had bad teeth hygiene and didn't appear to have eaten that night as their stomachs were empty. Alcohol and drugs were in their systems.

"Conway, have we got anything about the search for a buyer of a Sig Sauer Mark 25?"

"I know what you're going to ask. Done."

With that, he was on his phone calling Tucker again. It sounded like they had the information but someone forgot to get it to us. Shortly thereafter, he opened an email and printed out its contents. He handed me a copy. The homeless killed became less a focus considering what CSI sent us regarding purchase of the suspected weapon.

"Take a look at this!" as I reviewed the information from CSI.

Fifty-five names were on the list with purchases of the weapon from several area gun stores.

One name stood out.

"About 9 months ago, Tony Franklin purchased a Sig Sauer

Mark 25. The address given is south of Costco. His purchase was cleared after a background check and a waiting period of ten days. A lot of ammunition was bought at the same time, 300 rounds, and a silencer. You know me, Conway, I don't believe in coincidences."

"Concur."

We walked into the Sergeant's office.

"We have new information that should impact what we are doing with our 'persons of interest'. In fact, we may have a suspect," I began.

"So quickly, Kelly. What's up?" the Sergeant asked.

"CSI has confirmed the purchase of the Sig Sauer Mark 25 9mm with ammunition and a silencer by one of the names on our list, Sgt. Franklin. 9 months ago," I explained.

"What's your gut feeling on this?"

"I think Conway and I should interview Sledge, one of the last two names. Unless I am totally mistaken, we need to pull the tail on Sledge and double the tail on Franklin," I replied.

Conway added, "We've had a tail on Franklin, but we've also had two additional killings. As Kelly has said, either he is not our killer and someone else is, or he is our killer and able to lose the tail. Don't forget, we have the killer on tape with night goggles."

"Ok, I'll have the tails shifted to concentrate on Franklin," the Sergeant agreed. "Do you guys want a search warrant for Franklin's residence? You certainly have probable cause."

"May be a bit premature and might spook him if he's our killer. The gun in his possession doesn't necessarily mean he's the killer. He might have lost it and someone else is using it."

The Sergeant agreed with our observations. We left his office for our interview with Sgt. Sledge.

43

Though it was early afternoon, Conway and I arranged a face-to-face visit with Sgt. Travis Sledge. We agreed to meet in downtown Kent at a Starbucks. We told him we'd recognize him; he said look for the cowboy hat. He told us he would recognize the suits. There was no missing either of us. His height and large cowboy hat were a giveaway, as were our suits, as we both approached each other.

"Sgt. Sledge," I began, and he interrupted.

"Yes, Sir. Call me Travis. Prefer that. Sledge makes me sound like some sort of television detective. Sure, ain't one. Family said we migrated with the pioneers, and stopped in Nebraska, may even have our name engraved on some sand-stoned bluffs like other pioneers. Sorry, just like talking about my home."

"That's okay. Was your name the brunt of jokes in the Army?"

"Yes, Sir. Sometimes had to bust a few heads. Once that happened the others backed off. Of course, my size helped a little, too."

"We have a situation in which your VA group therapy leader suggested we visit with you."

"Have no clue why she would refer me to you. How is the PD involved with the VA? I do know I get loud at times, but man, cannot handle being cooped up. Maybe she felt threatened by my size and outbursts?"

"Why's that, Travis?"

"Don't like being cooped up. Have a ranch in Nebraska with cattle and my horse. I like the open range and skies with their stars. Do you know what it's like at night when there are no lights other than the stars? It's amazing how deep you can see into those heavens. The sky seems to wrap itself around you, the stars blinking, the Milky Way."

"What happened to you when you were in combat?"

"Oh, you mean the chaos and carnage of fighting? It wasn't a picnic. Got myself wounded by shrapnel from a mortar explosion. I was lucky but lost two buddies who're still splattered around over there. Gave me a Purple Heart and sent me home."

"Do you now ever have the urge to shoot anyone?" I hesitantly asked.

"Hell no! Did that stuff overseas. Crazy stuff, insane stuff. Just us bullying other harmless peoples in non-descript villages with bullets to their heads. Made no sense."

"And being placed in a therapy group?"

"The wound. Was told when being discharged I was referred to the VA to assist with what they called latent or post-traumatic stress, whatever that is. Therapy is to help me adjust to the invasion of my body, as they would say, which is nothing more than being shot and wounded. All I want to do is go home. Riding my beautiful stallion will be a challenge until I'm fully healed, but have got to get out of dodge, so to speak."

"What do you do evenings?"

"Sleep the best I can. I still have nightmares of what happened, the sounds and blood and dead bodies. Usually wake up in a sweat. They tell me it will decrease, but how do you stop hearing or seeing something in your head you've experienced?"

"Where in Nebraska do you live?" Conway asked.

"Farm and ranch country, western side of the state, a long way from those larger populated towns. Our cattle roam the range lands."

"How much longer before you return to your ranch?"

"I have no clue. Depends on the healing of my wounds and the therapy group. Nearest VA to where I live is either Denver west or Omaha east, both a long distance from my ranch. So, I guess I'll settle for here for the moment, but am bucking to get home as soon as possible."

"Travis, I don't think we need to take any more of your time. Our investigation continues, but you're no longer a part of it; I might say, though, you are an interesting person with your ranch and horse. Sounds like a fabulous lifestyle, like 'home on the range.'" I said.

"Thanks. You bet it is. Just waiting to get back on my horse and do some serious riding, rounding up cattle. That to me is freedom, not the bull I saw overseas."

Conway and I departed and crossed him off our list. That put only one name in our cross hairs. Maybe now an appropriate pun.

44

The first thing I did on getting into the office, was call Dr. Ward. I put the call on speaker so Conway could participate.

"Caitlin, we're down to one name. One suspect."

"You have a suspect?" asked Caitlin.

"Yes, and a strong one, too. All the others you referred to us have been cleared. However, Sergeant Franklin has not been interviewed and I'm not sure we should. He bought a Sig Sauer Mark 25 about 9 months ago and 300 rounds of ammunition."

"Whoa. That's pretty suspicious."

"He's been under surveillance, but we've asked the Sergeant to double it and make it round the clock."

"Can you tie him to the recent murders?" she asked.

"No. That's so far the disappointing part. Either he slipped our tail or he's not our killer. We're getting a photo of him. But I need your help in getting a more in-depth background on him. You know, begin with his current therapy and why his therapists flagged him. Do you think she'll cough up her analysis, you know, with all those confidentiality laws?"

"I don't know but I'll make her feel guilty if she doesn't."

"Slap on the fact there were two more killed last evening. Maybe that will drive home the urgency of your questions. The tails said he did not leave his residence. We're not sure that's correct."

"What are you looking for, if you even know?"

"Neither of us are sure, but we want to know his motive for killing and why just the homeless. Is he reliving his past combat encounters? Has he freaked out and gone over the edge? Anything that might give us some insights into who we're dealing with and how dangerous he really is, beyond the fact he may kill again, if it's him."

"I'll do what I can. When do you need this?"

"Yesterday," Conway replied.

"I thought you'd say that. I'll get back to you as soon as possible, if not sooner," said with humor in her voice.

Conway and I knew she was serious and driven, and we might well hear within the hour.

"We decided on Robert Junior for the boy's name," out of nowhere Conway offered.

"Did I miss something in our conversation?"

"No, just thought we needed to take our minds off the current quagmire with something different, some fun news."

"Congratulations to you and Cindy. How is Mommy-to-be?"

"As I've said before, more energy than I've ever seen. She loves being pregnant. Bigger every day."

"I'm so thrilled for you. Patti and I are thrilled. She had Neil Jr. and knows the thrill of his birth and the turmoil of raising him. Uncle John will get a chance to vicariously raise your son or daughter."

"Let's take a walk. I need the fresh air and something to eat," Conway suggested.

We walked downtown chatting about their plans for the baby's room and adjusting their lives when the baby arrives, and found a Chinese place to slip into. As always, the food was plentiful and delicious. While we ate, Caitlin called and informed us about what was being emailed. We figured another twenty minutes finishing our lunch wouldn't cause the world to implode.

Opening my emails at my desk, I found two pages of notes from Caitlin: her comments and analysis along with those of the suspect's therapist. No photo. We had elevated him to a suspect status, and for the right reasons. Now for the nitty-gritty.

CONFIDENTIAL

<u>Subject:</u> Anthony Franklin

<u>Vitals</u>: Male, 5'-11", 210 pounds, dark hair, Caucasian, not married.

<u>Rank:</u> Staff Sergeant, U. S. Army; 7 years in the Army.

<u>Specialty:</u> Delta Force/Special Forces. Service in Iraq and Afghanistan

<u>Injuries:</u> Severely wounded (multiple wounds), second tour, Afghanistan

<u>Decorations</u>: Distinguished Service Cross, Silver Star, Bronze Star, Purple Heart, Campaign Ribbons. Decorations awarded for exemplary service and for risking his own life while under fire to save members of his squad during an ambush.

<u>Psychological Analysis</u>: Suffers from severe traumatic events, PTSD. Therapist has considered having him hospitalized for observation and treatment. Holds his feelings close to his chest, not willing to share what is going on in his life and head.

<u>Action</u>: In PTSD group therapy, prescribed antidepressants. Calls in sick frequently and misses his therapy sessions.

<u>Comments:</u> An angry soldier, frustrated with life. Claims he cannot get the visions and sounds out of his head. Cannot sleep, wanders. Signs of severe depression. Not a strong participant in therapy group, often saying

nothing. Has angry outbursts seemingly disconnected with reality. Says his nightmares make him scream and wake up in a cold sweat. Says he's being stalked by the enemy and wants to strike first and not be ambushed. Unstable. Candidate for mental health care. Therapist reports he scares her, and she thought she had seen a lot. Cannot get into this guy's head to understand why he's so violent, angry and frightened. Believes he's dangerous to himself and others. Dr. Leslie Stevens is his VA therapist.

<u>Additional Background</u>: *Dysfunctional family. Only sister died of leukemia. Parents divorced. Father abusive, mother a waitress. Considered a bully in school, got in trouble in high school and given ultimatum at graduation, jail or Army. Excelled in the Army. Re-enlisted, opting for Special Forces training. Demonstrated expert shot with weapons and fanatical fervor that probably contributed to his being able to rescue squad members under fire. Wounded at that time. Returned to Lewis-McChord for resilience training and discharge.*

<u>Current employment</u>: *daytime greeter for Costco, Seattle. (9-5).*

CONFIDENTIAL

"Okay, we have an angry basket case walking around. Need to get this to the Sergeant." I offered.

"No kidding. I notice the therapist's concerns again; she mentioned that during our interview with her and she's a former combat Army veteran, too, and has seen a lot," noted Conway.

We walked into the Sergeant's office.

"Now what?" he gruffly barked.

We said nothing initially, handing him the psychological

profile; he slowly read it.

"I imagine we're prepared for his unpredictable aggressive behaviors?" he asked.

"We will be. Obviously, a mental case."

"Regardless, he's killed a lot of innocent people," the Sergeant responded, "if it's actually him."

"Sad a man becomes so lost he hurts others and hurts himself. He must be ready to explode and that scares me as he's totally unpredictable."

"What do you think needs to be done?" Sergeant Troy asked.

"We've got a 24/7 tail on him. But for Franklin's tail, it should be clear we don't wish any interception; when he's on the move, just a simple notification of when and where to. My thinking is if the tail sees him going places, we record those locations, especially if we see any homeless in the area, or where he goes is where homeless are hard to find. That being the case, it's reasonable to think he's stalking his intended victims. If we feel he has decided on a location, we'll assume he's identified his potential victims."

The Sergeant interrupted, "That's a lot of 'ifs' Kelly."

"Better to have 'ifs' than nothing. If we have an assessment that seems to make sense about a target and his victims, no doubt he'll plan a final move dressed in black. He'll be on his maneuver. And so shall we. If we assess a potential target, I want permission to have a tactical squad back up with snipers."

"That can be arranged," Troy inserted.

"We have a couple of options we'll need to examine. First, we need to tie him to the previous murders. I'm not sure how we'll do this. The only common thing among the murders is the weapon; if we capture him, forensics can go to work on whether the weapon he carries is our murder weapon. If not, back to square one."

"What are you other concerns?" asked the Sergeant.

"If he's on the hunt, we can get there ahead of him, be hidden and take him down before he kills. If he resists, well, we know what's likely to happen. If that happens, doubtful we'll know why he killed so many."

"I like the preplanning with a potential site. Work with the tactical command and see what they recommend and how fast they can respond. I'm sure Captain Jeffrey can provide a worthwhile strategy," responded Sergeant Troy.

Captain Michael Jeffrey heads the Seattle PD Tactical Squad, actually two squads of exceptionally well-trained officers, more like commandos. He's served with the department for over ten years and has several commendations for defusing volatile situations and rescuing kidnapped persons. Standing at 6'3", some 250 pounds, when in his tactical uniform, he's a formidable threat to those resisting. He, too, comes from a Special Forces background and can think like they do, as an asset when leading a tactical unit.

A meeting was set up.

"You said it was urgent?" Jeffrey asked.

"Yeah, it is. We have a suspect who may be behind the killing of the homeless men. If it turns out to be the current suspect, he'll try to kill more, and we'd like to prevent that. Franklin is decorated for his combat activities. He's former black ops and currently incredibly unstable. The psychological analysis does not make him a candidate for man-of-the-year. We've got a round-the-clock tail on him. And we know he scopes out his targets and target areas before he makes the kill, and uses night vision goggles to do that."

"I've seen your reports," said Jeffrey, "and those sites were well hidden. He reconnoitered and knew where he was going."

"We agree."

"Doesn't sound like he'll be cooperative?" responded Jeffrey,

"Particularly if unstable."

"Doubtful. If this suspect is our man, he bought a military Sig Sauer Mark 25 9mm, a silencer and 300 rounds of ammunition. That to me is a big red flag. If we can get him alive …"

"As I said, doesn't sound likely," responded Jeffrey.

"No, it doesn't. My gut tells me he will fight. I just don't want others unnecessarily injured."

"What are your thoughts? What do you need?" Jeffrey asked.

"The strategic implementation is your domain. Can you move on a moment's notice? Once a site is apparently scoped out, do you want to stake it out? Your domain, your planning," I said.

"We can do anything necessary to prevent further deaths. If we can get in ahead of him, into the site itself, we can surround him and stop him before he pulls the trigger. If that's not possible, we can stop him coming out, and hope he'll surrender. But there's another action that could happen and be even more scary."

"And what would that be?"

"He escapes. If he's Special Forces trained, he's black ops, and those crazies can disappear before your eyes. Then he's a big threat to neighbors and the surrounding area. We literally would have a massive manhunt."

"Well, I hope it doesn't go in that direction," not said with much conviction either.

45

The morning was quiet, routine catch-up stuff. I decided to focus on organizing the murder book with all the reports and information from CSI, the ME, Lewis-McChord, the Seattle VA and Dr. Caitlin's reports. We have a suspect and if it turns out the way we hope it will, the DA's office will need all our data. The process gave me an opportunity to think through what we had and whether we'd missed anything. I knew we'd missed our killer; he's been stealth-like, in and out, without any noise or anyone seeing or hearing anything. But now we have a suspect.

Not realizing the hours had drifted by feeding the proverbial "Purple Paper Eater", Conway suggested a sandwich at one of our favorite delicatessens, the Metropolitan Market in the Admiral District; I suggested we opt for something closer and found a nearby corner grill with great hamburgers.

"Sounds like we're getting close to the end," remarked Conway biting into his burger.

"Not sure I would describe it that way." I paused to take a sip of my drink. "We have this one single suspect who may or may not be who we're looking for," I responded.

"Assume he is our serial killer. Do you think this guy's going to be easy to take down?" Conway asked.

"I don't think so. He's pretty much into whatever's in his head driving him. He's irrational; we're likely his enemy and thus he'll fight."

"If that happens, there will be less of a chance to understand why he did what he's done?"

"Yeah, it leaves everything hanging. If he's taken alive, he'll be a psychiatric case and incarcerated, but not on death row. And even then, we might never know. He may not be able to tell us why he's doing what he's doing."

"I've been doing some thinking about locating and watching him. Time may be short and having Jeffrey's team on alert is good. Why don't we do a DMV registration check for his car - of course, if it's registered. If we locate the car, we can tag it with a tracker, and put a drone in the air to follow when the car's in motion. We could see where he's going," observed Conway.

"Great idea. I'll let you take the lead and run Franklin through DMV. Then a BOLO for his car," I said.

"Just thinking. It may account for missing him leaving at night if his car is not at his place of residence. Dressed in black, he slips out, walks wherever, and our tail is still sitting there sensing no activity," added Conway.

"Best explanation I've heard about prior movements being missed. I can hear you cranking those gears again. What're you thinking?" I observed.

"At present we know he's single, works at Costco. Just thinking again about the need to gain access to his digs while at work and even planting a tracker in his gear."

"Not a bad idea, but like I told the Sergeant when he offered to get us a search warrant, it might spook him if he gets a sense we've been in his place. Too risky, but a good idea."

We had a leisurely walk back to the office. It had been a good call to keep our lunch break close to home.

"Kelly," answering my cell; it was Tucker.

"Not good news. Two more dead. They were found hidden in Freeway Park by the Washington State Convention Center. Apparently found a nook which they thought was safe. The ME is on the scene. Same MO. Sorry guys."

"This just continues. I thought we had our suspect covered. Who found them?"

"An employee on a smoke break."

"Homeless?"

"As far as we can tell, yes. We'll give you more later when we know," clicking off.

First Tucker and then the ME was on the line.

"The victims were killed around 2am last night. Same MO, one shot to their heads, no shells, men and the way they were dressed and bundled up, apparently homeless," said our ME. "The pattern's the same, so the perpetrator has not changed what and how he does it."

He, like Tucker, abruptly disconnected; it was back to work. Conway and I decided we needed a conference with the Sergeant. He wasn't going to like this, nor would the Chief.

We walked into his office and found him deep into writing another report, to add to the collection he already had on his desk.

"We don't know what went wrong, Sergeant. Two more dead and our suspect apparently didn't go anywhere, or our eyes didn't see him take off."

"Has the tail reported in?"

"No, but we'll need to ask their routine and where they're stationed. If he has a car, which Conway is checking, it's either in the parking lot next to the apartment building or on the street somewhere. My take, I doubt it's parked in the lot. So, parked on the streets, it's possible he sneaks out under dark to get it."

"And."

"We're thinking if we can locate his car, we'll place a tracker on it. If he doesn't take it to work and we can confirm he's at his job, that might be the best time to place a tracker on it."

"Sounds reasonable. What about these two new homicides?"

"Same MO."

"How do you want to play this cat and mouse game?"

"Just like we've planned, except find his car, put a tracker on it and use a drone to track his movements."

"Do you think it'll help?"

"Sarge, it has to. We have a suspect who is black ops and can easily disappear before our eyes. Obviously, that happened last night. The tracker can let us know when he's on the move."

"I'll check with the tail and see what happened. Get us the vehicle info, Conway, as soon as possible and we'll tag it. Kelly, what if his car is not registered?"

"I don't want to think that's likely. Then I guess it's back to the drawing board and maybe upping the number of individuals watching for his moves. Conway even suggested we look at his digs, and you had offered a search warrant, but again I don't want to spook him. We really don't have much anyway to justify such a move. All circumstantial but nothing tangible tying him directly to the murders, except the purchase of a gun like what is being used for the killings."

"And if after we do all this, and we find he does not go out at night, what do we do next," asked the Sergeant.

"That's a haunting question. No clue. We'd be back to square one," I remarked as I was leaving his office.

46

Trying to be proactive, we were awaiting the DMV results. The more I thought about our conversation with Dr. Stephens, the more my gut was telling me to protect her and her family. She had described him as unbalanced and one who scared her. When my gut starts to growl, it's time to take note. It's usually valid.

I called Jeffrey. "Got a favor to ask you, actually more than that. I need an extra protection shield around one of the VA therapists and her family, specifically her home. She's the one who gave us the name of the individual we've discussed possibly being our killer."

"We can do that. Obvious or stealth?"

"Stealth. If this guy turns on his therapist because he feels betrayed for whatever crazy reason, he'll attack. If your guys are hidden, the protection is there as well as the capability to take him down, if it comes to that."

"What about our other plan?"

"That stays in place. Meanwhile, we're working on locating his car and having a tracker stuck on it. If he goes on the move, we'll have a drone following him."

"Okay with me."

"Remember, he was given the Silver Star for getting his squad out of a firefight and while wounded at the same time. He's not going to go down easy."

Conway handed me a piece of paper with Franklin's car information. We passed it to the Sergeant and had dispatch put out a BOLO. Once that damn tracker's on it, I'll feel better about our covering him. Of course, if the killer is not him, then who is he and how do we ID him? Of course, there are 54 others on the list who bought the Sig Sauer Mark 25 9 mm. That would be a task to crawl through each one of those names, but if it becomes necessary, it's what needs to be done.

"Do we have any reports from the current tail on Franklin," asked Conway.

"No, but CSI is sending some photos taken of him at work."

CSI said Franklin sat or stood at his station at the entrance to Costco, asking for identification from those entering. They said he was impeccably dressed in a starched white shirt and dark Docker pants with a crease. CSI said his appearance is certainly not that of a killer.

"Okay. We have his photo and he dresses well. What does that tell us if anything?"

"I don't know, Kelly. If he's the spook we're looking for, I'm not sure how we would expect him to dress. Neat, clean cut, probably left over from his military days."

The Sergeant called and told us how the tail missed Franklin's departure the night before. He was increasing the cover to avoid another fiasco. The car's been found, located on the street a block from his apartment, and a tracker was being put on the car as we talked.

"What if he has equipment to uncover the tracker?" asked Sergeant Troy.

"We'll have to assume he doesn't. We'll have to trust it works for us when the drone's activated. If he does find it, we'll know when the drone doesn't move."

"Suggest we keep officers in place to tail and respond to the drone's tracking results. We know the murders are taking place early morning so if nothing is happening, there might be a problem. I have Jeffrey setting up a stealth protection team at the therapist's home. The VA therapists don't use last names; her professional name is different from her husband's name, but if Franklin stalked her, he already knows where she lives. Jeffrey's team will be ready should Franklin show."

"Sounds like a wise move, Kelly. Keep me posted." Troy clicked off.

Conway and I had little to do but the proverbial waiting game. We told the officers on the detail watching Franklin there's a drone now supporting them, and should he make a move, Officer Bergen would notify everyone when the drone is on the move.

At this point, we had in place what was needed and we were little more than just waiting for Franklin's next move.

47

That night, or rather early morning, it began. The wave tone from my cell filled the otherwise quiet of my room.

"Kelly, this is Officer Bergen. We're in motion following the tracker at a distance. The drone is above as well. The suspect is crossing the West Seattle Bridge. We'll keep you posted," clicking off.

Bergen had been added to the surveillance team and had the drone controls in his car. The tracker alerted the drone and it was launched. Bergen has a visual screen from a camera on board the drone, showing the car it's tracking, along with providing street names, directions, and other related data. Kelly and Conway had talked with Bergen and knew, although the drone was new for the department, that Bergen's experience, controlling and monitoring its movements, was quite lengthy. Traffic had used the drone to monitor traffic movements, oversee highway crashes and backups. Its use was gaining wide acceptance within the department as it augmented what current personnel were able to do.

Not much to do at one in the morning; I laid the phone down and Patti rolled over and asked if everything is okay. I assured her it was and to go back to sleep. I tried to go back to sleep but couldn't shake the many scenarios dashing through my head as to what was likely to happen. My preoccupation was even interfered with by the warmth of Patti sleeping next to me.

The wave ringer sounded again. Officer Bergen simply stated the suspect had returned home. He would update later in the morning.

As promised, Bergen emailed us a report of the night before.

The suspect left his apartment around 12:45am and drove across the West Seattle Bridge, down Fauntleroy past the Vashion ferry dock, up the hill past Joe's Grill, and followed the road down and around the loop that becomes 35th Avenue heading north, back to Fauntleroy, across the bridge and home. It took him about thirty-five minutes including slowing down, almost to a complete stop, at the bottom of the loop.

Conway and I reread the report, looked at each other, and made a call to Jeffrey.

"Did your men sight a car passing the house between 12:45 and 1:15am?"

"Just a moment while I check. (pause) Yes, they logged a car had passed the house at an awfully slow speed. It didn't stop."

"Okay, be on the alert. What we suspected may be materializing."

"Meaning?" he asked.

"That car belongs to Staff Sergeant Franklin according to our tracker. He's made one pass which means he's reconnoitering his target, namely his therapist's home. He must have followed her some time earlier as she has an unlisted address. He seems to have turned on her for whatever reasons. My suspicion is he'll make another pass to ensure everything is clear, and either strike after he makes that pass, or wait another night. Just keep that family safe regardless of what happens."

"If he doesn't stop, what do we do if anything?"

"If we are so lucky tonight and he doesn't stop, get the family out as quickly as you can once the situation is clear, meaning the suspect has returned home. Get them to a safe house. Leave your men on the scene as he no doubt will be back, at which time you confront and arrest him," I said. "He'll most likely return the next night and that is when we will have our encounter."

Clicking off, I momentarily reflected on my statement and was truly hoping to be right, that the suspect would make another pass but not stop. I was debating on moving the family now, but again, didn't wish to alert the suspect to anything being abnormal.

48

Patti called me mid-morning and said she was being asked to fly to Washington DC regarding the two drug cartel leaders she'd captured, Eduardo Delgado and Carlos Ramirez.

"They've booked a flight for me, leaving in a couple of hours. It'll be night when I land; they have a room for me, and a meeting scheduled at headquarters at 8am."

"What's it all about, any clue?"

"I think they're getting nervous about our cartel heads and their pending litigation. They want to strategize handling their cases in Court and have relocated the prisoners to a maximum-security prison in the Midwest. We're getting ready for the formal indictments and trial that includes quite a laundry list of offenses, including murder and accessory to murder."

"Think you'll get those to stick?"

"Sherlock did a hellava job identifying that list of 40-some-odd names with murder dates and locations. Our overseas offices and Interpol have been able to verify most of those dates with known unsolved murders and the country in which they took place. Couple that with his analysis of emails between El and PP, and I think we have a lock on it."

"Sounds like they're going to occupy federal facilities for the rest of their lives?"

"Hope so. But DC is more concerned about protecting all those involved with their arrest and legal proceeding."

"Yeah, I imagine the long arms of the cartel can be a challenge, especially with the dismantling of their cash cows."

"You know what still intrigues me, Kelly? How they got away with it for nearly twenty-years across the street from your department?"

"I'm not sure either, but they deserve an award for camouflaging their web of deceit."

"Well I wanted you to know. I have my emergency bag here at the office and will be good for at least two overnights. I'll call you when I get there. I love you, miss you."

"Love you too. Be safe and await your call."

Around midnight, Patti called to tell me she had arrived and was booked into the Sheraton. Her meeting was at 8am; she would call me after it broke up and let me know what was happening and when she'd be home. Without her next to me, sleep would be difficult.

Then again, the evening would not be without its own drama.

49

Some 30-40 minutes after Patti had called to say she was in DC, the wave tone from my cell broke the silence of my room again.

"Kelly, Officer Bergen. Our suspect is on the move again taking the same route I reported last night. Still cannot tell whether he's planning to stop or continue around. Give you another call shortly."

"Let Jeffrey know he's on the move please. The drone can track while you lay back."

Clicking off, I decided it's time to wash my face and, since Patti was not with me, head for the psychologist's home in West Seattle. If he keeps moving and does not stop, that's one thing. But should he stop, Jeffrey's team will activate its protective shield on site and try to capture him. I had serious doubts about the latter happening. My concern was for Dr. Stephens and her family.

I had my cell and a radio, so I was reachable by anyone. I decided if I couldn't sleep neither should the Sergeant or Conway and called both to let them know what was happening. Both asked what they could do, and I affirmed, nothing, that Jeffrey had it under control.

Once on the road, I let dispatch know of my whereabouts and intentions. It dawned on me that the suspect could be monitoring a police frequency; I decided to use my cell phone instead.

At this hour in the morning, Seattle glimmers with lights from the many downtown office towers and huge white or green cranes, with their flood lights, loading or unloading the container ships. The Seahawk's stadium is lit with blue and green on its arched roof. And a light fog dusts the city and its surroundings. Pacific Northwest weather sitting on the Sound. I decided to cross the West Seattle Bridge and then take 35th Street South. It would lead more directly to the house and should he not stop, pass him in the opposite direction. I wouldn't recognize his car nor would he recognize mine, particularly since I wasn't driving a police car. The humorous thing about police cars is they all look alike, with or without stickers, lights and letters on their bodies. You can spot them a mile away, but my little BMW was like any other private vehicle.

The radio chirped. It was Jeffrey. Officer Bergen had notified him that the suspect had cleared the house and wasn't appearing to stop. The tracker had him heading north on 35th toward the bridge, his current distance from the house, a mile and growing. He said Bergen would continue the tail and monitor his movements and report back. I suggested we go to a tactical channel, not likely to be picked up by a police monitor, or use our cell phones. We shifted to the use of cell phones.

I decided it was time to not take chances and told Jeffrey I was about 10 minutes from his location. I wanted him to awaken the family now, get them out of the house as quickly as possible and take them to the safe house. I would be there shortly to talk with the family.

The family weren't particularly happy campers, especially the teens. I met them in their driveway as they were getting into cars with their baggage, driven by police officers who explained what was taking place to ensure their safety.

"You're saying he's turned on me?" asked Dr. Stephens, her husband next to her with his arms wrapped around her shoulders.

"Yes. Originally, as you know, we had a security shield placed on you and the other therapists. A couple of days ago, we were able to put a tracker on Franklin's car. We weren't sure if he was the killer or someone else. But there were two murders and our stake out said he had not left his apartment. We found his car a block from where he lived so we concluded he was able to leave his place, get to his car undetected, and do whatever he does."

"It sounds so strange to believe one of my patients actually would turn on me, but I told you, he scares me," she responded.

"We know. We spoke about his behavior and for the past two days, we've tracked him, and he's made two non-stop trips past your house, the most recent 25 minutes ago. We want you out of here. He might strike later tonight but more likely to return tomorrow. He's definitely targeted you and your family."

"What about the house?"

"Give us your house and car keys. We will switch the sides your cars are parked on but otherwise they remain in the driveway, so the house doesn't look particularly deserted. If he returns, he will check it before he tries to enter. Jeffrey and his men will have the house under surveillance and will try to capture him."

"And if he resists?" she asked.

"You know what that means. At that point he will have narrowed the options with little room to flex. Now, no more questions please. We need you out of here and will connect with you later. By the way, no one is going to work or school tomorrow."

The teens grumbled and said they had homework due and would be penalized; I quickly assured them we would take care of the matter and that I knew their Principal Dr. Day. I asked Dr. Stephens to call in and advise her supervisor she was sick and not coming in, no other information. We finally got them out of the area and took a deep breath of relief. Now the show was all in Jeffrey's hands, depending on what the suspect did or did not want to do.

Officer Bergen called my cell and said he had tracked the suspect back to his apartment. The drama for tonight was over, but tomorrow awaited. Meanwhile, it was early morning hours and I was bushed, so returned home to capture a few hours of sleep before any more excitement.

50

Her meeting had apparently turned into a series of meetings including one with the Director. As a result, she would not be arriving SeaTac until 6pm. We talked a little about her day but she didn't want to say much over the phone; she asked me how the case was going and what was happening. I told her what had happened last night and felt tonight might be a little tense.

"I don't want you taking any chances," with 'worry' in the sound of her voice.

"Not planning to do that. Conway will be with me; Jeffrey and his tactical squad are at the house and the family has been relocated to a safe house. The kids didn't like being moved so early in the morning, but we did not want to push our luck."

"What do you think is likely to happen?" she asked.

"Two nights in a row, two slow passes past the house. He must have shadowed her earlier to find out where she lives, as she does not use her last name at the hospital and she and her husband have unlisted numbers and an unlisted address. I'm figuring he's ready to strike."

"And where will you be?"

"I'm planning to be near but not at the scene. It's Jeffrey's show and his men are hidden and trained to do what needs to be done. Inside the house, he'll have a couple of his men, turning lights on and off as if it's occupied. We had the family leave their cars, but take their dog and cat. Those inside will stay inside after everything is darkened. Our suspect knows the house, its location and is aware of the security sign in the front yard. We suspect he'll disengage the security system, enter the house and, surprise, be confronted by Jeffrey's men."

"Sounds like a good plan and I trust it will work."

"We do too. His strikes have always been around the same time, early morning. We anticipate that will continue to be the case. If something occurs, if he doesn't appear or comes at a different time, Jeffrey said he can flex. They're the ones having to wait."

"Please be careful, Honey. I'll be home to cuddle with you when this is over."

"I miss you and really never knew how much I would."

"It's not that bad is it?" she said, and I am sure, smiling on the other end.

"Not at all. I'm happy we are 'we'. See you when you get home. It's going to be a long night for Conway and me. I love you!"

"And I love you too," she responded and clicked off.

51

The day was short, based on little sleep last night. Getting a cat nap was all I was able to do. Neither Conway nor I had gone home during the day to get any sleep. Our office time was nonproductive as our minds were focused on what was likely to happen this evening, or more accurately, during the early morning hours of the night. We grabbed a bite to eat at the Luna Park Café at the foot of the West Seattle Bridge, had our coffee thermoses refreshed and drove to our staging area. We let Jeffrey know of our whereabouts; we had other uniformed back up, beyond Jeffrey's team, staged in a church parking lot not far from the therapist's home. We sat waiting, frankly dozing off at times, tense with anticipation, while at other times, staring out our car windows, slowly sipping coffee from our thermoses. Just as we had anticipated, the inevitable began to unfold and our adrenalin started to kick in.

My cell played its ringtone, the sound of waves reverberating, pleasant yet alerting. It was 1:30 in the morning.

"Kelly, he's on the move," said Officer Bergen. "He's just begun his drive toward the West Seattle Bridge."

"Let Jeffrey know our cat is on the prowl," clicking off. Using my cell phone, I called dispatch and advised them of my location. Then I called the Sergeant to let him know what was happening.

"Officer Bergen here again, he's just passed Joe's Grill on his way up the hill toward the target. Jeffrey knows too," and he clicked off. I had told all personnel in this operation to stay off the radio and use only their cell phones. They knew why too. We don't need interlopers when we have a dangerous situation going down. Gawkers and media will have their opportunities later, once the situation is safe.

My phone rang again with its reverberating sound.

"He's passed the house and has stopped about four blocks down 35th. No visual yet but believe he'll be dressed in black and may have night vision goggles on. Heads up," was the message from Officer Bergen. Our timing seemed to work. Our suspect was confirming his elite status and we were ready for his maneuvers, whatever they were.

My phone vibrated again.

"We have a visual. He's in black and does have night goggles on. We do too and can see him trying to walk cautiously and stay in the shadows. Showtime." Jeffrey's 'heads up' meant just that. I wanted to be closer and a part of the action. However, I had a mandate to be safe, which I agreed with; as we were dealing with an unstable mental case, no telling what might happen. I continued sipping my coffee slowly. Damn, waiting is like time stops. Silence and anticipation grow with no frame of reference; what's happening? Is everyone okay? Is it going down like we had anticipated? Has our suspect surrendered rather than fight it out?

All these weeks of unexplained killings of the homeless boiling down to one very unstable combat veteran with severe mental issues, now making a move on his therapist, the one who understood his context having been a combat veteran herself. Someone trying to help him is now the object of his anger. Makes no sense but again, he's unstable and fighting debilitating demons.

Jeffrey and his men were on full alert. They had watched our suspect ease himself toward the house, then slide in where there were external electrical boxes. He looked around cautiously and carefully opened the security alarm box and disabled the alarm system. Once it was disarmed, he pulled out a little tool and unlocked the back door. He pushed it open slowly, crouching low using one hand while the other held his weapon. Once open, he slowly entered in almost a crawl.

A loud voice over a megaphone broke into the silence of the night.

"Stop where you are. Do not move or take another step. This is the Seattle Police Department and you're under arrest for breaking and entering."

Silence.

He froze, and so did Jeffrey's men. This was the pregnant decision moment. Was he going to surrender quietly or engage in a fight?

How did anyone know he would be here? Who had compromised his mission? He then made his move and it was all nonverbal, yet loud. Quickly turning around, he fired a volley of shots into the green bushes from where he thought the voice was coming from. Then ducking back inside, other voices were heard.

"Lay down your weapon and put your hands up over your head. Slowly walk out of the house."

That too was met with a volley of shots, shells clinking to the floor. He had taken cover and waited. From outside the same admonishment again, "surrender."

Never in his life had he surrendered, nor did he intend to begin now. If he got his squad safely out from under enemy fire, he could get himself out of this situation too. He had no clue how many there were, but he knew, or at least thought, he was invisible and could slip past their enemy lines. This was war and he intended to take it to the enemy. Slipping a full clip back into his weapon, he touched the other two full clips in the front of his black vest and felt he had enough ammunition to escape.

Then again, another command.

"Sergeant Franklin, you are commanded to surrender and

come out with your hands held high above your head, no weapons."

Silence.

How does the enemy know my name? No enemy knows my name. Who's the traitor? Are they crazy or something, he thought? When you're in a battle, you never surrender. MacArthur and his troops at Corregidor were weak, and they deserved their death march. You don't become a soldier to surrender. You defend to the death like Custer did. No giving up. Try your tries and figure a way to unbalance your enemy with an unexpected move.

The silence was deafening. The air was quiet, no movement, no sounds.

He was trying to control his heart rate and breathing, but for some reason it wasn't working. He had to admit some concern as he knew he was in-between and could face a crossfire. Of course, the enemy is taking a chance too, and could kill their own with any miscalculation. His night goggles did not reveal anything to him. He couldn't see who was in the house behind him. He couldn't see anyone in the backyard either. He paused, calculating his options. How many enemies hidden? Where? How far to clear their firing angles? He had done enough thinking how the situation might develop. He was out of ideas and time.

Now was the time to act.

Springing to his feet, he dashed out the back door, fired some shots randomly, made an instantaneous turn around the side of the house, fired more shots, and began to race toward the front. So far so good. No return fire from the enemy.

"We command you to stop and surrender," was the loud voice again from behind him. He kept focusing ahead and saw through his night goggles the enemy finally rear their heads, at which point he began to shoot. The fighting was short. His mission was not completed. He never felt the bullets. He was dead before he hit the ground. His agony was over.

52

Jeffrey called me to let me know the curtain had dropped, the show was over. I told him Conway and I would be there shortly. We called the other officers at the church parking lot to join us and start to secure the perimeter.

On both sides of the street, house lights came on. Jeffrey's men moved their tactical wagon into the front driveway and surrounded the scene with red and yellow "crime scene" tape. I made a call to the Sergeant and suggested he, and maybe even the Chief, would want to be here. We knew news vans and reporters were already on their way. The Sergeant asked to be called back as soon as the suspect had been officially confirmed. CSI and the ME were also called to the scene.

The air now felt nippy, as it usually is at 3 in the morning in Seattle. With the neighboring houses all lit, people gazing at what was happening from their front porch or windows, one of the officers was assigned to visit the neighbors and let them know what had happened, then ask them to return to their homes and remain inside. They would know more later, on the news. The suspect, now the victim, was on the ground, covered, pending arrival of the ME. Nothing was being moved, not the weapon nor the shell casings. CSI needed to take photographs and mark the locations of everything, as did the ME need to look at the victim before wrapping it in a body bag. Jeffrey continued to record verbally into the microphone clipped on his shirt, the actions of his men, the sequence of events, the warnings, and the finale.

Franklin had done what we expected, fought. No doubt in his head, the situation had turned into a combat setting, himself against the enemy. No Silver Star for these actions this time. Not even a Purple Heart. He was now the casualty.

CSI began to search the area to mark the locations of and recover shell casings. Each magazine could handle 15 shots, so we were aware that he used one full clip and was working on the second. The third and fourth clips were found on his body, unused. The weapon was confirmed as a Sig Sauer Mark 25 9mm, bagged and tagged. Forensics would confirm the slugs previously recovered from the victims, and the slugs and shells recovered this evening, were from the same weapon. We were sure the homeless killings had come to an end. Why they had been his target would remain shrouded in mystery.

The ME would conduct his autopsy, but whether he could see anything in the victim's head that made him so crazy might never be answered. The ME pronounced the victim dead at the scene and was having the body bagged and removed. He would confirm with fingerprints and DNA who the victim was, anticipating that it would confirm him to be our suspect, Staff Sergeant Anthony Franklin, a decorated Army veteran crippled by PTSD.

Sergeant Troy did not come to the scene, but called and advised me he had informed the Chief who said she was holding a press conference later in the morning. She was pleased this nightmare was over and expressed her thanks to the team. He requested CSI and ME expedite their findings based on the Chief's pending press conference, and that Conway and I be present at it as well.

It wasn't too long before news reporters were in our face, lights, camera, action. We detained them a fair distance from the house, indicating that it was a crime scene and an investigation in progress. They weren't happy but were aware the Chief was holding her press conference later in the morning. Of course, the news channels were having a ball with their "breaking news" story of the shoot-out in West Seattle. They had little else to work with except being told it was one shooter brought down and the family was okay; beyond that we were deferring all inquiries to the Chief's planned press conference later in the day.

I made the call to Dr. Stephens informing her of the situation. The house could be reoccupied as soon as CSI cleared it. There was some bullet hole damage inside, no blood.

"He wanted to fight back, made a dash outside firing his weapon, and was killed. Fortunately, his aim tonight was poor, and no police officers were hurt. Your house is still a crime scene, we're collecting evidence."

"Was it Sergeant Franklin?" she asked.

"The ME will absolutely confirm, but based on who we were tracking, I'd say yes."

"He's done a lot of damage in our community; maybe his actions will help us in our screening processes and the care we wish to give our returning veterans. This one will be a lesson I wish to learn from so I can better help others."

"I commend you, Doctor. And I don't envy you when you have to confront the faces of your patients." I told her she would be notified when the house was clear to re-enter.

53

It was late morning; the media had been advised of the Chief's press conference regarding the shooting in the early morning hours. Their "breaking news" reports earlier in the morning had been rather anemic, as the department was not confirming who the victim was nor whose house it was. They had had their haggard reporters standing next to the yellow tape at 3 in the morning, when the air was cold coming off the water. Television screens at home were occupied with their "breaking news" red banners and the announcement of the pending press conference.

The City I love had been jarred, with the murders of homeless men, and a shoot-out in a quiet West Seattle neighborhood. The setting was now ready for the Chief and her performance. In her uniform with ribbons decorating her chest and stars flashing on her collar, she was in charge and everyone knew that, as she stepped to the podium. The Press Conference had drawn reporters from AP, CNN, and *Real Change*, in addition to all the local papers and news stations. Reporters were poised with their notebooks and recorders while cameras lined the side and rear of the room. Technicians were checking their equipment to ensure it was functioning properly, and taping a barrage of microphones on the podium, almost building a barrier between the Chief and her audience. Everyone was fighting for the proverbial scoop.

She adjusted the microphones and paused. Now you could see her face. Cameras flashed, then the room went silent.

"Ladies and Gentlemen. I'm Seattle Police Chief Carol Flanigan. I wish to thank you for coming and am hoping that with this announcement, our community will rest easier. When I have finished with my remarks I will take some questions, but do not wish to be interrupted while I make this presentation." She paused. "For several weeks, our department has been engaged in an intense and frustrating investigation to find the person or persons responsible for so many homeless deaths, the unnecessary loss of valuable lives. Regardless of who they are, what they are, what they do, what their ethnic background, gender or religious affiliation might be, those murdered were deprived of their lives, their futures, their ability to ultimately make a contribution to our community. Each of those killed has a name. Many have families and friends. There has been a lot of suffering and grieving. We have suffered an irrational loss of those who needed us the most, and we failed to protect them. We're asking *Real Change* to include a memorial in their newspaper with the names of those who lost their lives these past weeks."

"You, the media and our citizens, were also frustrated thinking we were not making any progress in finding a killer, let alone caring about the homeless victims. There wasn't a day without calls to my office, asking us what we were doing and why there had been no results. Some of those asking were not so nice in their phrasing or demands. Let me assure you we were working hard. At first, reasons for the deaths were not known, there was no idea as to who might be committing them, and no one had seen or heard anything. Finding pieces of the puzzle took time, commitment, and a lot of legwork. We told you the victims suffered one shot to their head, no shell casings left behind, the victims well-hidden and homeless. To help in our search and to not spook a suspect, what we had not reported was the type of weapon used to commit these murders. This sounded like a highly trained professional who knew what he was doing. That was confirmed." Another brief pause. "Our forensics lab was able to identify, from the slugs recovered from his victims, a military Sig Sauer Mark 25 9mm handgun with a silencer. Based on a profile from our Forensic Psychologist, we began to work with the U.S. Army at Joint Base Lewis-McChord and the Seattle VA, to identify those with such lethal training who might be suffering from post-traumatic stress disorder, PTSD. From the Army and the

VA data regarding recently discharged veterans under therapy was obtained, data showing veterans with special forces training, special lethal training. Our focus continued to narrow down, and ultimately, our Forensic Psychologist working with the clinical staff at the VA, was able to identify a handful of veterans whose behaviors were abnormally angry or irrational. Some of those were wounded, their bodies violated. That, in itself, is a trauma, but when coupled with the life and death struggle of combat, then being wounded, and having to return to a society that has no understanding what you've experienced or how you're continuing to suffer, it's a tragedy. It was a sad reality to acknowledge that one might be our killer, working out his irrational behaviors."

"During this process, we learned a lot about post-traumatic stress disorder, and what our returning vets are tossed into after having served their country. They're home but in their heads, they continue to relive the dark traumas of what they did and saw. Their battlefields returned with them, causing them to constantly re-experience the sounds and horrific pictures of battle."

"Homicide Detectives Kelly, a former Army MP, and Homicide Detective Conway have relentlessly pursued this evasive killer, visiting with some incredible war veterans. These are brave individuals, courageous, challenged by what they've experienced, but each with a hopeful story. And before you even ask, no, we're not revealing their names. Except for the killer, who died this morning in an attempt to kill his VA therapist, the others were cleared and deserve their privacy and our public 'welcome home' for serving our country."

"There was no pattern to the killing of our homeless, which only frustrated our detectives. However, they persisted and built a scenario that made sense, and followed it to last night's unfortunate conclusion. The killer, officially identified by our Medical Examiner as former U.S. Army Staff Sgt. Anthony Franklin, was recently placed under 24/7 surveillance. Sgt. Franklin had served in Iraq and Afghanistan, was awarded the Distinguished Service Cross, Silver Star and Bronze Star for exemplary performance of duty in rescuing his team members and squad while under enemy fire, himself wounded, and was later awarded a Purple Heart. He was a patient with the Seattle VA. His behaviors, described as bizarre and irrational, seemed to set him apart as one to watch. We did. The instincts and analysis of those involved were critical in saving the lives of a family. Having been trained as Special Forces, he reconnoitered his targets, thus accounting for his finding many of his homeless encampments that were so well hidden. He used night vision goggles so he could see his victims and their settings clearly in the dark. He did the same with his final target. Sgt. Franklin had presumably come to a point of feeling irrationally betrayed and went after his therapist. Again, that family is safe."

"Early this morning, Sgt. Franklin fought his last combat engagement. Our tactical team had removed the family from their home and staked out the house inside and out, for the past few days. He reconnoitered the house twice before he made his assault. We don't really know what was going on in his head, but when confronted several times with an order to surrender, he refused and decided to stand his ground. He was killed by our Tactical Unit in a gun battle, firing more than 15 shots at our officers. No one else was injured, for which we are grateful."

"You may want to ask a lot of questions about Sgt. Franklin. Our Public Relations office will provide you with the names of those innocent homeless victims killed, and a brief background on Staff Sgt. Franklin. His medical records are confidential and closed. We know he suffered from a severe case of PTSD and are not sure, nor will we ever know, what was going on in his tormented head. Whatever it was, it must have been the source of enormous pain, so much so that he played out whatever was going on, with the brunt being 18 homeless in our community murdered and a lot of fear spread around."

"Two final thoughts. First, all the officers and personnel who are with your police department are sworn public servants; we protect all who live within our community regardless of race, ethnic or religious background, gender, sexual orientation or economic strata. Each of you are valued for being who you are, and the many contributions you make within your homes, schools, neighborhood, the community and so many other places. What happened is regrettable and a terrible loss of human lives which we will remember for a long time. Murder, regardless of who commits it for whatever bizarre reason, is inexplicable and irrational."

"Second, if by chance you're a veteran suffering from a trauma, the result of being in combat, please ask for help. Go directly to the VA and ask for help. You don't need to feel you're alone. There are trained professionals ready to guide you and provide you with support to address your agony. We tried, and wish we'd been able to reach Sgt. Franklin, but he was so unwilling or unable to face his own agonies and demons making it difficult for us, or anyone, to give him the resources he needed to rebuild a better life. Now I'll take questions, but in an orderly fashion. Please identify your name and who you are with before you ask your question."

"Chief, Alan King with AP. In the final act of this incredible drama, was anyone hurt beside the death of the Sergeant?"

"No, as I said, no one was hurt. The victim unloaded his clip but did not hit any of the officers surrounding the house or inside it. The family had been evacuated so they were not in harm's way."

"Chief. Kathy Moss from CNN. Didn't anyone suspect the victim was seriously ill and likely to commit murder, in this case, multiple murders?"

"We knew the killer was irrational. All killings are irrational. As I said, the victim suffered from PTSD, and was in a VA therapy group. His behavior was not unlike other patients suffering from the same unfortunate and debilitating effects. We had no clues or persons of interest until we were given access to the Army's and VA's information; correlating their data on special forces trained soldiers, recently discharged but assigned to a PTSD therapy group, the VA clinicians were able to give us names we needed to interview, vets that seemed angry and struggling with adjusting to a society they were thrown back into but now as strangers. It was only then we had names to work with, individuals we needed to interview, Sgt. Franklin among those names. As we narrowed down the list, Sgt Franklin emerged as the prime suspect. Why he chose the homeless as his victims remains a mystery that went with him to his grave."

"Chief. Alfred Knolls from KING 5 news. Why did it seem to take so long to find the killer of the homeless men? Was there discrimination against the homeless men because they were homeless?"

"No. In fact, as I already said, we are sworn public servants and it doesn't matter to us who the victims are, their color, sex, background, etc. We treat all victims equally and their being homeless was never considered an issue. The best our detectives were able to piece this together, without the input from the murderer himself, was a psychological profile based on the slugs taken from the victims. The killer was obviously suffering significantly from the disease that gripped his soul. Again, I repeat, everyone deserves and receives equal respect from our department as we address criminal behavior, whether murder, robbery or something else."

"Chief, Frederick Gopher from NBC. Was there any attempt to take the killer alive?"

"Yes, our Tactical Squad was prepared and would have preferred to take the killer into custody had he surrendered. But when ordered to surrender, several times, his response was to fire at the officers. It was sort of clear at that point our hope of taking him alive had literally disappeared. He wanted to fight. He was given several opportunities to surrender before even one shot was fired by our officers. When the killer made his final dash for freedom and fired at our officers, it was apparent to our Tactical Team that he had to be stopped and not be allowed to escape. I can assure you proper protocol was followed; the killer had already expended some 15 shots and thankfully, no one else was injured. And one other thing. Having to bring down our suspected killer also closed the door on our homicide team learning what his reason was for targeting the homeless. That was not what we wanted. We can only speculate now but have no firm understanding."

"Chief, Susan Archer, with KOMO news. You've mentioned the severity of PTSD; what is being done by the VA, or anybody, to address this challenge among our vets?"

"What we've learned about PTSD during this investigation has been incredibly revealing. Homicide Detective Kelly is a former Army MP and saw a lot of our vets returning home while he was stationed at Joint Base Lewis-McCord. But even he admits, as a result of his many interviews with the clinicians and vets, that it's a debilitating disease and so difficult to treat. We can be proud of the efforts the VA is making in trying to address constructively those challenges and to provide our vets with support and assistance."

Chief Flanigan took several more questions, mostly questions asking about what she had already reported. She was patient, but had to repeat just about everything she had originally said. There were a couple of questions she refused to answer on the grounds of medical confidentiality. The Chief finally thanked everyone, turned to Conway and me, and said "When will the media ever ask questions that don't repeat information already given."

I was a little surprised when the Chief shook our hands and asked us to join her in her office.

Conway and I were feeling the long night, now daytime fatigue. I called Patti and told her I'd eventually meet her at home. She'd been given the very abbreviated version of what had happened, and had no doubt watched the Chief's press conference.

We walked into the Chief's office and were met by Sergeant Troy and Assistant Chief Marshall Plummer of our Investigative Bureau. The Chief began.

"Bluntly, I didn't think we'd find this crazy. Kelly and Conway, you are to be congratulated for your persistence once again. I heard a little about your encounter with the VA Administrator and can happily report he was relieved of his position, that is fired, last week. The VA has sent a message this morning congratulating the department on finding the killer, apologizing for the arrogance of their former local administrator and is looking at adding funds and resources to help their therapists working with vets suffering from PTSD. So, job well done, and thank Patti too (said with a slight smile). Gentlemen, (looking at the Assistant Chief and Sergeant Troy), will you do the honors."

With that I was a bit taken back. What honors?

The Assistant Chief and Sergeant Troy stepped forward and handed us a commendation and medal for the work we had done. For me, it was a little embarrassing. It's my job. But I wasn't going to resist the recognition.

"Thank you, Chief. I'm embarrassed but appreciate the recognition."

Conway likewise thanked the ranks. Handshakes again, then we were dismissed.

54

Though I was tired, I asked Tucker when they were planning to go to Franklin's apartment. They were about to; I told him Conway and I were coming along with Dr. Ward and Dr. Stephens. We all wanted to see what the apartment looked like and whether there were any clues as to what was going on in his head that drove him to kill 18 innocent men.

CSI was awaiting our arrival at Franklin's apartment. They had spoken with the manager and asked to be let into the apartment. Apparently, the manager was reluctant, saying we were invading his privacy. Tucker told her it didn't matter, he's dead. CSI was then guided to his apartment and with her key, she opened the door. We were right behind Tucker and his team by that time.

At first look, the front room and kitchen were immaculately clean and neat, almost compulsively neat. The refrigerator had food but not a lot. Dishes were clean and put away, magazines lay neatly on the coffee table, and cushions on his couch fluffed. You wouldn't suspect, based on just this portion of his apartment, Franklin was a killer.

Then Tucker opened the bedroom door; he looked around and turning back to his photographer, asked him to go in first, take pictures of everything and try not to disturb anything.

"We'll go in together, but I want to get photos first. From what I could see, his bedroom is an operational center with all kinds of maps, charts and newspaper clippings on the walls. The materials inside might give us all some insights into his mental state and why he was doing what he did."

"When we get in there, will you let us touch anything?" asked

Dr. Stephens. "I need to try and figure out what was going on in his head. Those clues may be on these walls."

"I have no problem if you don't object, Kelly. He's dead, so we're not looking at any court trial," said Tucker.

"It's okay with me and, in fact, Dr. Ward needs to be in on this with her colleague. Maybe their analysis of what's in there will define why he did what he did."

When both finally entered the bedroom, they gasped! Their hands came to their mouths; you could see they were visibly shaken. Their eyes could not take in what they saw posted on the walls: clippings of the murders reported, maps showing each of the kill sites in red, other sites circled in pencil. He even drew a black line around much of Seattle and designated it "enemy territory." Where he lived was outside that demarcation and labeled "base." Dr. Stephens shivered when she realized Franklin had put a bull's-eye over her house and marked it "enemy headquarters." There were pieces of paper with rantings about dreams, orders given to carry out missions, and the pain in his head. There were no bright lights in the room; in fact, he had removed the overhead light bulbs and relied on a small, low wattage red light on a small table pushed against the wall on which he had tacked up the map and other items. He didn't even have a double bed, but what looked like a surplus Army cot, a twin bed, canvas bottom holding a thin mattress with camouflage bedding.

Dr. Stephens asked Tucker for copies of the photographs taken. He looked at me and I nodded it was okay.

Dr. Stephens began, "I need to study all this stuff. Kelly, if it's removed, I'd like copies. I need to understand what pushed him over the edge. I'll review my own case notes, but I need to find an answer, if there is one. This is shocking!"

"You may have copies of everything. Tucker will arrange that for you. The originals must go into our forensic files tied to all the other stuff we've collected on and about him. No question, Sgt. Franklin was in a lot of pain, and delusionary."

The stuff we looked at was irrational. It made no sense, at least from a sane perspective. He designated the homeless as "the enemy" for reasons the psychologists would have to surmise. We'd found the additional ammunition; CSI took charge of it. His combat decorations, hanging on the wall, would no longer be displayed but put in a box in our archives.

"Look at this item, Tucker," I stated. I handed him what appeared to be a green covered notebook with the title "Log" written on its front cover.

"You've got to be kidding," was his first response as he opened and began to read its contents. "There are random notes, dated, that seem to detail his operations. He's giving us a road map of his killings, an admission of guilt for our purposes, and the anguish of his feelings."

Dr. Stephens stepped in and asked to look at the book. "This is most revealing, as he never shared this stuff in his therapy sessions. I can learn a lot from what he writes."

"Where did you find this?" asked Tucker.

"On the table with the red light. My guess is he would return from whatever he was doing and jot down what he had done, where, and his reactions. Makes no sense other than a log of his actions," I stated. "Probably something he imagined, irrationally, he was preparing for his imagined superiors."

Several hours later, we were about ready to seal up the apartment. I asked Dr. Stephens her thoughts.

"I'm stunned, and shiver at what I see. Yes, I told you he scared me; yes, he was irrational, angry and irritable, flew off the handle and vented his frustrations, but at no time had he ever indicated he was doing anything like this. I'll be checking my notes from our therapy sessions for any clues. In fact, I still don't see an explanation of why he targeted the homeless. It may be buried in all these materials or buried with him. This is incredible, scary and tragic."

I had to ask, "Why tragic?"

"We lost him. Even though psychotherapy groups seem to be the most effective way of addressing PTSD, obviously it didn't work in his case. I'll be doing my own research and, working with Caitlin and others, maybe we'll find a hint of an explanation. Maybe we'll find some insights to share with others treating vets with PTSD on how to better offer our services."

"We interviewed nine other vets with PTSD, four from you. Their individual stories are insightful and encouraging. No question, some have physical wounds that will not let them forget their experience. Others have chosen to live their lives recognizing the wound will not go away."

"And you can see what we therapists are contending with. Getting our patients past their emotional reactions to recognize they're alive and how they wish to live their lives is totally up to them."

"Conway and I saw some surprisingly good examples of success, if that word can even be applied. My take is, you've got the context which makes you a great therapist, thus credible. Letting those you work with know this, and even the vets in your groups, is no doubt an enormous asset."

"Thanks, Kelly. And I almost forgot to ask you amid all this excitement, how did he find out where I lived?"

"He was a master at black ops, and tracking people was easy for him. How and when he did it, we don't know. Conway and I had a gut instinct we needed to protect you and, beyond that, can't say why we reacted that way. I know when my gut says something I've learned to listen, and this was a good call."

"That makes me shudder."

"You're safe and so is your family. Let your kids know if they need Conway or me to go and see their Principal about missing homework or class, we're available. However, if she saw the Chief's press conference, she'd understand and appreciate you're all safe."

With that, Dr. Stephens departed. Much to think about and much to be relieved about.

Conway and I returned to the office, made our official report and fed it to our "Purple Paper Eater." Tomorrow, the ME and CSI would have their official reports and conclusions. The Chief was happy with her press conference and shutting up the outcry from the do-gooders. We had done our job and done it well.

Before we left, I told Conway I had one more call to make, to the editor of *Real Change*. The Chief, in her news conference, had asked them to publish a memorial to those who had died recognizing their value as humans. I wanted him to know a list would be sent from the ME's office with their names, based on fingerprinting and DNA tests and any other relevant information the ME might find. He agreed it would be appropriate.

We called it a day.

55

Patti was home ahead of me and had dinner planned, but the two glasses of wine on the deck were more enticing. It had been a couple of long days and nights with little sleep. Relaxing, looking at the activity on Lake Union, was just the right setting to refresh me.

"Got your killer, I hear."

"Yes, and he was certifiably crazy. When we inspected his apartment, we found he was using his bedroom as a command center. A lot of maps and notes hanging on the walls. He labeled his victims as the enemy. He labeled his therapist's home as enemy headquarters. He labeled our city as enemy territory and where he lived as some sort of 'base'. A lot of irrational rambling notes hung on his wall. He even kept a log which we hope will reveal more about what he was doing and why. And he did what I expected him to do, not surrender but fight."

"What's the next step, if there is one?"

"Too tired to think straight yet. The therapist and Dr. Ward are going to put their heads together over the stuff we recovered from his apartment. It was scary; maps with targets circled, newspaper clipping, notes, orders and so much more. It was quite sobering. What about your junket to DC?"

"Well, the meetings, and there were quite a few, all addressed what and how the FBI wanted to proceed with the prosecution of the cartel heads. They also reported what Sherlock had found was enormously helpful to Interpol; ships have been boarded and port security enhanced as they dismantle the cartel's web of smuggling. Our overseas offices are staying in touch with Interpol and keeping

DC up to date on developments as they unfold."

"Do they have concerns?"

"Yeah, in a manner of speaking. Delgado and Ramirez are incommunicado. They've been relocated to Leavenworth, isolated and kept away from anything electronic or walking on two legs, except the guards, and there's two of those at a time, a check and balance. The Bureau is concerned about the length of the cartel's tentacles and who is likely to be eliminated or paid off. The penitentiary, judges, lawyers, etc., are within reach, as well as you and me. They are strategizing how best to address these concerns. I told them my thoughts, bluntly."

"And how did they react?"

"They listened. They were taken off guard by my bluntness but took it under advisement. We've got international killers and the situation is more than just the FBI, but needs Homeland Security, Customs and the CIA involved. I also reminded them we were a nation of law and had processes to provide protection for our people, and we should use those on behalf of all of us. Call it profiling if you wish, but as we dismantle this incredible twenty-year web of money laundering, drug smuggling, and killings, I think they'll see what needs to be done and react quickly."

"Anything said about Neil?"

"I didn't expect anything to be said, but when I was asked to visit with the Director, he congratulated me on my promotion and expressed his condolences about Neil's death, and how grateful he was that you, you big bloke, were able to find the murderer."

"He knows about Flores, then?"

"Oh, yes. He's amazed how dumb he was tagging his victims, keeping records on his computer and hiding the murder weapon in his own home. Obviously, he wasn't hired because of his quick thinking. Then the surprise. He asked several other department heads and my regional SAC to join him in his office whereupon they recognized Neil's service, awarded him the Bureau's valor decoration, and gave me a commendation for the arrests of Delgado and Ramirez."

I got up, set my wine glass down, and took her into my arms and held her.

Whispering in her ear, "I'm so proud of you and how much they appreciate you, your talents and skills. You deserve the recognition, and for Neil, too."

"Thanks," she said with a scratchy voice.

She didn't resist, holding me tight. She was crying and so was I.

We may be in law enforcement but it's draining, at times. We've stepped forward to stop the irrational, illogical, rash and inexcusable and thus are always in harm's way. Pausing to feel the warmth of one another gives us reassurance and renews our faith in one another, in our careers, and in life.

It's funny how a little time in the hot tub stimulates your juices. We had our wine, our tears and adjourned to the hot tub. We both were tired yet stimulated, and you can imagine which one won, well maybe at first. Another night thin on sleep, sitting up in bed at the crack of dawn, Patti nestled in my arms with her head on my chest, looking through the sheer curtain at the Lake and its awakening activities. We needed to move and get to work, but not at this moment or the next.

"Guess our next project is attending our son's and Susan's graduation. I'll take the time off," I remarked. "Conway is more than capable of holding down the fort while I'm away."

"Let's go in a day or so early. It'll give us a chance to see San Diego and the kids as well," she replied.

"Since we're planning a post-graduation reception, we can

book our stay at the same hotel. Make it a little easier on us."

"Good idea. Need to get together with their catering staff to lay out what we want in food and drinks."

"How about a flat cake with their names on it, not only congratulating them on their graduation, but also their engagement and new careers? Think that would be fun and totally unexpected," I offered.

The graduation exercises at the University of California San Diego are held by schools at different times and days over the weekend. The site was their RIMAC field, Recreation, Intramural and Athletic Complex. Neil promised us tickets to access his graduation, and directions to the RIMAC field.

She lifted her eyes toward mine and asked a surprising question.

"What would you think if I gave Neil the award the Bureau gave his Dad?"

"I'd think he'd be surprised and appreciative. But what about you keeping it?"

"It was an honor to have Neil recognized. He's on the Bureau's 'Wall of Heroes' honoring those agents who have paid the ultimate sacrifice in the line of duty. I'm appreciative that he hasn't been forgotten. For me, it really doesn't have that much significance. Neil's gone, but his son will always remember him and the times they were together. And now he's entering the academy. I'm thinking of giving him his dad's yellow brick, too. Just a thought."

"I think he would welcome having those remembrances; he's well aware of what his dad did and what it cost him."

"Then it's done. Part of his graduation gift is that award and the brick. It'll be a huge surprise."

56

The wave tone of my cell ringer filled the air; I so wanted to ignore it. But the screen showed it was Charlie, our ME. I took the call and put it on speaker so Patti could hear as well.

"Boy, this is unusual having you call this early in the morning," I began.

"Good morning to you too, Kelly. Sorry to bother you but thought you should know what I found in the detailed autopsy of Sgt. Franklin."

"You've been up early to do the autopsy?"

"Yep. I got the superficial one done to accommodate the Chief yesterday. But I needed to be more thorough before I closed the case entirely."

"Knowing you, it must be important for you to be up this early and making this call."

"You're right. Had breakfast yet? Don't want this to be messing that up if you're sitting at the table."

"No. Go ahead," I replied.

"I continued my more detailed part of the autopsy this morning. Cause of death was multiple gunshot wounds. No questions there. But as I began to look at his brain, I recognized a growth, a glioblastoma."

"What's that, Charlie? I don't speak Latin or whatever."

"A brain tumor. It's the most aggressive cancer that begins in the brain. It's hard to diagnose, but symptoms might include headaches and personality changes."

"Could the tumor have contributed to his bizarre behaviors?" I asked.

"It might have. Its growth might have exerted pressure on the brain which contributed to his irrational behavior, and verbal outbursts. The cancer is fast growing and may have caused excruciating headaches. Unless he was aware of or had a medical diagnosis that the tumor existed, he would be unaware of its presence and the affect it was having on his brain and personality."

"He's dead, but it sounds like he was dying without knowing it."

"He was. The common length of survival following a diagnosis is no more than fifteen months. We have no idea when it began but I'm thinking he was about halfway through those fifteen months."

"He was walking a tight rope, reliving his combat traumas, having been wounded, and now as you say, Charlie, an undiagnosed growth in his head killing him."

"No question he was one messed up vet. It just wasn't the traumas and PTSD; the tumor was also his unknown, vicious enemy. The lab tests will officially confirm the tumor. It's difficult to say how it started or when, and without any family, we cannot assess whether other family members had the same growth."

"I know a short profile report I received on him said he had a younger sister die of leukemia. Nothing was noted about the date, when or where," I commented.

"That's interesting, but not necessarily applicable. I'll make a short reference to that in my final notes," responded Charlie.

"I need to ask you to contact Dr. Leslie Stephens at the VA and Dr. Ward. Dr. Stephens was his therapist and is trying to wade through all the stuff we found in his apartment. Your information may provide her with a ray of hope that it wasn't anything she wasn't doing, but well beyond anyone's control. Dr. Ward had helped with the killer's profile. She needs to know the same information. I'll have Conway email you their numbers later this morning."

"Can do. I don't know if they MRI the vets suffering from PTSD, but it would seem to be needed when a patient is so extreme in their behaviors."

"Long guess on my part, but a reasonable assumption they don't. Tickle Dr. Stephens with that idea, as she oversees the therapy groups handling vets with PTSD. Treatment varies with each patient and if they have a standard checklist, I doubt a brain MRI would be on it," I said.

"It doesn't excuse what he did whatever his reasons. It's just sad so many had to die."

"I'll agree with you on that, and thanks for the call, even if it is early."

Clicking off, I lay there thinking about Franklin's command center, his irrational behaviors and his willingness to die thinking we were all his enemies. He was sick, yet many were trying to help him.

"What are you thinking, Kelly?" Patti asked.

"You heard the ME. I know Dr. Stephens is beating herself up trying to figure out where she went wrong. I don't think she did anything wrong. She was not aware of the physiological changes inside his head, possibly contributing to his bizarre actions. Several questions come to mind. How long after he was discharged did his bizarre behaviors begin? Was he always the way Dr. Stephens describes him, irrational and angry from day one in her therapy sessions? And can a timeline be developed that demonstrates when the brain tumor might have begun to impact his behaviors?"

"Sounds like you think maybe the brain tumor was the possible cause of his irrational behaviors and not just PTSD?"

"With what the ME found, it makes me think, maybe, maybe there is some sort of explanation, beyond just PTSD, that explains or contributes to his outrageous actions."

"Do you think talking with Charlie will help her gain insight?"

"I do. Her husband is an MD as well and when they talk, no doubt he will affirm her and assure her the brain tumor was a contributing factor. I'll get Dr. Ward to chat with the ME too, and she and Dr. Stephens can have coffee and mutually discuss their concerns and observations. This may also be the beginning of a new friendship between them."

"It's over?" she asked.

"For me, yes. Conway and I wrote up our report, but will amend it to reference the ME's findings. I will have his report before I get to the office; then will amend ours and have Conway send a copy to the Sergeant and Chief Flanigan as an FYI, and to the others."

She rolled over on top of me and began to run her soft hands through my hair. She bent down, began kissing me with her sensuous and moist lips, slowly, then deeply; the rhythmic beauty of traveling to the moon and back consumed our every being.

Going into the office was delayed.

57

"Caitlin, this is Kelly."

"Top of the morning to you too. What can I do for you?"

"I wanted you to know about the ME's autopsy report and his plans to call you."

"Dead from gunshot wounds, I imagine," she inserted.

"Correct. But he called me a little while ago to share a rather interesting finding that might explain, in part, Franklin's irrational behaviors and outbursts. A brain tumor."

"You're kidding me. What kind of tumor?"

"He said it was a Glioblastoma tumor. He believes it was exerting pressure on the brain therefore potentially contributing to his exaggerated behaviors. After you've spoken with the ME, I'd like you to chat with Dr. Stephens. He's planning to call her as well. She did everything she could. She wasn't, nor was anyone, aware and probably neither did Franklin know he had a tumor. The ME did say it was a fast-growing cancer; when diagnosed most people don't live much longer than fifteen months. She might need some affirmation."

"Yes, I'll call her and arrange to visit. But wow! That's an interesting discovery. You said cancer, a tumor, so I wonder how it happened?"

"The ME can clarify those details. Franklin has no known family so the ME is not sure how it might have developed or whether there's any history of it in his family. He said he wasn't sure when it began nor how far along it was, just that it was an aggressive cancer usually giving patients fifteen months to live. But along those lines, it raises questions about when he began to act irrationally and angry, whether it was immediately upon discharge or later. You two will need to explore timelines assessing the impact of both the PTSD and the tumor. Sounds like I'm trying to do your job, yea, right. No way," chuckling.

"What a surprise. And your questions are good ones, good for thought and explorations. You've given me much to think about and I appreciate your input. Thanks for calling." She understood and clicked off.

Conway and I were again at our desks finishing up the amendment to our reports. He was surprised when I showed him the ME's report for our murder book. I asked him to email the ME the numbers for Dr. Stephens and Dr. Ward, and a copy of the ME's report to Chief Flanigan as an FYI.

"Let's go chat with the Sergeant and give him the latest," I suggested.

We wandered into his office unannounced. He looked up from his computer screen where it appeared he was playing with numbers again. We slid a copy of the ME's report in front of him.

"Are you kidding?" said Sergeant Troy after a quick glance at the ME's report.

"Wish I was. The ME says this kind of cancerous tumor is fast growing, probably giving Franklin less than 15 months to live. The tumor could have been exerting pressure, thus his exaggerated irrational behaviors. I suspect Franklin was not aware of it."

"What does this mean, if anything?"

"Not much. It didn't kill him directly. But it probably interfered with his behaviors, making them rash, and his outbursts irrational and threatening. I asked the ME to call Dr. Stephens directly, as she was Franklin's therapist; he can let her know about the tumor and explain better from a medical perspective. She did everything right in treating him but was unaware, as everyone was, that he had a debilitating brain growth. I've asked Dr. Ward to talk with the ME as well and then visit with Dr. Stephens. This new development may help them in analyzing the circumstances surrounding Franklin's behaviors."

"That's about all you can do, from what I see," commented the Sergeant.

"Yeah, I guess so. I know Dr. Stephens is sorting out the stuff we found in Franklin's so-called 'command center.' She is really trying to figure out what she missed and how she failed to reach him. You know, Sarge, she's been in the Army and in combat, too. She really does have that empathy, that understanding, and insight needed to address those struggling with PTSD and those feeling no one understands them. She's doing good work."

"I commend you, Kelly, for giving her the information and support."

Leaving the Sergeant's office, I suggested to Conway we walk to the Chinese Place for lunch. We called Sherlock as well and wanted to hear how he's transitioning from being immersed in his technology to finding a real life with Clarice. I called Patti and left a voice mail inviting her to join us. We would be heading to San Diego shortly for Neil and Susan's graduation ceremonies. We also needed to catch up with the pending event that would be causing an expansion in the Conway family. Death, murder and the interviews Conway and I had had with the vets had taken its toll for the past few weeks. It was time to decompress from the adrenalin that had pumped through my body.

It was time to have an enjoyable lunch with close friends, nothing more than that.

Epilogue

Graduation day for Neil and Susan was one of those special-order sunny days in San Diego. The RIMAC Field was swarming with parents, and graduates in their iridescent blue and gold robes with other paraphernalia hanging around their necks. The students had marched in to the proverbial tune used for such events, been seated, listened patiently to a bunch of boring speeches from faculty and a keynote speaker they cared even less about, continued to hear the announcements of special awards and recognition, and then marched across the stage like cattle being herded as their names were read and diploma covers presented. Patti had about 4 seconds to get a photo of Neil on stage receiving his degree, and about the same for a photo of Susan. She was so proud, as were they. When the event was officially concluded, the graduates shifted their tassels and threw their hats in the air, a traditional celebration ritual. I always wondered how they found their own hats again, if ever. Whatever, they had their degrees and their debt. But who cared about the latter, or the hat?

Patti and I arranged a special celebration at the Marriott Hotel on the waterfront. We invited family and friends to drop by to greet and congratulate the latest bachelor's degree recipients in Computer Science and Pre-Law, along with other surprises. Nearly a hundred showed up, which thrilled Patti. Even her former colleagues from their LA and Orange County offices came.

The tinkling of a knife on a wine glass sounded, gaining the attention of everyone in the room.

"Thank you for coming to celebrate Neil and Susan's

graduation. I'm Patti Hancock, Neil's mother. I am taking the prerogative to say a few words and hope you will bear with me. Several years ago, my agent-husband and Neil's father, was murdered on an FBI undercover assignment. For Neil and me, it's been a long road of recovery. Three things are significant today. My fiancé Homicide Detective John Kelly (pointing to me), my high-school sweetheart, had a murder case in Seattle. That's a long way from Southern California. But he had a hunch, and the outcome was that the murderer he caught for the Seattle crime was the same person who killed my husband. Coincidence? No, we don't believe in those. So, Neil and I had some very tearful moments after finding the murderer of his dad, the man he adored. The second item is Neil will be leaving in a few weeks to attend the FBI Academy in Quantico." There was a moment of light applause. "Talk about surprises! He shows up in Seattle a few weeks ago, engaged, and introduces Kelly and me to Susan. Then he says he's going to the Academy while Susan attends law school. I couldn't be prouder of both of them. Welcome to our family, Susan."

There was more light applause; she then continued. "Now I'm going to embarrass him a little. A short time ago, I was called to Washington D.C. It was related to the case Kelly had solved. The Bureau Director called me into his office to congratulate me on the case having been solved. But there was a surprise. Neil, would you join me?" She pauses for Neil to join her. "The Director announced that Neil Young, deceased FBI Agent, was being added to their Wall of Honor, recognizing the ultimate sacrifice he made in the line of duty. Then, they presented me their commendation of valor, recognizing Neil's contribution and sacrifice. Son, Kelly and I discussed this, and with you departing for the Academy shortly, and considering your love for your dad and your following in his footsteps, we felt this commendation should be yours. And so, you should also have his yellow brick."

With that, she took the plaque, medal and brick from me and

handed them to her son, who was in tears. She hugged him and kissed his cheek. He didn't know how to respond. Meanwhile, Susan had come up and put her arm around his waist, she too in tears, and said thank you to Patti. She knew her son was overwhelmed and did not push him to say anything. It was his time now to hold the recognition his dad had received. It was his time to realize he was following in the steps of a man recognized by his colleagues and loved by his family.

Patti continued, "Now that I got all of us in tears, let's celebrate life, and the hopes and dreams held by Neil and Susan." There was loud applause and the guests started moving toward the kids.

Patti meanwhile stepped off the small riser, walked over to me, fell into my arms shivering, and cried her heart out, the emotional release of years of pain finding resolution in a moment of celebration.

Acknowledgements

Thank You

To the Veterans who shared with me their stories and battles with Post Traumatic Stress Disorder (PTSD).

To Sergeant Steven Paulsen, Lieutenant Michael Kebbar, Sergeant Gary Nelson, Homicide Detective Rolf Norton, Homicide Unit, Violent Crimes Section, Seattle Police Department.

To my readers and editors, Sidney Green and JoFrances Calk.

To Bruce Polvi (Weapons Expert), and Binaya Dangol (Computer Specialist) for your technical support and advice.

To Kim Stafford and Jennifer Lauck, for encouragement and coaching me in your writing seminars.

To Brando Skyhorse, Amy Bloom, Amity Gauge and Salvatore Scribona at Wesleyan University, for teaching me so much in your creative writing classes.

To Word-2-Kindle.com, Kindle Direct Publishing and Amazon Books, thank you for your assistance with publishing this novel.

Looking Ahead

"The Snake Has Two Heads" is the third in a series of detective murder mysteries with Homicide Detective John Francis Kelly and his partner Homicide Detective Bob Conway, which finds them in harm's way. A phone call from his Chief disturbs the romantic dinner with his wife, as they watch their houseboat blow up across the harbor. Met by his Sergeant, Kelly and his wife Patti are taken to the Seattle Coast Guard Station where they're told of the attempts made on the Conway's, the brutal assaults on Assistant Prosecutor Jennifer Hunter and her husband and the assassination of a federal prosecutor. Sherlock and his fiancée are murdered, and an airborne attack is made on Leavenworth Federal Prison. Being kept out of sight as part of the Chief's charade, Kelly and his wife Patti, the SAC for the Seattle FBI office, along with Conway, work with a specially assigned federal agent to unravel who's behind these despicable criminal acts. Their investigation startles everyone when they find out why they've been targeted, by whom and that the police department has a mole - not one but two.

Also, you may wish to read "Under Their Nose"
Book I in the Homicide Detective John Francis Kelley series.

About the Author

Richard Gartrell is retired and lives with his wife on the Oregon Coast. Previously he's written a tourism marketing textbook and numerous professional journal articles during his career as an educator and tourism chief executive. A Vietnam Veteran, "Reliving the Dark" is the second murder mystery in the Homicide Detective John Francis Kelly series.

Made in the USA
Columbia, SC
22 October 2021